As soon as his wife's — — — — — Zeus, the remarkable creature was his wife!—Galen hurried out of his box and down the stairs before anyone could come to poke and pry. He found his way backstage and was waiting for Margot as she made her last bows and ran into the wings. He scooped her up and twirled her around, not caring who saw. "You were magnificent, my Margot." And he kissed her while the applause thundered on from the audience and the stagehands cheered nearby.

"Oh, my," she said when she could breathe again. The walls were still spinning and her feet did not feel the ground beneath them, not even when Galen put her down. "You . . . you liked my song?" she whispered, as the play was about to recommence behind them.

"I loved your song, madame wife," Galen whispered back, "and I think I am falling in love with you."

Coming next month

LADY JANE'S NEMESIS
by Patricia Oliver

Roger Hastings' long-awaited proposal to Lady Jane Sinclair comes at a price: the devious plans of his mistress to destroy their love....

0-451-20069-1/$4.99

A PRUDENT MATCH
by Laura Matthews

A hasty wedding between a debt-ridden baron and an innocent beauty turns from a marriage of convenience into a marriage of surprising passion....

0-451-20070-5/$4.99

A PERILOUS ENGAGEMENT
by Emily Hendrickson

After the untimely demise of his reckless cousin, Jordan Robards inherits a barony, his brother's bereft fiancée, and the terrible suspicion that his cousin's death was not an accident at all....

0-451-20071-3/$4.99

To order call: 1-800-788-6262

Saved
by
Scandal

Barbara Metzger

A SIGNET BOOK

SIGNET
Published by New American Library, a division of
Penguin Putnam Inc., 375 Hudson Street,
New York, New York 10014, U.S.A.
Penguin Books Ltd, 27 Wrights Lane,
London W8 5TZ, England
Penguin Books Australia Ltd, Ringwood,
Victoria, Australia
Penguin Books Canada Ltd, 10 Alcorn Avenue,
Toronto, Ontario, Canada M4V 3B2
Penguin Books (N.Z.) Ltd, 182–190 Wairau Road,
Auckland 10, New Zealand

Penguin Books Ltd, Registered Offices:
Harmondsworth, Middlesex, England

First published by Signet, an imprint of New American Library,
a division of Penguin Putnam Inc.

First Printing, June 2000
10 9 8 7 6 5 4 3 2 1

Copyright © Barbara Metzger, 2000

To the second Siegal sibling, Jillian Rose. Hooray!

Chapter One

Whoever said that it was better to have loved and lost than never to have loved at all had not consulted Galen Woodrow, Lord Woodbridge. How, the viscount wondered, could he be better off with his heart wrenched out of his chest, carved into tiny pieces, then ground under the dainty feet of Lady Floria Cleary, in full view of the entire *ton*? Twice. The conscienceless witch had jilted him. Again.

The first time two years ago hadn't been so bad. He'd been a mere four-and-twenty, and relieved to have his bachelorhood extended a few years while Florrie matured. Bridal nerves, her father had said. Wanting to enjoy a few more Seasons as an Incomparable, Galen had supposed, without being tied to a husband who criticized her flirting, lowered necklines, and cropped curls. At eighteen, Florrie hadn't been ready for marriage or motherhood, and Galen had gladly accepted the note she'd sent a week before the ceremony. The viscount had also patiently accepted the gibes and the gossip of the Polite World—for two weeks. Then, since he was free of the immediate entanglement if not the engagement, Galen joined the forces against Napoleon. He served on the Peninsula until a minor injury sent him home, at which his father insisted the marriage go forth, with heirs forthcoming, to ensure the succession. One hint of Cousin Harold as Duke of Woburton had been enough to have His Grace calling the banns. Galen might be a viscount in his own right, inheriting from a deceased uncle, but he still had to answer the duke's call.

But this time, this very morning, Lady Floria hadn't de-

veloped cold feet. She simply had a cold heart. She had pur-
posely wounded him worse than any French artillery shell.
Worse than a saber gash. Worse than being blown off his
horse, trampled, and left for dead, which Galen was wishing
he was. This time Florrie had left him at the altar, and not
just any altar, but the vast, echoing altar of St. George's. At
least three hundred pairs of laughing eyes had been fixed on
him, with Lud knew how many lesser folk watching from
outside. The uninvited spectators, at least, caught a glimpse
of his bride, which was more than Galen did. She'd arrived
in her father's coach, all strewn with ribbons and roses, and
stepped out to cheers and well-wishes. She'd waved, they
told him after, right before climbing into Sir Henry Lytell's
barouche. Then she'd tossed her wedding bouquet to a
dressmaker's apprentice come to gape at her betters.

Better, hah! The little seamstress would not have run off
with a rake of the first order, a fortune hunter, a gambler, a
wife-stealing worm.

Florrie's father had come rushing into the church, white-
faced and trembling. "You have to go after her!" he shouted
on his way down the white-carpeted aisle, loudly enough for
everyone to hear, if they hadn't already been informed of
the bride's taking white-gowned wing by those nearer the
doors.

"Go after her?" Galen had shouted back. "Why, so I can
strangle her? Let Lytell do it when he is tired of her fits and
starts. I would not marry your daughter, my lord, if she were
the last woman on earth."

Lord Cleary had gone after the jade himself, but not before Galen's father had made him swear to return the settlements, but not reclaim the dowry, unless he wished a
breach-of-promise lawsuit. Trust His Grace to worry about
pounds and pence when his son's pride was being put to the
stake.

Galen's sister Harriet, meanwhile, was setting up a screech
that now she had no one to present her next Season. One of
the other bridesmaids thought that if she swooned into

Galen's arms, he might choose her to take Lady Floria's place. Galen let her fall. The duke stormed out of the church, dragging Harriet with him, declaring London no place for a well-mannered chit. He was returning to the country, His Grace declared, to his orchids and his books. Harriet was turning purple. The bridesmaid was moaning, the bishop was clucking his tongue, and everyone else was laughing. Everyone except Galen, of course. Dredging forth what dignity he had left, the viscount had raised one arm and addressed the congregation, those who had not rushed out to spread the word to the newspapers, the clubs, the four corners of the kingdom.

"My friends," he had lied. He despised every one of the snickering, snorting dastards. "I am certain Lord Cleary would want me to repeat his invitation to the wedding breakfast. The food would only go to waste otherwise, and the drink. So go, and help me celebrate my lucky escape."

He had no intention of facing the grinning crowds, of course, but in the bustle of emptying the church, Galen was able to flee out the side door and flag down a passing hackney carriage. He ducked beneath the coach windows till they were well away.

The staff at Woburton House in Grosvenor Square had all been sent to Lord Cleary's to help with the reception, which suited the viscount just fine. Laughter was bad, pity was worse. He barricaded himself in the library, locking the door behind. Now he was alone with three good friends: brandy, Burgundy, and blue ruin. Galen fully intended to enjoy their company to the last drop. Better a bottle than a bitch for a bride.

The realization that he felt more anger than grief was a good sign, Galen decided after the second glass. Perhaps his heart was not broken after all. It wasn't as if he had any grand *amour* for Florrie; he was just accustomed to thinking of her as his, his to protect from importunate puppies, his to tease out of the sullens, his to buy trinkets for, and his to escort to innumerable dull parties. More like a burden than a bride, he reflected. The occasional kisses they'd shared were more pleasant than passionate, but he'd accepted that too, since a man did not want his wife being so warm-blooded she'd worry him. Florrie was a lady, not a ladybird, he'd thought. And she was beautiful, with her auburn curls and green eyes and luscious figure. He'd been proud to have her on his arm, once she outgrew the spots and stubby legs of girlhood, and proud that other men seemed to admire her. He didn't have to pretend to play the love-sick suitor, not with so many mooncalves worshiping at her feet. Or so he'd thought.

They'd known each other since the cradle, and had been engaged nearly that long. Their fathers had decided on the match: a duke's son, an earl's daughter, fortune to fortune. What could be more suitable? Galen had been raised knowing his duty, knowing Florrie was his fate. He'd assumed she was as resigned. Obviously, he'd been wrong, again. Well, good riddance to the heartless harlot. She would have made a wretched mother to his children anyway, with her need to enjoy the newest gossip, the newest fashions, the newest flirtations. Why, staying home by the fireside of an evening was torture for Florrie—and for anyone unfortunate enough to be sharing such quiet entertainment. Galen tried to recall if he'd ever seen her read anything besides a ladies' magazine. He gazed around the book-filled room, thinking of all the hours he'd spent here, lost in the wonder of words.

He raised his glass—his fourth or fifth—to the portrait of the elegant lady hanging over the mantel. Her Grace had been gone for ten years, and Galen missed her still. His mother had been a governess before becoming a duchess, so she was wise in the ways of young females and would have seen Florrie for a strumpet long since, and saved him from making such a fool of himself. Damn, but now he was weeping for his mama like a homesick, runny-nosed schoolboy. His mother could not help him now. No one could. He was going to be grist for the gossip mills.

So his heart was intact. So what? He'd never trust it to another woman. Cousin Harold would have to provide the heirs, if the nodcock could figure out how. And Galen would . . . what? He would not dare show his face outside this door. He couldn't go to White's or his other usual haunts, and he couldn't go abroad, not with the war on. The family had property in Jamaica, but Galen got seasick. He could rejoin his army unit, but that would likely send his father into apoplexy. Besides, word of Florrie's ignominious abandonment would reach Spain with the next despatches. He'd rather put a bullet through his head and get it over with, than fall victim to his fellow officers' merciless teasing. No, he would not give Florrie the satisfaction of knowing he was so distraught he'd done himself in. Besides, Galen Woodrow was not a coward. A few more glasses and he might even be brave enough to face his own valet.

No one died of a broken heart, and no one died of embarrassment, the viscount told himself. In a few days, some other scandal would arise, and his wedding-day debacle would be relegated to a footnote to the Season. "Oh, yes," he could hear the dowagers' tongues clacking, "that was the year Lady Floria left young Woodbridge at the church door, right before Lady Witherspoon married her butler and Lord Hammermill gambled away his wife's dowry." Besides, with the Season soon ending, the *haute monde* would be leaving Town for their country properties or the seashore. They'd have better things to think about than Galen's ghastly affairs.

Affairs—that was it! Amazing what brilliant ideas lurked in the bottom of a bottle. He'd cause a scandal, that's what—a major, epically proportioned scandal, one to make Florrie's defection seem like a schoolgirl's mischief. No one would pity him, and no one would wonder what he was so lacking that his bride chose a rake over a respectable marriage.

His idea would work, Galen just knew it would, if he could get Mademoiselle Margot Montclaire to cooperate.

Miss Montclaire was the current comet of the theater world, the entr'acte singer at Drury Lane. She was the daughter of Simone Montclaire, a famous French chanteuse of the previous generation who'd run off to Italy with her lover. Galen didn't care who fathered the chit or who trained her to sing like a husky nightingale. He simply wanted Miss Montclaire, to help stir the scandal broth, of course.

A whole page of the betting book at White's—nay, a whole chapter—was devoted to Mademoiselle Margot, to who would win her favors and how much blunt it would take. Perhaps the most beautiful woman in all of London, the willowy singer was certainly the most elusive. No one had yet to claim the title of her protector, although scores of admirers had offered and been refused. They beseeched her in the Green Room, tossed her bouquets and baubles as she made her bows on stage, and waited outside the theater for a glimpse of the blond beauty. She always smiled, waved, and went home alone, leading speculation to run rampant as to a secret husband in France, a married lover in the country, a teasing game to drive her price higher. Galen had lots of money, whatever it took. He even had Florrie's dowry, by George.

The viscount had not been among the legions of Miss Montclaire's devotees. He admired her, of course, but only from his box at the theater. What man wouldn't lust after the golden-haired beauty, with her slim but gracefully rounded figure and come-hither voice? A dead one. Lord Woodbridge was very much alive, but he'd been an engaged man, a gentleman who would not betray his bride-to-be. He'd had women in Spain, of course, and the occasional paid companion, but so near to the wedding he would not dishonor Florrie, for all the good it did him. Thunderation, he could have been keeping a harem for all she cared. While he was taking cold baths, Lady Floria was likely taking Lytell to her bed. Galen emptied another bottle, then pushed the glass aside. No, he needed a clear head for the coming negotiations. He lit a cigarillo instead and blew smoke rings over-head. He thought of wedding rings, like the one in his pocket. Miss Montclaire's price could be as high as Prinny's debts, but Galen Woodrow, Viscount Woodbridge, had something a lot richer to offer.

Chapter Two

Whoever said that dog was man's best friend had never encountered Mademoiselle Margot's mongrel. The rack-ribbed cur stood waist-high, with tufts of hair here and there on its reddish-colored body, as if a greyhound had mated with a shaving brush, with a bit of moth-eaten fox thrown in. The huge mutt's teeth were as long and white as a pirate's ivory peg leg, and those leathery lips were not curled up in a smile. The bare floor under Galen's boots was vibrating, shaking from the rumbling growl that issued from the dog's cavernous maw.

Galen liked dogs. He held out his gloved hand to be sniffed, to make friends. His glove disappeared down the overgrown beast's gullet. Better bare hands than bare bones, he considered, putting his other hand in the pocket of his hooded cloak, fingering the loaded pistol he'd put there before venturing into London's less luxurious neighborhoods at nighttime. He could not suppose Miss Montclaire would be amenable to his offer if he shot her pet, however, so he addressed himself to the woman holding the dog's collar. She was nearly as homely as the mongrel, and just as surly.

"I don't care what you want, *mademoiselle* ain't receiving this evening. An' she ain't receiving the likes of you any time."

Waiting till dark, Galen had crept out of his own house with the hood of his cloak pulled up to hide his face, then hurried down the street, keeping to the shadows, until he could hire a hackney carriage to drive him to Drury Lane. The theater was closed on this Sunday night, but the manager was there, counting receipts. The dastard demanded half of Florrie's dowry, it seemed, just to reveal the singer's direction.

"*Mademoiselle* ain't no light-skirt to be giving her address to every jumped-up jackanapes, you know," the manager declared.

If she were, Galen wouldn't be here. He put another stack of coins on the man's cluttered desk.

"An' she better be here to work tomorrow night. I have a contract, I do."

More coins had changed owners, until an address was scribbled on the back of a playbill. Nichol Road was just a few blocks away from the theater, so Galen walked. The streets grew narrower and darker, with more filth in the gutter. Some of the filth scuttled away when he passed, some held out emaciated hands for a coin, and some offered their bodies for the night. Miss Montclaire would be happy to leave such a neighborhood.

Galen kept walking until he reached Number Ten, which was slightly more prepossessing than its neighbors. At least this building did not have boards where windows should have been, nor drunks huddled in its doorstep. A neat sign in the front window proclaimed ROOMS TO LET, LADIES ONLY. Ladies of the night, Viscount Woodbridge assumed. He raised the polished brass knocker, wondering that it had not been filched ages ago, and let it rap against the door. The resulting roar told him why the house was not burgled or overrun by beggars. A bark that could make the thick wooden door tremble ought to discourage most criminal intent. Since Galen was not bent on any mischief, he stood his ground and rapped the knocker again.

The door was finally pulled open, though only a crack, by a stooped female draped in black. "No gentlemen callers after dark," she rasped. "House rules." The hag would have closed the door in his face, if Galen hadn't had his foot in the way.

He hid his disbelief—and his pain—with a nod, handing

over another king's ransom in coins. "Could you please take my card to Miss Montclaire, anyway? I am sure she will see me."

Then again, he'd been sure Florrie would be at the church this morning to say her vows. He tried to look unconcerned and inconspicuous as he waited outside Number Ten, Nichol Road, as if a tall, broad-shouldered, well-dressed viscount could fade into such a derelict neighborhood.

A different woman opened the door a few minutes later. This one was not so old, not so stooped, but she had the same man-hating sneer on her hard-lined face. She held his card in one hand, ripped in two, and the slavering dog's collar in the other. "*Mademoiselle* ain't in. She'll have a thing or two to say to that weasel of a manager for giving out her address, asides. Now get."

"But I have a proposition to put to Miss Montclaire," Galen protested, not anxious to force his way past the dragon or the dog.

"I'm sure you do, just like all the other randy young bucks, and the randy old goats, too. *Mademoiselle* don't entertain gentleman callers, 'specially at her house, after dark, and she don't entertain lewd offers, never. Now go on with you, or I'll set the dog loose."

Galen doubted the dog would let him pass, and he couldn't shoot the beast for doing its job, so he backed away. "But I will be returning, you can tell your mistress that. With an offer she'll want to hear."

He was glad, in a way, that he'd been turned aside, for his dismissal meant that Miss Montclaire was no ripe plum, ready to fall into any man's hands. Of course, she might have a man upstairs already, but he could not think about that now. He had too much to do to convince her to see him and to listen to his offer. More firmly convinced than ever that he was on the right course, that Miss Montclaire was his salvation, Galen hurried back into the night. The walk through the cool, dank air to find a hackney, rare in this neighborhood, did not bring about a change of heart or mind. He might be above par, Galen confessed to himself, but he was not so castaway that any of his other options appealed in the least. His liquor-laced logic might be saying he needed Miss Montclaire, but his loins were, too.

There was nothing for it, then, but to pay a call on his old schoolmate, Skippy, "Skip the lecture," Skidmore. Since he and Skippy had been out celebrating the end to Galen's bachelorhood last evening, right into this morning, the viscount was fairly confident Skippy would be at home, making an early night of it. Galen knew for a fact that Skippy'd been up betimes this morning, for his old friend had been standing right there in his robes, next to the bishop, ready to assist at the wedding that wasn't.

Lud, he still had a hard time thinking of old Skipper in orders. In jail, perhaps; in the arms of some doxy, likely; in Dun Territory, always. But in holy orders? The Lord most decidedly worked in mysterious ways, choosing such an addle-pated apostle. Of course, the Lord hadn't precisely chosen young Skidmore, nor had Skippy willingly taken the cloth. The cloth was all that was being offered, however, by a family out of patience with such a debt-ridden, decadent dunderhead. He wasn't even the second son, the spare heir, who got to go into the Army. Galen silently thanked Baron Skidmore. They'd all be speaking French by now if Skippy had taken colors instead of clerical collars.

The rattlepate had barely made it through university, but his powerful father had bought him a position as aide to the bishop. No one let him minister to the congregation, thank God. Galen supposed God should be thanking the bishop for not inflicting Skippy on His innocent believers. Still, Skippy looked a treat in his flowing robes, until one smelled the liquor on his breath, and he had not been arrested once since joining the Church. The brother who had signed up with Wellesley returned missing a limb or two; all Skippy missed were a few, a very few, parties when the bishop needed his assistance. He might be a man of the cloth, but he was still a gentleman of fashion, and he had wits enough to figure betting odds.

Galen reached for the key nailed to the bishop's back door and headed toward the servants' stairwell. He was fully familiar with the house, having dragged a stuporous, senseless Skippy up those same back stairs to his rooms many a time. Galen scratched softly on the door, then pushed it open. Skippy leaped out of his armchair and snatched up the Bible from the table next to it.

"Put that thing down, old man. I know you've got the racing forms glued to the inside pages anyway."

Skippy staggered over to the sideboard and poked around until he found a bottle and two glasses. Then he held one of the glasses, the unchipped one, out to Galen, saying, "Gads, do I look as awful as you?" He settled his lanky frame back into the worn chair, leaving the equally dilapidated sofa for Galen, and dragged his other hand through his sandy-colored hair, managing to make his thinning windswept look more tornado-tossed. "Devil take it, I must have been so drunk I slept through your wedding. I am truly sorry, old chap, you know I am. But if you think I've dishonored your bride or betrayed our friendship, you can skip the lecture and just hit me."

Galen gritted his teeth, shoving a pair of gloves and a garter to the floor so he could sit. "There was no wedding, Skippy."

"No wedding? That wasn't a whiskey dream then, you sending everyone to the earl's for an unwedding breakfast?"

"It was a nightmare, all right, but it didn't come from any bottle. Floria flew the coop, did a flit, fled to Gretna Green with a feckless fortune hunter." Saying the words out loud didn't hurt quite as much as Galen expected, most likely because his old friend was madly searching through some scraps of paper on the table, the mantel, and the floor, and not listening.

"Damn, I know it's here somewhere." He finally found the slip of paper he was looking for, then cursed again.

"Blast, you just cost me a quarter's wage. That's what I get for standing by you. Couldn't bet against m'old friend, could I, not when they were giving such good odds against that flighty filly coming up to scratch?"

"Confound it, you were betting about my marriage?"

"I was betting *for* it, old boy. I figured I couldn't lose, not with your fortune and title and elegant phiz. And her father pushing for the match. Why, chits have been dropping their handkerchiefs at your feet since we were in short pants. What more does that peagoose Lady Floria want? Uh, sorry, old chap, if I've struck a sore spot."

Galen brushed that aside. Labeling Florrie a peagoose was mild compared to what he'd been calling her. "I suppose she wanted adventure and excitement. You know, high drama like those ridiculous novels females are always reading."

Skippy kicked a purple-covered book under the sofa. "Yes, well, if you're here for advice and consolation, I know a new house that just opened near Covent Garden. We could—"

"No, I am here for a favor."

"Oh?" Skippy fingered the gambling vowels and tried to look innocent. He failed, but Galen took the chit anyway.

"I'll make good on this, and pay off the rest of your debts, too, if you can get me a special license."

Skippy grabbed the paper back. "If you were to marry the chit, then I won and you won't have to pay it off. I wagered on the marriage coming off, not the wedding."

"I am not going to marry Lady Floria Cleary, you nodcock. She is halfway to Scotland by now, anyway."

"Didn't think you needed a license for getting hitched over the border. Don't know if the fellows at White's will accept that."

"Dash it, Skippy, will you listen! I would not marry Lady Floria on a dare, much less over an anvil. Nor am I haring off to Scotland after her. You lost the bet, fair and square, because we were both fools, but I will make it up to you if you can get me the blasted special license."

Skippy stroked his unshaven chin, thinking, an exercise in futility as Galen well knew. "But if she ain't here and you ain't there . . . ?"

Galen took a sip of his drink. "I am going to offer for— No, I am going to marry Miss Margot Montclaire."

Skippy fell off his chair. Picking himself up, he drank straight from the bottle. "Sorry, I thought you said you were going to marry the Magnificent Margot."

"I did. And do not say a word about the dust-up the marriage will cause. For once you can skip the lecture, for I've thought it all out. M'father can't fly too far up in the boughs, because he married the neighbor's governess. My sister can stay with Aunt Matty in Bath till all the gossip dies down. It's the least Aunt Matty can do, after bringing Cousin Harold into the world. As for everyone else, they were going to chew me up over morning chocolate anyway. I'd rather they choked on this morsel."

Skippy's mouth was hanging open. Galen feared the gudgeon had swallowed the cork or something. He started to pound him on the back, but Skidmore held up one hand. "I . . . I . . ."

"You won't change my mind, dash it, if that's what you are trying to say. I am going to marry Miss Montclaire, as soon as possible, and I'll need you to officiate. You do know the words of the ceremony, don't you?"

Skippy bobbed his head frantically, joyfully. Then he grabbed for Galen's hand and started pumping it, a huge grin lighting his face. "Change your mind? Zeus, that's the last thing I'd try. You've got to be the second luckiest man on earth. Mademoiselle Margot in your arms, you sly dog, you."

Galen could not confess that he'd never spoken two words to the woman. He simply accepted his friend's enthusiastic congratulations. "Then you'll get the papers? Everything has to be aboveboard, you know. I don't want anyone

questioning the legitimacy of my marriage or my children."
If there should be a marriage, and if there should be children. But he wasn't going to overburden poor Skippy's brain with any doubts.

Still shaking the viscount's hand, Skippy said he'd clear the whole thing with the bishop in the morning. There would be no problem.

Galen reclaimed his hand while he could still use it to sign the documents. "But tell me, Skippy, why am I the second luckiest man in the world? Who's the first?"

"Why, I am! I wagered you'd win the lady's favor as soon as you came back from your wedding trip. Two weeks of Lady Floria ought to have cured you of any foolish notions of fidelity. I'm rich, man, I'm rich!"

Chapter Three

Whoever said that fools rush in where angels fear to tread would have been mowed down by Galen's head-long dash back to the Nichol Street rooming house. The sun was almost up by the time Skippy finished with the papers, and folks in this neighborhood would be starting off to work. They would not recognize Viscount Woodbridge either, so Galen pushed the hood of his cape back. The sun on his head felt right, felt good. If he were the poetic sort, his lordship might have taken the clear dawning as an omen, leading him from darkest despair. Galen took it as a help in avoiding the offal in the streets.

This time, he was better prepared to call on his would-be wife. He had his pistol in his right pocket, a meat pasty in paper in his left pocket, a nosegay of violets in his left hand, and his *bona fides* in his right. The special license was carefully filled in, leaving extra space for Miss Montclaire's real name in case she was using a stage persona. False names would invalidate the marriage, and his father, or Florrie's, would have the marriage annulled before the ink was dry.

Wrapped in the folds of the official document was a gold band studded with diamonds, brand-new, never used. Galen had been going to present it to Florrie on their wedding night, knowing how she loved jewelry. She'd deemed his mother's plain gold band hopelessly outdated, but agreed to wear it for the ceremony, to please His Grace. The viscount supposed the ring still reposed in his father's pocket, where it could stay. He did not think that he could offer his mother's wedding band to an unknown entertainer. His name and fortune and courtesy title, yes. His mother's ring, no.

Outside Number Ten, Nichol Road, Galen juggled the flowers and the license, straightened his neckcloth, a hastily donned fresh one from Skippy's wardrobe, and smoothed back his dark hair. Then he took a deep breath and raised the brass knocker.

Before he could give an extra tap, the dog started barking. Galen wondered if the beast had breakfasted yet, and if one meat pasty would be enough. The hunched old hag opened the door an inch or two, peering out with red-rimmed eyes. She was wearing the same shapeless black gown and black lace cap whose ends trailed down her shoulders, as if she had a bat perched on her skull. Galen shook himself and pasted a smile on his face. "I have come to call on Miss Montclaire. Would you see that she gets these"—he handed over the flowers and the folded document—"and say that Viscount Woodbridge requests a moment of her time." With his hands free, he could reach into his waistcoat and extract a coin, which disappeared down the front of the black sack.

"I'll say you're persistent, if nothing else. Missy ain't going to listen to a word you say, but I don't mind getting rich meantime if you don't mind wasting the ready. I'll take her your tokens, for all the good it'll do you." She sniffed at the violets, obviously disdaining such a paltry offering. "You can wait in the parlor. I don't allow no gentlemen callers above the first floor."

The parlor was clean and tidy, with signs of wear, but with no signs of a man's presence, no racing forms or snuff-boxes, no misplaced gloves, riding crops, or pipes. Perhaps the place really was a respectable boardinghouse and not the bordello he assumed. None of the furnishings was of high quality or new, and the only picture on the wall was of a poorly executed bowl of fruit. Overall it was a pleasant room, especially with sunshine streaming through the opened curtains, highlighting the pianoforte in the corner. He went over and plinked a few keys, picturing Miss Montclaire in his own music room, singing to him alone. He smiled at the vision and sat down to wait. He could afford to be patient now, for at least his foot was in the door. One hurdle was crossed.

The second hurdle hurtled at him from the doorway, pinning him to the pianoforte bench, drooling on his fresh neckcloth. Picket fence teeth snapped just inches from his nose, daring him to make a move. Galen stopped breathing. "Good doggie," he lied, then gingerly reached into his pocket. The gun? No, he'd try the bribe first, wishing he'd thought to lace it with sleeping powder, or arsenic.

The dog took the meat pasty from his hand, paper and all, and swallowed both. He left the hand, to Galen's relief, then showed his gratitude by swiping at Galen's face with his tongue. The animal collapsed across the viscount's feet with a sigh, and began to snore. Two hurdles leaped. But would the beast get hungry again before Miss Montclaire deigned to make an appearance? Judging from the creature's prominent rib cage, the mutt must always be on the verge of starvation. Afraid to move, Galen looked around for a dish of bonbons or comfits to hold in reserve. There was nothing. Suddenly time seemed to stretch ahead like an endless cord. He drew his pocket watch out, and the dog raised its head to snarl. Where the deuce was the woman, anyway?

Margot was upstairs in bed. Where else should she be at seven o'clock of a morning? Besides, she had a performance this evening and needed as much rest as possible.

"Go away, Ella. It's much too early. Tell Rufus our walk will have to wait."

Ella, her friend and dresser at the theater, pulled the curtains aside, letting in bright sunlight. "The dog can hold his water. I don't know about that swell down in Mrs. McGuirk's parlor."

Margot pulled the covers over her head, hiding her eyes. Then she poked her head out and squinted at Ella. "What swell?"

"That nob what called last night came by again, with that." Ella jerked her head toward a bouquet of violets on the nightstand. "And this." She tossed a thick folded packet onto Margot's pillow. "Deuced libertine couldn't wait for a proper hour to make his improper offer again." She clucked her tongue at the wicked ways of man. "Seems he sweet-talked Mrs. McGuirk into letting him sit in the parlor. Now we'll never be rid of him until you hear the blackguard out."

Margot's curiosity was fully aroused, to think of some Town buck winning over her crotchety landlady. She sat up in bed, letting her night braid hang over her shoulder, as she reached for a pair of spectacles by the bedside. "I suppose I shall have to see what he wants, then."

Ella hissed between crooked teeth. "You know dashed well what the dastard wants. It's what all of them wants."

But Margot had unfolded the thick papers. "It . . . it seems to be a special license, and a wedding ring."

"His lordship's up to some tomfoolery, I don't doubt. Last night you said you didn't even know the toff when I brung you his card."

"I said I'd never spoken to him. I know which box is his at the theater, though. Lord Woodbridge is never rude enough to be talking during my performance, or walking about." Margot was turning the paper over and over, holding it to the light. "It seems official, with all these seals and signatures. And those look like real diamonds around the ring."

"Then the man must be castaway. I told you, he smelled of spirits last night. I misdoubt he ever took to his bed to sleep it off."

"I suppose," Margot agreed. "But I'll have to go talk to him, at any rate, and return these."

"Something else you ought to see." Ella tossed a newssheet onto Margot's bed, folded to an article entitled: *Viscount's Wedding Woes.* Yes, she read, it was the very same viscount whose names were inscribed next to hers on the license, the same gentleman who was sitting in the shabby parlor.

"Oh, dear," Margot murmured, instantly feeling sorry for the poor man. She had a glimmer of his intentions now, and they would never do, of course, but he did deserve a hearing. And breakfast. A man always felt better with a full stomach. "Why don't you bring the gentleman a tray while I get dressed? Perhaps Mrs. McGuirk made scones again today. And be sure to bring a pot of coffee. I don't think tea will suit Lord Woodbridge this morning."

Muttering that what her lamb knew about gentlemen could fit in her thimble, Ella clomped off down the stairs.

As Margot dabbed lukewarm water on her cheeks, she tried to picture the viscount's face. She held only a faint impression of dark hair and broad shoulders. Well, if nothing else, she'd get to chat with a real live lordship, in Mrs. McGuirk's parlor. Margot couldn't help the chuckle that escaped her lips, to think of a top-of-the-trees Corinthian taking tea with her landlady. If he thought to perpetuate any evil designs, Mrs. McGuirk and Ella would set him straight. Or Rufus would. But that special license did seem authentic. . . .

The next hurdle was going to be harder, Galen decided; someone kept raising the bars. The other old woman, not the ancient one, marched into the room, bearing a tray. "Mistress be dressing. She said to feed you betimes."

In truth, Galen could not remember when he'd eaten last. He'd bought the meat pie on the way from Skippy's, before remembering he had a better use for it. Now the scones looked inviting, and the strong coffee smell was making his mouth water. It was a good thing that he drank his coffee black, though, for the scowl on the servant's face would have curdled the cream. Her arms crossed across a boney chest, she was watching him as if he were going to steal the silverware.

Galen turned on his most ingratiating smile. "Thank you, Miss, ah . . . ?"

"That's Mrs. Humber," she said, her raised chin daring him to challenge the existence of any Mr. Humber, the poor sod. "But folks just call me Ella. I'm a costume seamstress at the theater. And I am *mademoiselle's* dresser here."

And watchdog. Galen would wager Ella Humber was more vigilant than the four-legged one, the one who was drooling on his fawn-colored breeches, begging for a scone. The dog could be bribed with food, the landlady with gold. He wondered what it would take to win Ella Humber's approval, and decided to try the truth. "I don't mean her any dishonor, you know."

"Humph. Fine nob like you can't mean anything else. You're up to some rig or row, I swear." She settled in the chair near the window with her sewing basket, obviously intending to stay for the duration.

Galen buttered another scone for the dog. He needed all the allies he could get. He sipped at his coffee and said, "But what if there is no trickery, only a grand opportunity for Miss Montclaire?"

Ella jabbed her needle through the hem she was sewing. "Missy's doing fine on her own."

"Is she?" The viscount let his gaze roam the tiny parlor, from the threadbare carpets to the faded curtains, the earthenware coffee cup that did not match its saucer. His eyes fixed on the still life with blotchy fruit, and he grimaced. Either the fruit was all rotten, or the artist hadn't bothered cleaning his brushes. Even the servants' quarters at Woburton House had more appealing artwork. "I can offer her a better life."

"That's what they all promise. A cozy love nest, servants, a carriage of her own. Two weeks or two months later, a girl finds herself out on the street, with no choice but to find another so-called protector."

That sounded to Galen like the bitter voice of experience. "Yes, unfortunately it often happens that way. I cannot excuse the conduct of some men. But if the woman was married, no one could toss her out. She'd be cared for and respected and protected. Even if the marriage was not a success, she'd have security. Solicitors can have such things written into contracts, with settlements put aside for the future."

Ella glared at him through narrowed eyes. "I don't hold with any contracts and lawyers. Marriage, is it, that you're offering? Humph. I'd need to hear it from the bishop himself, before I'd believe a silver-tongued devil like you."

Galen drank his coffee and smiled. At least she hadn't asked to hear it from God's own lips. The bishop he could manage.

Chapter Four

Whoever said look before you leap could not have meant staring through the keyhole, but that's just what Margot did before entering Mrs. McGuirk's guest parlor. She could get a good peek at his lordship, sitting as he was directly opposite the door, at the pianoforte bench. His shoulders were even broader than she'd recalled, and his hair darker. He needed a shave, too, giving his complexion a somber cast. With the cape thrown over his back he looked like a pirate, or a bird of prey. But his fingers were idly rubbing Ruff's ears, and he was smiling at Ella. No man ever smiled at Ella, but this one did. What a smile it was, too, all flashing white teeth and crinkled eyes and a dimple. No wonder the broadsides called him Galahad.

Viscount Woodbridge's appearance was magnificent, but what was truly overwhelming was his appearing on her front doorstep at all. And the words he was telling Ella! Words like settlements and security and solicitors, words Margot had even stopped dreaming about. No one mentioned marriage in the same sentence as actress, yet here he was, swearing to love, honor, and protect—well, he hadn't mentioned love, but that was all right—in the rooming house parlor, and here she was, holding a license and a wedding ring. Margot had to take her eyes away from the keyhole to look down at the papers in her hand again. Yes, that was her name spelled out, with a space for her real last name, right above his: Galen Collin Spreewell Woodrow.

No gentlemen ever came to her rooms; Margot made sure of that. Accepting a gentleman's *carte blanche* was expected for a female in her position, and it might even have been the answer to some of her pressing problems, but Margot was not interested. She was not tempted to set her feet on the primrose path, not tempted by any of the libertines who pressed flowers and poems and damp kisses into her hands in the Green Room. But, oh, she was tempted now by that piece of paper, whatever it was his lordship had in mind.

While Margot was building air castles, Rufus had gone to the parlor door. His mistress was on the other side, and she was always willing to share her muffins and toast, so he whined. Since Ella was encumbered by her sewing, Viscount Woodbridge got up to let the dog out. He pulled on the handle to open the door, then had to jump back as a slim, golden-haired young female wearing spectacles tumbled at his feet.

First he reached for her hand, to help her up. Then he reached for his quizzing glass. Lud, the chit was even lovelier up close than she appeared from his theater box. She seemed younger, fresher, more innocent, which made her more alluring to him. Now he could almost imagine he wasn't taking a soiled dove as his viscountess. With her wide-eyed stare and embarrassed blushes, Miss Montclaire looked as if she'd never even been kissed.

Usually her hair was coiled into a topknot; now it flowed down her back, held off her face by a cornflower blue ribbon that matched her incredible eyes. Usually she wore stage makeup; now he could see that she had a clear, rose-tinged complexion under the suddenly reddened cheeks, enhanced by a sprinkling of freckles across her nose. Usually he admired a pretty woman as a dispassionate connoisseur of artwork; now he was ready to fall at *her* feet.

Margot stuffed the spectacles into her gown's pocket and tried to will her blushes away. Goodness, such hoydenish behavior would frighten the poor man off before he even met her. Please, please, she begged, don't let him turn his back and walk out. The dream was too sweet not to savor as long as it lasted.

He didn't leave, but guided her to a seat instead. With a glance in Ella's direction, he said, "Miss Montclaire, I am certain you have gathered that I have something of a personal matter to discuss with you."

She could not help her unruly tongue from blurting out: "I don't see how, since we have never met. And I cannot think it proper to—" Ella was already gathering her sewing together to leave.

"I'll take the dog for his walk, then, Miss Margot."

What, they were both going to desert her, along with her wits? Margot folded her hands in her lap, trying to feign a poise she was far from feeling. Goodness, she mentally shook herself. She faced hundreds of strangers every night as she sang; surely this one was not going to discompose her. She'd listen to what he had to say, and later she and Ella could have a good laugh over the antics of the aristocracy.

He was still standing, too tall in the little room. "Won't you please sit down, my lord?"

He went back to the pianoforte bench, then decided it was too far away, so he dragged it toward her chintz-covered chair. Then he brought the breakfast tray to a closer table, saying he regretted causing her to miss her meal. One slice of dry toast remained, and half a scone. The water for tea would be cold by now, besides. "Dash it, I am sorry." He looked around, as if seeking the bellpull to make a legion of servants appear with a fresh tray. There was, of course, no bellpull, and no servants. The viscount flushed and cleared his throat.

He was nervous, Margot realized. Amazingly enough, this top-drawer gentleman was ill at ease over his errand. As well he should be, she supposed, if he was trying to invent some faradiddle to dupe an innocent female into taking part in an immoral, illegal, or impossible scheme. Still, her good manners demanded she make her guest comfortable, so she said she'd already had chocolate and a roll upstairs. "Please, be seated. I admit to a raging curiosity, my lord."

The viscount sat on the bench, crossed his legs, then uncrossed them. Finally he leaned forward, swallowed, and managed to declare, "I should very much like to marry you, Miss Montclaire."

Margot tapped the papers in her lap. "So I gathered. But why?"

Dash it, the minx was making this harder than it had to be, Galen thought. He'd offered; she ought to accept. But she was looking at him expectantly, every inch the polite hostess. She might have been asking why he preferred coffee to tea, instead of why he was sitting in her parlor, making a total ass of himself. And he was too busy listening to her slightly husky voice, with its slight French accent, to pay attention. Why did he want to marry her? Galen dredged the shoals of his wits for an answer: "Because I find myself in need of a bride. The one I had seems to have had a change of heart."

"Yes, I read about that. My sympathies, Lord Woodbridge."

"No, no. That was for the best. No regrets, I assure you. Lucky escape and all that. But it was a bit of an embarrassment," he vastly understated.

"And you thought to marry someone else, to divert the gossip's attention?"

"Precisely." He was relieved to find her so astute.

"But why me? You do not know me, or if we would suit."

Galen was on firmer ground now. "But I do know a great deal about you, Miss Montclaire. Your beauty and talent are obvious." He watched as she lowered her eyes at the compliment, charmed at her modesty. "And all of my friends and acquaintances constantly sing your praises, saying you are well-spoken and refined, more intelligent than most of them."

She smiled. "That is not hard, my lord."

"Ah, met Skippy Skidmore, have you? He said he'd won

an introduction, for all the good it did him. And that's another factor in your favor—your virtue. You never go home with any of those who seek your companionship, never let any of the mooncalves or the moneyed lords call on you here. You even refused to see me last evening."

She looked down again. "You have too high an opinion of your own worth, I think, my lord."

"Not if you were a woman who earned her living pleasing men. Everyone knows I am warm in the pockets. No, if you were looking for a lover, you would have at least met with me."

If she were looking for a lover, Margot thought, she'd drag this nonpareil off to her bedchamber before the cat could lick its ear. But she was not seeking a lover, a patron, a protector. "Fie," she said, "for all you know I could already have a gentleman hidden away in my dressing room this very moment."

He nodded. "You could have. But if you are not virtuous, at least you are discreet, which is another advantage. Do you?"

"Do I what?"

"Have a lover stashed away somewhere? In the country, if not upstairs? Out of Town or with the Army, perhaps?"

Her blush told him enough, but she replied, "That is none of your concern, my lord."

"It would be, if we married. Fidelity is one of the few things I would require of you. I could not bear to be cuckolded again."

Margot raised her chin. "You may be sure I would honor my wedding vows, if I ever gave them. How do you know I am not already married?"

"Because no decent man would keep his beautiful wife in such squalor, and you are too downy to wed a scoundrel."

"Thank you, I think. What are the other requirements for this hypothetical bride of yours?"

At least she was interested, Galen thought in relief. "Not many. I do not expect a dowry, naturally, for I have no need of one." And he still had Florrie's. "I would not expect you to give up your career, if that is a worry."

Margot hated her career, hated having to perform for all those cold-eyed strangers, hated being considered fair prey by the rakes and roués. She might have to sing for her supper, but that did not mean she was a strumpet. His lordship seemed to appreciate that fact, treating her like a lady instead of a ladybird. "What else?"

He brushed a dog hair off his superfine sleeve. "I would not demand my husbandly rights, for, oh, six months or so. That way if we decide we cannot suit, I am sure a large enough donation to the church will convince the bishop that Skippy filled out the papers incorrectly, and the marriage can be annulled."

Margot's brow knit in concentration. No consummation of the marriage for six months? But all noblemen were expected to provide heirs. That was the only reason most of them bothered to get married at all. Then her forehead cleared as she reached comprehension. "Ah, in six months you would be sure I am not carrying another man's child to inherit your title."

He nodded. "You see, we *do* understand each other. You have everything to gain by such an arrangement, my dear." He held up his fingers to count off the advantages, in case she had not tallied them for herself. "Wealth, with widow's benefits and a generous allowance written into the marriage settlements. A title that will grant you respectability and open doors now shut to you, if you wish to enter. You could be a duchess someday, a day long in the future, God willing. Numerous houses and properties, so you can have an independent existence if you'd rather. Children, I hope. And a grateful husband, of course."

A home, children, respectability, and security, Margot mused. What more could a woman ask? Unfortunately they came with the last, the husband. Margot held up her own five-fingered reasoning. "Husbands have been known to keep mistresses, gamble away their fortunes, demand total obedience, and drink in excess." She stared right into his brown, bloodshot eyes as her smallest finger joined the others. "And beat their wives."

Galen took a deep breath. "Yesterday was an exception. Perhaps I could be forgiven for overindulging since it was, after all, my wedding day. As for your other concerns, you are right to be cautious. First, I have never wagered more than I can afford, and a great deal of my fortune is entailed besides, not mine to gamble away. Second, I want a wife, a companion, not a servant to do my bidding and agree with my every opinion. Third, I, too, take the marriage vows seriously, but if we find we cannot rub along together, I would never embarrass my lady wife with my other interests."

"Ah, discretion again?"

"Quite. As to your last worry, I would demand satisfaction from any man who dared suggest that I might hurt one who is weaker than I, one whom, moreover, I have sworn to protect."

Galahad indeed, Margot thought, somehow believing in this man's integrity. He might be attics-to-let, making her this insane proposal, but at least they were honorable attics. "I apologize if I have given offense."

"No, I am glad to have things open between us. You have to know what you are getting into, of course."

Margot did not need Lord Woodbridge to tell her what she would be getting out of: this house, this neighborhood, a hand-to-mouth existence fraught with indignities and insults, a future as bleak as Mrs. McGuirk's black dresses. "Very well, the advantages to me are considerable. But, my lord, I need to ask where is the benefit to you? You could have any lady of the *ton* you wish, attractive young women with fortunes and titles and sterling reputations, trained from birth to take their place in your social circles. Marrying an actress can bring you only scandal."

"Yes," he said with a boyish grin, "a wondrous, magnificent scandal. The biggest this year. Even more scandalous than Lady Carew and her husband's valet. That's the point, my dear."

"You'd marry me to thumb your nose at the gossips, to spite your former fiancée?"

"Tomorrow. No, it's already tomorrow. I would wed you this morning, Miss Montclaire, if you would do me the honor of accepting my hand."

The notion was preposterous, but a soft, warm what-if was wriggling its way into Margot's thoughts. She could do this, she told herself, marry a charming Bedlamite for his money and position. She'd done more outrageous things in her life, for her brother's sake.

Chapter Five

Whoever asked, am I my brother's keeper? should have asked Margot Montclaire Penrose first. Now the answer to her prayers for Ansel just might be sitting on the rickety pianoforte bench, if Lord Woodbridge was willing to take on this additional responsibility. The viscount was ready to wed a socially unwelcome bride, but Margot could not marry anyone not willing to welcome her brother. For an instant she thought of accepting his lordship's lunatic offer, explaining about Ansel later and relying on Lord Woodbridge's code of honor, but she had her own scruples. They were being honest, weren't they? Even if the viscount was dicked in the nob, he deserved to know what else he was getting along with a wife. Margot needed to know that he would shoulder this weighty burden she'd been carrying.

Convinced that he was serious about wedding her—the license alone must have cost him a fortune—Margot also decided that it was not fair to let his lordship go on thinking she was some totally ineligible female. "What if this marriage would not be such a total misalliance, my lord?" she finally asked.

Galen had been giving Mademoiselle Margot time to decide, watching her weigh all the factors, certain that any rational female—if such a creature existed—would come to the correct conclusion. Now he was confused. "I don't understand. The last I knew, young women who sing at Drury Lane are rarely granted vouchers for Almack's."

Margot bobbed her head in acknowledgment of his polite phrasing of her circumstances. "Especially those whose mothers were unwed French opera singers who ran off to Italy to give birth." That was the common assumption, as they both well knew. Trading on her mother's famous name had been necessary for Margot to gain an audition, so she had never corrected the sordid story. "But what if my mother was legally married, and she and my father left England to escape the narrow-mindedness of my father's family? And what if that family held an old and honorable title, a barony that eventually passed to my papa? Would I still be unacceptable enough to suit your purposes if I were Margot Montclaire Penrose, daughter of Baron Penrose of Rossington, Sussex?"

"Intriguingly, my dear, like tossing more delicious crumbs to the rumor mills. We'll have an easier go of getting you invited to the drawing rooms of the highest sticklers, where you would not want to go anyway, trust me. But you'd still be the Magnificent Margot of Drury Lane, the most sought-after female in Town, only now you'd have a fascinating background to go with your fame. May I ask what happened to your baron-father?"

"He died shortly after returning to England to claim his inheritance. My mother had succumbed to a congestion of the lungs some years before."

"I am sorry. But what happened after your father's death that left you penniless, taking to the boards to support yourself? Did the title revert to some vile distant relative who stole your dowry? My own heir presumptive is no great shakes, but at least I trust him to look after my sister."

"No, my brother Ansel inherited. He is only eleven now, though, and . . . sickly. My father's younger brother was appointed guardian. He is not a kind man." Margot was twisting at the blue ribbon that tied the high waist of her muslin gown. These were hard words to say. "I fear Uncle Manfred is an ambitious man, moreover, who does not have my brother's best interests at heart. If Ansel should not survive to his majority . . ."

"Your uncle would inherit," Galen finished for her. "So

you have to worry that the boy is not getting the proper care and treatment, correct? Would the lad not have done better under your supervision?"

"Perhaps, if I could have afforded specialists and consulting physicians. But my uncle gave me no choice except to leave. Uncle Manfred decided I should marry his neighbor, a pox-ridden old miser who had buried three wives before. Uncle Manfred owed him money, you see, and Lord Grinsted was willing to forgive the debt, for my hand."

Galen leaped to his feet. "Grinsted? That loose screw?" The very idea of that filthy old man touching his wife—he was already thinking of Miss Montclaire, no, Miss Penrose as his wife—was an abomination.

"Uncle said I could marry him or leave. I think he knew I would leave, which was all he wanted. I could not take Ansel, of course, for I had no way to support him, nor the legal right to his wardship. I could have gone for a governess, I suppose, keeping my reputation, since I am fluent in three languages and know music and the globes and some mathematics, but that would have availed Ansel nothing. By singing, I can earn enough to send money back to the Penrose Hall housekeeper, to keep me informed, to buy whatever my brother needs that Uncle Manfred refuses to provide. I was hoping to earn enough to purchase a cottage somewhere, so that I could eventually have Ansel with me if I could steal him away from my uncle."

Galen bent and took both her hands in his, prying the mangled ribbon out of her fingers. "Miss Penrose, Margot, listen to me. If we marry, your brother becomes my brother. He will never want for anything."

Margot had to reclaim her hands so she could wipe her eyes. Galen offered his handkerchief and waited while she blew her nose. "Uncle will not give him up easily. He threatened to send poor Ansel away if I interfered."

"I promise you, the boy will be at your side within the week, with the best physicians in London in attendance, and your uncle be damned. I doubt he'd want to face me at twenty paces otherwise."

"You would do that, for me?"

She looked up at him through blue eyes glistening with tears, like a spring day after a rain shower. Galen would have done anything for her at that moment, adopted seventy sickly waifs, despatched a hundred heinous uncles. The extent of his newfound dedication shocked even himself. Hell, he was supposed to be offering the chit a bargain, not his life's blood. To lighten the tenor of the conversation, he quipped, "Of course you'll be getting my sister in return. You're definitely getting the worst of the deal."

"There's more."

"What, an evil uncle and a maltreated heir and a selfless sister aren't enough? Are you sure you are not writing for the Minerva Press?"

"I only wish I were making this up. Uncle Manfred swears he will have Ansel declared unfit to hold the title."

This was no laughing matter. Galen could have supposed her maunderings the imagination of a doting sister wanting to coddle the boy, although his own sister had never shown anything resembling such tender feelings. But to steal the lad's heritage? And just what was wrong with the little baron that his uncle could declare him incompetent, as Prinny kept trying to label his poor, mad father? "Sickly" could mean a great many things. "Is he fit?"

"What, to take his place in Parliament? To oversee his estate? Of course not. Ansel is eleven years old, my lord, a little boy who has lost both his parents and now his sister. He is naturally upset, finding himself at the mercy of a bully. But he is bright and well-mannered. He can converse in Italian as well as English, and he is remarkably talented." Margot stood and moved toward the fruit painting. "That is one of his works."

"It is certainly remarkable," was the only comment Galen felt able to make, praying she did not insist on hanging the monstrosity in his town house. Gads, if her taste was so poor, perhaps he should reconsider his offer after all. Or insist she wear her spectacles.

She touched the painting fondly. "He was eight years old at the time, and the drawing master said he showed great promise. Uncle dismissed the man, of course, saying such skills were not manly. He also put a stop to Ansel's music lessons, although my brother was already proficient at the violin, the pianoforte, and voice. Then he turned off the tutor and the nanny, sending Ansel to the vicar for Latin lessons, before the dastard decided my brother was too feeble to attend classes."

Galen stood next to her, his eyes averted from the rotten fruit. Miss Penrose was a much more pleasing sight anyway. He thought he would never get tired of looking at her, which, he also thought, was an excellent prospect in a prospective bridegroom. It was all he could do to keep his hands at his sides, instead of touching the long gold hair that trailed down her back in shining waves. He ached to see if those curls were as soft as they looked, if her curves were as generous, her skin as silky as they appeared. He had not expected to want the woman as a woman, only as a wife. Now he wanted it all. If straightening out one little boy's life was what it took to make this glorious female his, Galen was ready to give the nipper Latin lessons himself. Hell, he might even try teaching him to draw.

"My dear," he said now, "you can stop worrying over your brother. I will petition the courts to be named one of his trustees if I have to. I will kidnap him from your uncle if I have to. I will do whatever it takes to see him happy and healthy. All you have to do is say yes."

"I am tempted, my lord. So tempted you will never know. But I fear you would regret such a hasty decision. You might relish the talk now, but the disgrace of your marrying an actress will linger. Think of your family. I would hate to be the cause of a rift between you, the way my parents' marriage divided my father's kin. Or see you ostracized from your friends."

"Never fear, my father will accept you. If you give him a grandson, so he does not have to worry about Cousin Harold inheriting, he will adore you. And he married his neighbor's governess, so cannot preach propriety at this late date, especially after the behavior of his choice of a bride for me. His own brother was shot by a jealous husband, and one of his uncles was hung as a highwayman. That's where the viscountcy came from. Why, there have been so many scandals in my family, His Grace will never notice another. My relatives have committed every disgrace imaginable except treason and the crime without a name, although I fear Harold is working on that one." At her look of confusion, he added, "Never mind. No one will object to your joining the family. And my friends will all be horrified, but only that I managed to snabble you out from under their eyes. Anyone who is not happy for us, who cannot celebrate our marriage or welcome us to his home, was never much of a friend to start with and will not be missed. But my father is a duke, Margot. No one is going to offend him by slighting his daughter-in-law. I apologize for the familiarity, but calling you Miss Penrose or Mademoiselle Montclaire seems absurd under the circumstances if we are about to wed. And I am Galen."

"Very well, Galen. But why don't we both think about it, spend some time getting to know each other, and then decide? I am contracted for two more weeks of performances anyway, and could not let the cast down by disappearing."

"So we shall have our honeymoon in London before traveling to my father at Three Woods in Woburton. You see, I am not a difficult man to please."

"You are everything kind, but I fear that tomorrow, with a clearer head, you will see the obstacles better. I might never be accepted in your circles, no matter what you think. My uncle will fight you for Ansel's guardianship. We might find we have nothing to say to each other."

"Now you are acting like a peagoose, my dear. I am not drunk, and I will not regret our marriage. I will not stay in London without you, however. I am sorry, but if you won't have me, I'll be sailing for Jamaica on the next ship. I'd rather be leaning over the rail than listening to all the laughter at my expense." He took her hand in his and brought it to his lips. "Be brave, my dear Margot, say yes. That is all you need ever say to please me."

"I can bring Ruff?"

"Ruff?"

"My dog. His name is Rufus, for his color, but I call him Ruff, so he can say his own name."

"If you wished the beast to speak his name, ma'am, you should have named him Grr. Whyever would you keep such a mean, mangy creature?"

"Because he loves me, and protects me. And *I* think he is beautiful."

"Very well, I will hire Ruff a cook of his own, and buy him a dozen pairs of leather gloves."

"And my dresser? Ella has fallen on hard times since her husband was arrested, for a theft he did not commit."

"The dragon Ella?" He shuddered, but nodded. "And I suppose you expect me to see him exonerated and brought home?"

Margot simply smiled.

It was enough. "Very well. You can bring anyone and anything. Except I think you should leave the fruit bowl for Mrs. McGuirk. Ansel shall paint us another."

"Then . . . then yes, my lord . . . Galen. Yes, I would be honored to accept your wonderful, generous offer."

"You have made me the happiest of men, my dear."

"No, but I promise to try!"

With that, she threw herself into his arms, where she fit very snugly indeed. Galen pressed a kiss onto her forehead, sealing their bargain, before setting her aside. "As delightful as this getting better acquainted may be, we have a great deal to do, sweetings. I shall give you two hours to pack and change your gown, although this one is delightful, but I know how females set great store by such things. I'll send a baggage cart for your things, along with a crew of footmen

to help. Meanwhile I shall shave and see my solicitor to
draw up settlements for you, and write the notices to be sent
to the newspapers. And send a note to make sure Skippy and
the bishop are ready for us. Better make that three hours before I get back with my carriage."

Three hours to prepare for her wedding? Margot had to
laugh. Some girls took an entire year to purchase their
trousseaus and plan their wedding breakfasts. But she had
few enough belongings to pack, and few enough gowns to
choose from. Besides, given more time she might find more
reasons to change her mind . . . or fall into a mindless panic.
"Here," she said, handing him the diamond-strewn ring and
the license, "you better take these with you."

Galen paused in his mental list-making: fetching a bouquet, ordering champagne iced, seeing that the rooms ad-
joining his were aired and ready to accept a new mistress.
"The ring? Why?"

"So you can present them at the church, of course."

"Of course." She was not reneging already. Relieved, he
slipped the ring and the document into his pocket, adding
them to the roster of details to be remembered. Then he
pried off his own gold signet ring, with the three trees
carved into its onyx face, and pressed that one into her palm.
He folded her fingers over the ring, then kissed them. "You
hold onto the family heirloom, Lady Woodbridge-to-be, so
you know I'll be coming back."

Chapter Six

Whoever was about to say marry in haste, repent at—never got the chance to finish.

The baggage wagon and three sturdy footmen arrived in less than an hour. Ella put them to work hauling trunks and boxes, and hot water for *mademoiselle's* bath. Mrs. McGuirk had them turning carpets while they waited for further instructions, and waited for a glimpse of their new mistress. If any of the viscount's men thought to comment on the bride's lowly dwelling and meager possessions, such notions were instantly quelled by Ella's scowls and Ruff's growls.

Lord Woodbridge himself arrived thirty minutes early, after having his coachman drive around the block a few times. He wanted to come back two hours early, to make sure Margot had not changed her mind. Devil take it, he should never have left the woman alone. Permitting a female time to think was like giving a toad a road map. He should have carried her off, married her in all his dirt and disarray, and worried about her trappings and tender feelings later, when the deed was done and she could not withdraw her consent. But a girl was entitled to some consideration on her wedding day. Since this was the only wedding Galen hoped Margot would ever have, he'd given her the extra few minutes. Of course, if she did not come down soon, he'd go scoop her out of her bath or whatever, and the footmen and frowning maids could go hang.

Luckily for what remained of his lordship's fraying nerves, Margot shortly descended the narrow stairwell, nodding to the bows of the waiting servants and smiling brightly at her betrothed. He was looking every inch the wealthy aristocrat, confident and commanding in his perfectly tailored blue superfine and the buff pantaloons that hugged his well-formed, well-exercised body. His hair was neatly arranged, still damp from his bath, and without the shadow of a beard, he was like a prince from a fairy tale, except for a very slightly crooked nose. Heavens, he ought to be wedding a princess, she thought, not a needy Nichol Road ragamuffin. Perhaps he was coming early to tell her he'd reconsidered. Perhaps his friends had made him see reason, or threatened to commit him to an asylum. Perhaps she was marrying a madman! Oh, dear. Margot forced herself to smile. She had never let the vast audience of Drury Lane know she was quaking in her slippers, and she would not show the viscount how terrified she was now. With her head held high, crowned with her hair twisted into a golden braid encircled by a wreath of silk roses, Margot held out her hand to Galen, praying he would not notice the trembling.

She hadn't run off with one of his footmen, was all Galen could think, as he brought her gloved hand toward his mouth. She was going to go through with the marriage! Lud, his hand was shaking in relief. He hoped she wouldn't notice, this golden goddess in her ivory gown. He'd double Ella's salary, if she'd created such a masterpiece to complement his bride's slim elegance. This must be one of the Magnificent Margot's theater costumes, he realized, but the pearls around her neck looked real.

"My mother's," she whispered, touching the strand when she noticed his glance. Then she cleared her throat and spoke louder. "I sold everything else, but I was holding onto them for an emergency."

He squeezed her hand and presented a bouquet of orange blossoms. "And now you shall never have to part with such a precious reminder of your parent. Are you ready, my dear?"

Margot was as ready as she would ever be. She let him lead her to his waiting carriage, to another life.

Galen Woodrow, Viscount Woodbridge, was celebrating his nuptials at St. George's after all. This time, however, the ceremony was taking place in a narrow antechamber, more an office than a chapel. Skippy, the Reverend Mr. Skidmore, by George, had managed to waylay a floral tribute destined for the funeral being conducted later on in the actual church. The fact that the funeral was for one of the noble patrons of Epsom Downs, and the tribute was in the form of a horseshoe, had not fazed Skippy for an instant. He turned the horseshoe so the opening faced upward, to keep the luck in, he whispered to Galen. So what if such superstitions had no place in the church? So what if the flowers were now all wilting with their stems out of water? So what if Skippy was sneezing? He'd never been good out in the country, either. He'd done what he could to make his friend's marriage less of a skimble-skamble affair, and what was what mattered. Galen was about to thank him, when Skippy ruined all of his good intentions by dropping to one knee and proposing to the bride.

"You don't want to marry Woodbridge, you know. Just because he has money and a title and looks, he's really not at all the thing. Why, he cares more about his paintings and his horses than you'll like. His house is a veritable museum."

"Get up, you nodcock," Galen hissed, hauling on Skippy's arm, "before I knock you down altogether. The lady is bespoken. And go fetch the bishop. I promised Miss Penrose's maid."

"Who is Miss Penrose? If you ain't getting hitched to Miss Montclaire, then she is still available." He started to drop to his knees once more, but Galen had not let go of his arm, which he now twisted behind the gudgeon's back.

"Montclaire is the lady's stage name. Her legal name, for as long as it takes you to fetch the bishop, is Margot Mont-

claire Penrose, daughter of the late Baron Penrose of Rossington, Sussex. I already entered it on the license."

"She's well-born, besides a raging beauty?" Skippy's wa-
tery eyes grew wider. "You lucky dog."

"No, the lucky dog is in the carriage with a steak bone.
Now shut your mouth. You look like a carp the cat dragged
out of the ornamental pool."

Ella did not believe the bishop was anything but an actor,
paid by the villainous viscount to hoodwink her poor mistress. Swells didn't marry opera singers, not in this life. "My
Eminence, my arse."

"Hush, Ella, look at his ring. He really is the bishop. I saw
him once in the queen's box."

The bishop was beginning the service despite the mutter-
ings, since Lord Asplenall's funeral was due to begin
shortly. He had decided to conduct this ceremony himself,
considering that such a shocking, sudden mismatch needed
more heavenly intercession than his gambling-mad young
assistant could provide. If Skidmore had more than a nodding acquaintance with the Almighty, he'd be astounded.
For sure the clunch must have skipped every divinity course
at university. Nevertheless, the bishop trotted out every
blessing and every lesson on marital bliss he could recall in
a hurry, before he had to send Lord Asplenall to the Great
Racecourse in the Sky.

While the bishop droned on, Skippy, standing next to
Galen as his best man, whispered, "How did you convince
her? She never even let a fellow escort her home before."

Galen was trying to appear attentive to whatever the old
windbag was nattering about. Fidelity, obedience—Yes, yes,
they had already covered those issues. He whispered back to
Skippy, "Charm, that's the ticket." Charm and a fortune and
influence, he added to himself, and swearing away his honor
to defend a child who might prove indefensible. But he
would not regret his choice.

Margot was listening to every word the bishop spoke.
Well, maybe every other word, between stealing glances at

her handsome fiancé. She swallowed a nervous giggle. Theirs had to be the shortest engagement in history. Not even a day. Was it just this morning that he had come with his outrageous proposal, looking sad and pleading? Now he was looking every inch the bored gentleman of fashion, not even listening to his own marriage rites. What had she done?

She'd found a way to safeguard her brother, that's what. And she would not regret it. Why would she, when she could never have picked a more perfect *parti* if she'd been shopping the marriage mart at Almack's? And she vowed to be the best wife the viscount could every have, despite disagreeing with some of the bishop's pronouncements as to a wife's duties. Not even Margot could be a worse wife than the fickle female who'd taken flight. That woman had cared so little for his lordship that she would trample on his pride, on her way to join another.

Of course, when it came time to make her actual vows, Margot found her mouth so dry and her tongue so numbed with nerves, she could barely pronounce the words.

"That's all right," Galen said. "She's just saving her voice for her appearance at the theater tonight."

At the end of the ceremony, when the bishop declared, "You may now kiss the bride," his raised eyebrows seemed to imply that Galen already had, repeatedly. So the viscount placed a chaste kiss on Margot's lips, as a mark of respect. His inclinations were screaming otherwise, but he would let no one treat his lady like a light-skirt, not even himself.

Then the bishop left and Skippy produced a bottle of wine for a toast that was almost as long as the bishop's service. Blushing at all the praise he was heaping on her, Margot tried to thank the reverend.

"Oh, no. You have to call me Skippy, ma'am. Skip the formalities, don't you know. Everyone does."

"Thank you, ah, Skippy. And you may call me Margot, but not for a week or so, if you do not mind. For right now I think I need to get used to being addressed as Lady Woodbridge."

Skippy tipped his glass back again. "Well spoken, my lady. Deuces, but you'll make a grand duchess some day. Woodbridge couldn't have found himself a better 'un, and I'll challenge anyone who says otherwise! Couldn't be happier, ma'am. Unless, of course, you'd married me instead."

Then Skippy couldn't be more eager to head to White's to spread the news and collect his winnings. Of course no one there believed a word he said, not Skip-brain Skidmore.

Lord and Lady Woodbridge took the carriage back to Woburton House, Grosvenor Square. Since coming to London, Margot had barely glimpsed the stately homes of the upper classes. Now she was to live in one of them, and one of the grandest at that. Before she could begin to wonder how many times Mrs. McGuirk's little house would fit into this imposing edifice, the front doors were thrown open, and a bewigged butler was bowing her inside with enough formality for visiting royalty.

"This is Fenning, my dear. You'll get used to him," was all Galen said.

In the massive hall, scores of menservants in their navy and gold livery and maids in their navy uniforms with crisp white caps and aprons were waiting to welcome Margot to her new home. She would have faltered on the doorstep, but for Galen at her side.

"Don't worry, my dear, I understand they are all thrilled to have a new mistress." He did not add that they were especially thrilled their new viscountess was not to be Lady Floria Cleary. He'd just learned from his valet, Clegg, this morning, over deliberations on the correct attire for an impromptu wedding, how much the staff had been dreading Florrie's ascendancy. She was a demanding enough guest the few times they'd entertained her, a pretty enough gel with a grande dame's hauteur. No one would have dared criticize her to their employer, of course, no more than they would show his new bride any disrespect. "They will adore you." He was not sure about the dog, hearing shrieks from the kitchen regions.

Clutching her bouquet in one hand and Galen's arm in her other, Margot made her way down the line of servants as Fenning intoned each name and position. She tried to match names to faces, but gave up midway. When the butler was done and bowing to her again—Heavens, the man would get a permanent crick in his neck if he kept this up—she thanked them all for their welcome and begged them to forgive her if she could not recall their identities at first. "My head is still too full of his lordship's string of names." Even Fenning smiled at her, which made her feel better than when she'd passed her first audition at Drury Lane.

"Tea is served in the Crimson Room, milady. We were not certain if you wished to dine before the theater or later."

Fenning made it sound as though she were attending the playhouse as Lord Woodbridge's guest. She would not let him pretend such a thing for the staff, even if the truth offended his sense of dignity. "Oh, after. I could never face an audience on a full stomach. Where would the butterflies go?"

She could not tell if she had lost the high-stickler's regard as he bowed again and left them, his back as rigid as a lamp pole. Galen patted her arm as he led her down the hall. "Don't worry. Old Fenning disapproves of me, too. But he'll come around. I'll send him to the theater one night so he can see what a gift you have, to be shared. I cannot help noticing, however, that you do not seem to enjoy performing in public. If your nerves are overset at facing the theater audience, you do not have to do it. I can pay off your contract, you know."

"What, because I suffer foolish stage fright? No, a replacement is too hard to find at such short notice. Besides, how could we make that big splash in society's fishpond if I do not perform?"

"I am thinking that you'd cause enough of a ripple if we drove in the park. No one could conceive that I'd be wearing the willow for Florrie, not when I have you on my arm. The newspaper announcements are enough, though, so you do not have to put yourself on display." Suddenly the idea of all the other men in London ogling his bride was not as attractive. "But the choice is yours, of course."

"I sing." Margot had left his side to examine the paintings that filled the niches between the crimson draperies of the vast drawing room. She'd seen the artwork of Italy, of course, and visited the Royal Academy in London once, where the pictures were so badly displayed that she could not see the half of them. But this was a veritable treasure trove of masterpieces—Italian, French, Flemish, like a huge illustrated book of great artworks. Skippy had been right, Galen's house was like a museum, only better. Now she could admire the paintings whenever she wished, with her spectacles on. "My brother will be thrilled."

He nodded, studying her as she walked around the room, delighted that she seemed to admire and appreciate his collection. "We'll start with the solicitors tomorrow about changing his guardianship. I'd like to have the law on my side before I confront your uncle, but I will not leave the boy with him either way."

"I have every confidence you will do what is best for Ansel." She was too rapt in the artwork to notice that Galen had poured tea and filled a plate of elegant cakes and tarts for her. She nibbled at what he put in her hand as she moved around the parlor, asking about this artist, that school. He couldn't wait to show her the portrait gallery and the paintings in the rest of the house. Unfortunately, she would not be viewing the Vermeer in his bedroom any time soon.

"We'd better save the rest of the collection for another day, my dear, if you are determined to perform tonight. I am sure you need some rest after this eventful day. Meantime, I will try to decide which of our own artists I should approach about painting your portrait to join the other Viscountesses Woodbridge." He thought he just might commission a few, for he doubted he'd ever get tired of looking at his beautiful new wife. Hell, he might even try painting her himself.

Chapter Seven

Whoever said that all the world's a stage would have been particularly proud of the cast that evening.

Margot entered the theater by the stage door late that afternoon on the arm of her new husband, followed by two sturdy footmen who were to stand guard outside her dressing room. This earned her dark looks from the male actors, who felt she'd sold her favors to the highest bidder after summarily scorning their offers of a free but honest tumble. Half the female members of the cast snickered, that Miss Prunes and Prisms was no better than she ought to be, and no better than the rest of them after all. The other half were too busy trying to attract his lordship's notice. He, however, glowered at them all and announced the marriage. Ella swore she'd seen it with her own eyes, and had a piece of stationery with the bishop's own letterhead to prove it.

Suddenly, everyone remembered what a lady their Margot had always been. They knew all along that she was fated for a gentler life than treading the boards. And if she could better herself to such a degree, their happy shouts and applause seemed to say, then so could they. Someone found a bottle of champagne, and the lead actress, Mrs. Martin, was so relieved that the popular songstress would be leaving in two weeks, she sent out for a cake.

The theater manager was as obsequious as an underbutler. Not only was Ryder leery of incurring such a well-connected and well-muscled nob's displeasure, but having a viscountess as a warbler could only help ticket sales. The pit was already starting to fill on rumors from the gentlemen's clubs alone. The mingle-mangle marriage was sure to be the most talked of event in Town, and the world would want to catch a glimpse of Woodbridge's second bride in two days.

Finally, everyone recalled that they still had to don costumes and makeup for the evening's performance. The show would go on, even if the audience only wanted to see Margot. She went off to change, escorted by Ella and the two footmen, and his lordship went off to gloat. His whiskey-risen idea was working even better than he'd planned, and his hastily chosen replacement bride was proving delightful, as nice as she was notorious. The only worry Galen had, as he returned to his house to change to formal evening wear, was how he was to survive two weeks of letting every loose screw in London ogle his wife. Perhaps he could convince her to cut the engagement short. But no, he had promised not to interfere with her career. He'd also promised to leave her untouched for six months, damn it. Surviving that could be deuced harder.

Margot's function was to entertain the audience during the intermission between the second and third acts. Acrobats and jugglers had the other intervals, and a chorus sang somewhat bawdy lyrics between the drama and the farce. They were all supposed to captivate the theatergoers enough that they would not grow impatient while the stagehands and cast changed scenery and costumes. The wealthy box-holders took the intermissions as an opportunity to visit back and forth, promenade in the halls, or send for refreshments. They were there less to see the play anyway, and more to be seen in their silks and satins and sparkling jewels. The patrons in the pit, however, had been known to grow rowdy when they were bored, hard to control once the actors had retaken the stage.

Not tonight. No one left their seats, not the Quality in the tiers, not the choice spirits in the cheap seats. Every pair of opera glasses was trained on the stage, every tongue was whispering the question of the night: Was it true? The Duke

of Woburton's box was dark, as was Lord Cleary's, not unexpected for two families suffering such a disgrace as a publicly misfired marriage. But if the viscount had fled, where
were all the rumors coming from? And could he actually
have committed such a shocking, stunning, shameful sin of
marrying a common singer?

Well, she was not precisely common, they conceded after
Margot stepped from behind the curtain. Those who were
seeing her for the first time—or paying attention to her for
the first time—admitted she was more than passably pretty.
And she was dressed in the first stare of fashion, showing
less bosom than many of the *beau monde*'s beauties. That
bright gold of her hair could not be natural, some of those
same belles complained to one another. And surely she wore
cosmetics, the coquette. Their own judicious use of the
hare's foot could not be compared. If a few of them pinched
their cheeks to add a touch more color to their complexions,
or bit their lips to emulate Mademoiselle Margot's rosy
glow, no one noticed. The boxes were too dark, for one, and
their escorts were too busy gazing worshipfully at the stage,
for another.

Then Margot started to sing. She sent a regal nod to her
accompanist in the orchestra, then took a deep breath and
began with a popular country ballad. The disgruntled females could find nothing outstanding in her voice, surely no
cause for their male companions to be hanging on every
note as if it were the Heavenly Choir. The women detected
the slight French accent, but they could not hear the somewhat throaty, yearning tones, as Margot sang of a lost love
gone to war. The men could. They were ready to console her.

Galen frowned, alone in the back of the family's box.
Why, she might have been inviting those blackguards to her
bed, with that sultry voice. He'd said she could keep
singing, not keep seducing every poor sod in Town. They
applauded madly when she was done.

Her next piece was an Italian aria. Her voice was not quite
of operatic quality, but it carried to the far reaches of the

vast hall. Most of the audience could not understand the words, but they knew enough that the heroine of the song was dying, deceived and betrayed by her lover. She always was. Even those who could not pronounce the King's English, much less a word of Italian, were soon dabbing at their eyes. The *grande dames* in their diamonds nodded their approval, wishing their own progeny could acquit themselves half so well when called on to entertain at those hideous musicales. They'd be hiring new music instructors in the morning.

The applause was louder, nearly covering the crash of a fallen backdrop and the curses of the stagehands. Such a distraction might have unnerved a lesser performer, but the thunderous acclamation from the audience seemed to have given Margot confidence and cured her stage fright, at least for this evening. She joked with the bucks and beaux sitting close to the stage about the considerate cabbage-heads, for waiting until she had finished the piece.

Then, when everything was almost quiet again both on stage and in the audience, Margot said, "My friends, I have an announcement to make."

Not even the orange girls shouted their wares into the silence that followed. Galen sat forward, although still in the shadows. He did not like having no idea what the female was going to say; they had not discussed any public statement. She was supposed to look beautiful, making him the envy of every man in the hall, and she was supposed to sing like a nightingale, that was all. She was not supposed to improvise on his script.

"*À regret,*" she was saying, the French accent that was part of her stage role more pronounced, though Galen knew from their talk this afternoon that she'd been educated in Italy by English governesses. "With regrets, I am announcing my retirement from the stage in two weeks. You have been so kind, and I will miss my friends in the cast, but this will be my last engagement."

Boos and catcalls rose from the pit, and feet started stomping in protest. Margot held up her hand for quiet. "No, no," she insisted, "you must not be angry. You must be happy for me, *mon amis,* especially on this, my wedding day."

Hysteria almost broke out in the theater as reporters rushed forward to catch every word, and a few punters ran out to check their wagers at White's. One tulip in the pit stood on his neighbor's shoulders and cried, "Say it is not so, Margot. I love you!"

Galen, from his box, promised himself a bout at Gentleman Jackson's with the sprig of fashion. See how pretty he looked then.

The fop toppled onto a Bird of Paradise, flattening a feather or two. The audience howled. One of the players off stage struck a cymbal, and quiet was restored.

Margot was smiling. "I am honored by your regard, *monsieur,* but my heart and my hand belong to another. You see, I have been waiting my whole life for the man of my dreams. He, alas, was entangled in one of those silly family arrangements, a tiresome technicality, you might say, *un petit* pother." She made shooing motions with her hands. "Now it is swept away like a dust ball, no? And *mon cher* is free to marry where his heart leads."

"Who is he, Margot?" The bloods in the pit were less polite than the equally eager listeners in the boxes. "Tell us his name so we can have him drawn and quartered for stealing you away!"

Instead of answering, Margot stepped to the edge of the stage, carefully picking her way past the flambeau lights. When she was almost under Galen's box, she held one arm extended, with her palm up, in a gesture of giving. Knowing he was somewhere hidden in the shadows, she said, "From now on, *mon amour,* I sing for you only."

Amid the loudest applause yet, Galen stepped to the edge of his box and leaned over the railing. He tossed her a single long-stemmed rose, without thorns, of course. Margot caught the flower and brought it to her lips. Then, facing him, and only him, she began to sing the English rendition of Robbie Burns's tender lyrics: "Oh, my love is like a red, red rose, that's newly sprung in June. Oh, my love is like the melody, that's sweetly played in tune."

Galen sat back, awed at the gift she had given him. In one short speech, Margot had made their marriage seem a love match, not a face-saving act of retaliation. She'd relegated Lady Floria to a dust ball, and removed the sordid stigma of a purchased bride. She'd left them both their dignity, and left the audience in tears at the triumph of true love. Lud, the woman was brilliant! He was brilliant for finding her! Even Florrie was brilliant for knowing their engagement was a soulless financial transaction.

When the papers came out, with the news that the new Lady Woodbridge was a baron's daughter, even the old tabbies were bound to approve their wedding. There'd still be a scandal, of sorts, with rumors that he'd been carrying on with an opera singer behind Florrie's back, but no one would blame him, now that they'd seen Margot. By Harry, he was almost tempted to send Florrie her dowry back for doing him such a favor.

As soon as his wife's last song was finished—Zeus, the remarkable creature was his wife!—Galen hurried out of his box and down the stairs before anyone could come to poke and pry. He found his way backstage and was waiting for Margot as she made her last bows and ran into the wings. He scooped her up and twirled her around, not caring who saw. "You were magnificent, my Margot." And he kissed her while the applause thundered on from the audience and the stagehands cheered nearby.

"Oh, my," she said when she could breathe again. The walls were still spinning and her feet did not feel the ground beneath them, not even when Galen put her down. "You . . . you liked my song?" she whispered, as the play was about to recommence behind them.

"I loved your song, madame wife," Galen whispered back, "and I think I am falling in love with you."

Oh, my.

Chapter Eight

Whoever said that two's company, three's a crowd, never tried to count how many people could squeeze into one private dining parlor at the Clarendon.

Having decided to dine out when word came that Margot's dog had eaten the capons, the veal roulades, and the chef's slippers, Galen thought they'd have a pleasant meal at the luxurious hotel. He'd worry about hiring a new chef tomorrow. This way, Galen reasoned, he'd avoid an intimate *tête-à-tête* with his bride, a goal to be highly desired in light of his own alarming statement.

He did not love this woman. He admired her courage, her wits, her talent, her beauty, and her loyalty to her brother, that was all. He did not intend to love another woman, ever. What if they decided to end their marriage in six months, either legally or in a *tonnish* separation? How could he go on with his life with his heart missing? No, he did not, would not, love his wife.

Half the chaps in London seemed to, though. If one more gudgeon slapped him on the back in congratulations, he'd be black-and-blue by morning. And he thought this was a private parlor! How could he deny his friends, though, when they were sending in bottles of champagne and bouquets for the bride?

Since he could not lock the door to keep them out without incurring more talk, and less food, Galen gritted his teeth and made the introductions. The gentlemen made no mention of previous acquaintanceship with Lady Woodbridge, and Margot made no mention of previous propositions tendered and rejected, although Galen knew from Skippy that many of these same fellows, married or otherwise, had sought Margot's favor. He hated them all, and their champagne tasted like dishwater.

Margot was starved after her performance, having, in fact, eaten little all day but some poppyseed cake at tea this afternoon. She let his lordship banter with the many callers, accepting their well wishes and the usual nuptial innuendoes, while she did justice to her meal. Then she began to notice that all of their callers were men, except for one widow in a dampened skirt and one young miss on her brother's arm. He'd get a bear-garden jaw from his mother in the morning, Margot had no doubt. His lordship was about to discover what a misalliance he had made. He might think he was falling in love, although Margot was wise enough to recognize his declaration as gratitude and glibness. Galen must tell all his brides that he loved them, and all his ladybirds, too. His lordship's infatuation would wither away when he realized his new viscountess was damned as a *demi-mondaine,* no matter her ancestors or her innocence. The meringue tasted like mud.

Margot was beginning to look deuced uncomfortable, in fact, and Galen was tempted to land a facer on the next nodcock who poured the butter boat over her. When he noticed that she'd stopped eating and stopped smiling at the men who called at their table, he signaled to the waiters to leave the room and see they were undisturbed. "They'll behave more respectfully when their wives are around," he told her. That must have been the wrong thing to say, for she choked on something and had to swallow a hurried sip of wine. She grew paler, too, leaving those faint freckles more visible across her just-scrubbed cheeks.

"They won't come," was all she said, pleating the napkin in her lap.

"Who won't come where?"

"The women, your friends' wives. What, did you think they were all at home with the headache this evening, sending their husbands out to dine alone? They are all tittering over their tenderloins, just outside this dining parlor. Did you not notice how the ladies turned away when we were escorted past their tables? They will not be calling, I assure you."

"Gammon. They were all staring, I swear. Once they hear of your connections, they'll be eager to leave their cards. I'll prove it to you. What do you say we hold a reception at the end of your theater engagement? Two weeks ought to be enough to do it up right. No grand ball, just a dinner and some dancing or cards. No one who is in Town will refuse, I promise." Galen would call in every marker he'd ever been owed if that's what it took. Hell, he'd call on Princess Esterhazy and Lady Drummond-Burrell and Sally Jersey if he had to. He'd danced with enough platter-faced chits at Almack's for them; they could come dance at his wife's party. Once they conversed with Margot and saw she was more of a lady than half the members of the *beau monde,* they would welcome her to their ranks. If they did not, well, the viscount could not see any great loss. Who needed stale bread and orgeat and unfledged chicks every Wednesday night?

Margot was still worrying her napkin. "And what of your father? Will he come stand on the receiving line with his son's new wife?"

"He will if his gout is not bothering him. I'll likely have to fight him over the first dance with you. Stop fretting, my dear."

Margot couldn't. He refused to see the truth. She stared at her plate, knowing that the sooner Galen saw reality, the less disappointed he'd be. And the sooner he stopped building air castles, the sooner she'd stop wanting to move into them— with him. "What of your sister?"

Now there was someone who did need those Wednesday night ordeals. Harriet was due to make her come-out next fall, and Lud knew the hoyden would have a hard enough time attracting an eligible *parti* on her own. The thought of having Harriet on his hands for the rest of her days was enough to make Galen reach for his wineglass.

Margot stopped his hand. "You see? You know her chances will be hurt by association with me."

"I cannot lie to you, Harriet is liable to be labeled fast with or without your company. The chit's been without a mother too long, and my father cannot say nay to her. Why, it would be just like her to waltz at our party without being approved. Zeus, she's never even been presented. And I fear there are those who would blame you, so no, she will not be invited to our party. I was thinking of asking Aunt Matty to leave Bath to chaperone the brat after the summer."

"I . . . I see."

"Do you? I was hoping you'd agree to stay in the country with me, avoiding the whole mare's nest of Harriet's Season. Not because I don't think you could be a sterling example to her, or that you'd hinder her chances of making a decent match, but she would run you ragged, and I prefer to have you to myself. Besides, I want to spend more time with my horses and the estate. My father is not as young as he thinks, and I would relieve him of some of his duties, as well as cataloguing the family's art collection. Then there is the land and cottage I inherited from an uncle, which I seldom get to visit. I thought you might enjoy helping me redecorate it."

"A home in the country? That sounds heavenly."

"We'd come to Town for Harriet's come-out ball, of course, and to refurbish our wardrobes, see the latest plays, and such. But I am tired of the City and its empty entertainments. Besides, the country is much more healthy for children."

"Children? But I thought—"

"Your brother."

"Of course."

Then Skippy came to their table. Closed doors meant little to him, in his altitudes. He'd been celebrating the wedding and his winnings since Margot's announcement, and now he was literally overflowing with good spirits. Neither Galen nor Margot objected, since so many awkward subjects lay between them like so many untouched dishes.

Skippy pulled up a chair at their table and proceeded to finish the asparagus Margot hadn't cared for, the poached salmon, and the rest of the rolls. "Skipped dinner, don't you know."

When his hunger was slaked—that is, when the table was empty—Skippy raised a glass, Galen's, for yet another toast. "To connubial bliss, to betting on a sure thing, and to setting the *ton* on its collective ear, my dears. You've done a bang-up job, I say. No one is speaking of anything else but the love match of the decade. Your performance at the theater was inspired, madam. Your singing too, of course. And you, Woodbridge, had the females all berating their lovers for not being half so romantical. I knew you two were perfect together. Told everyone, I did." He raised Galen's glass again. "To love and marriage, which so seldom go hand in hand."

In his usual skitter-witted fashion, Skippy must have forgotten that Galen and Margot had met and married on the same day. But if the Polite World wanted to put a polite face on their wedding, Galen would not contradict him.

"Do they seem disapproving?" Margot wanted to know, vaguely waving her hand to indicate the throngs outside.

"Not by half! Some of the hostesses are upset that everyone will be leaving for the country or Brighton before they get a chance to toss a ball or two in your honor. Others of 'em are talking about inviting you to their summer house parties. Think what a coup it would be—the latest tittle-tattle and some decent music for once, instead of some caterwauling, calf-eyed miss. And the gentlemen, well, they are talking about starting a new page in the betting book, to do with your first son and all that."

Skippy was being diplomatic, for once. The worthless wastrels at White's were likely wagering on when the child would be born, with odds in favor of a very premature birth. Galen pounded his fist on the table. "Dash it, I will not have them gambling on the arrival date of my heir. You may tell them that if I see my wife's name in the betting book, I shall tear the page out and shove it down the throat of whomever's name appears there."

The reverend nodded. "I'll tell 'em, but that won't stop the wagering, don't you know. They'll just use initials. It's too good a bet, and your getting as prickly as a hedgehog over it will just keep 'em speculating."

"He's right, Galen, and such foolishness can do us no harm if anyone wishes to waste his money that way."

"Just what I said." Skippy swallowed a forkful of apple tart. "Had to remind 'em wagering was a sin, too. After all, the bishop was there, soothing his throat after the funeral."

"Did you bet, Skippy?" Margot asked, which brought a blush to the cleric's thin cheeks. He looked around for one of the waiters to save him, or another caller, or an act of God. This was a hell of a time to get religion, though, he conceded. "I, ah, may have indulged. Weakness of the flesh, don't you know."

"Weakness of the mind, more like," Galen said with a growl. "Tell me, before I toss you sorry excuse for an ecclesiastic out of here, how did you place your bet? And if it was less than nine months from now, you better start running."

"What, show such disrespect for your lady wife? I never would! In fact, I figured you'd make sure no one could cast aspersions. I mean, stands to reason a chap don't mind talk about him winning the hand of a beautiful woman, but he don't want his son being taunted with it all his life. I took the twelve-month spot."

"Thank you, Skippy. I appreciate the vote of confidence." Margot pushed the bowl of fruit closer to him. "Perhaps we'll even name the baby after you. Unless of course he's a girl. Uh, what is your name anyway?"

"Skidmore. Skidmore Skidmore. The parents ran out of names before I came along, so they skipped that part. Makes it easy to remember, don't you know?"

*   *   *

By the time they were finished with coffee and more congratulations, the evening was far advanced. Margot was
yawning, and she still had a rehearsal in the morning. Ordering the carriage home, Galen pulled her into his lap for
the drive, so she would not bump her head when they hit a
rut. "Rest, my love. We've had a busy day," he said.

"Can you believe it's all been less than twenty-four
hours? I keep thinking I'm dreaming, that I'll wake up back
in Mrs. McGuirk's house."

"No chance, sweetings, I like you right here." And he did,
more than he'd have thought possible for such an innocuous
embrace. She simply felt right in his arms.

As for Margot, she had a million questions yet to be re-
solved, and as many worries, but for this short interlude she
was content to listen to the sounds of the horses' hooves on
the cobblestones, and his lordship's heart beneath her cheek.

All too soon they were at Grosvenor Square and his lordship was handing Margot down from the coach. The front
door opened—Fenning always watched for the master's return—and Margot's dog bounded out. Rufus danced around
them, barking loudly enough to frighten the horses, getting
his muddied pawprints on Galen's white satin unmention-
ables, and snarling at the footman who came to lead him off.
The footman and his length of rope faded into the shrubbery.

Staring over his lordship's shoulder, the butler courte-
ously inquired as to their evening.

"Delightful, thank you, Fenning." Galen handed over his
hat and gloves and Margot's wrap.

"Here, too, milord. The canine attacked your valet whilst
Mr. Clegg was polishing your boots. The beast won. Your
boots lost. Then he chased the housekeeper's cat into the or-
angery."

"Clegg?"

"No, milord, her ladyship's animal. I fear we shall not be
serving oranges soon. The housekeeper is no longer on our
payroll."

"Well, I never cared much for her sour puss anyway."

"The cat, milord?"

"No, the housekeeper. But her ladyship is tired. We'll deal with all of this in the morning, Fenning. Ah, you will be here in the morning, won't you?"

The butler sniffed at the viscount's levity and stalked off. He'd been majordomo to the Dukes of Woburton since taking over the position from his father, who'd replaced his father before him. No mongrel was going to force him to desert his post. Why, the family would never manage without a Fenning in charge.

Galen led Margot—and the dog—up the stairs and down the corridor to her bedroom. He opened the door and nudged the dog inside with his knee so that he might properly say good night to his bride. This was not how he'd imagined spending his wedding night, on the other side of his wife's bedroom door while a scruffy, overgrown sack of bones got to share her bed, if the blasted dog did not *eat* her bed. He'd worry about that in the morning, too. Right now, all he could think of was how good Margot felt in his arms, how sweet her perfume—before the dog licked her face—and how much he wanted to kiss her. But did that count as intimacy, which he'd promised to delay? He hesitated, until Margot stood on tiptoe and shyly placed a gentle kiss on his lips. "Thank you. For everything, my lord."

Confound it, he did not want to be her benefactor; he wanted to be her lover. Galen wrapped her in his arms and gave her a real kiss, a senses-stealing, toe-tingling, tongue-touching kiss. He might not be the man of her dreams, dash it, but, by George, he'd be the man *in* her dreams tonight.

Chapter Nine

Whoever said, first, let's kill all the lawyers, should have started with Samuel Hemmerdinger, Esquire. The prosy old pettifogger was provoking Galen into wishing he had a pistol to hand.

Lord Woodbridge had gone to see the family solicitor shortly after breakfast, which consisted of yesterday's rolls and scorched eggs and tepid coffee, since the second cook, who would have taken over from the departed chef, had not stepped out of the dog's way fast enough this morning when the coal wagon had arrived. Luckily, they would not be needing another delivery soon, Fenning reported, with the weather so clement. Luckily the second cook's leg was merely bruised, not broken. Luckily there were a great many employment agencies in London. Fenning would call on one where the family was not known, which circumstance, he sniffed, would doubtless soon change.

After the meal, and a stop at a coffee house for another, Galen had escorted Margot to the theater for her rehearsal. He'd left her with Ella, two footmen, and the dog, to Fenning's relief. The actors were used to Ruff; they used him to discourage bill collectors. Galen thought she'd be safe from any insult, but he could not like Margot out of his sight.

He was already in a foul temper before he reached Hemmerdinger's offices. He had hardly slept a wink last night, after that kiss. What the devil was he about, rousing passions he was promised to postpone? And how was he supposed to rest easily, knowing his beautiful wife was just on the other side of the connecting door? His mind joined his body in protest that the blasted dog was keeping her company, not her besotted husband. It was hard not to batter the confounded door down, vows and vermin-infested mongrels notwithstanding. Hell, if it wasn't hard, it would have been easy.

Then she'd looked so . . . so fresh at breakfast, all sunshine and rainbows in her yellow gown, delighted with the flowers Fenning—not he, dammit—had placed at her plate. She'd had a wonderful night's sleep, she told him, followed by an early morning walk in the square with her dog, trailed by the footman reluctantly assigned to the creature's comfort. The dog reluctantly permitted the poor chap to follow, since the servant's pockets were stuffed with the ham that was supposed to grace the viscount's breakfast table. Fenning had wrapped the slices in paper himself, telling his underling the meat was for emergencies only, if, for example, the dog tried to swallow a small child, or a medium-sized drayer's cart.

Margot was laughing as she told Galen of her walk, confident the footman and her pet were now on good terms. She was so pleased with her new circumstances, in fact, she did not even notice the sparse breakfast fare. Of course it was not so meager, by her previous standards. "I think I could grow used to such a life of luxury, my lord," she told him, her eyes twinkling at the understatement as her glance encompassed the waiting servants, the shining silverware, the huge Zepporini hunt scene on the morning room wall. She felt years younger, stones lighter, without the weight of an uncertain future on her shoulders.

She was so deuced grateful, Galen cursed just thinking about it. He did not want her gratitude, by Harry. She was the one who had pulled his chestnuts out of the fire. Hell, he'd be casting up his accounts right now on a ship bound for the tropics, if not for her. Or he'd be suffering the laughter of his friends and the pity of their wives. Worse, he'd be new prey on the marriage mart hunting grounds. Instead, he was the envy of London. And Margot thought she had something to be grateful about? Besides, thankfulness might be a stepping-stone toward affection, but he wanted much more than that.

Margot had wished to accompany him to the solicitor's office, but Galen did not want to wait till she was done with the rehearsal. He'd rather spend their short hours of free time this afternoon doing something pleasurable, like showing off his prize in the park. That's what he'd do, he planned, drive her in his curricle through Hyde Park at the fashionable hour. Unless, of course, she needed to rest for the evening's performance. Deuce take it, he wished she would give notice at the theater. She no longer needed the money or the acclamation, not with every male in Town falling at her feet. What she did need was to see that she was restored to her rightful place in the *haut monde,* now that the wedding notices had been published and her lineage revealed.

Galen knew the *ton.* No one was going to turn his or her back on the Duke of Woburton's daughter-in-law if she was halfway acceptable. Oh, some might not acknowledge Margot; Zeus, some of the high-sticklers did not acknowledge Galen because his mother had been a governess. He could not care a whit about those. He did care about anyone treating Margot like an opera singer.

By all that was holy, he ought to be at the theater, Galen fumed, making sure no one accosted her. That acting troupe was a scurvy lot, and the swells who hung around the Green Room were not to be trusted to keep the line. The dog was some protection, but the long-toothed mutt's loyalty was purchased with a lamb chop. Galen would rather trust in Ella to look after Margot, but the crusty costume-sewer would be busy about her own tasks in the wardrobe department. Were two footmen enough to fend off advances? Or were the nodcocks making sheep-eyes at her themselves? Dash it, Galen wished he were at the theater.

Instead, he was sitting on an uncushioned bench in the corner of a room full of curious clerks, waiting for Mr.

Hemmerdinger. The fact that he had not sent ahead for an appointment, nor even given notice that he was coming, did not make the hard wooden seat any more comfortable. If Hemmerdinger was closeted with anyone less than a cabinet minister, Galen would find another solicitor.

Perhaps he should anyway. When the lawyer finally deigned to have Galen shown into his private office, where the seats, incidentally, were all covered in plush and leather, Hemmerdinger was not helpful.

For one thing, the solicitor did not offer his felicitations on Galen's nuptials. If the old fussbudget had not drawn up the marriage contracts, then the match was not proper, his throat-clearing seemed to say, even if the wedding were sanctioned by the archbishop of Canterbury and King George himself. The legal mind did not embrace spontaneous, spur-of-the-moment love matches, nor dowerless brides.

Hemmerdinger would not write up the settlements for Margot's future, not without consulting Galen's father. Granted, the viscount could not promise away parts of the estate he had not yet inherited, such as the Dower House, but surely his wife was entitled to a generous allowance and an annuity if Galen died. Except for some minor income, his own monies had never been separated from the dukedom's, not since he was at university on quarterly allotments. To teach him to live within a budget, His Grace had said, as if Viscount Woodbridge were ever going to need to count pennies. He counted now, trying to recall his personal bank balance. All of his bills were met by the estate, his art collection joining the entailment, his horses included in operating expenses for the Three Woods stables. Perhaps it was a good thing that Margot had not stopped singing after all.

Hemmerdinger harrumphed a few times before agreeing to transfer to Margot and her possible future progeny the deed to the small Kentish estate Galen owned outright from his uncle, the previous viscount. At least she'd have a life tenancy there if Galen should die or if the marriage should not work.

After snorting as if he had an out-of-season oyster lodged in his throat, Hemmerdinger next refused to go to the courts to change Margot's brother's guardianship, not without proof of any wrongdoing or an irregularity in the late baron's will. Mr. Manfred Penrose was little Lord Penrose's blood kin, next in line to the title and estate, and lawful trustee. A mere brother-in-law had no claims. Of course Hemmerdinger would be willing to consult with the Penrose family solicitor concerning a visit to the lad's sister.

Like hell he would. If Galen wanted to consult another man of affairs, it would be to replace this one. And the boy was not coming to visit his sister on some solicitor's sufferance; he was moving in with them, permanently. Furthermore, Galen Collin Spreewell Woodrow, Viscount Woodbridge, had never been a mere anything. Hemmerdinger could go hang.

Margot was disappointed, of course, when Galen picked her up at the theater in his curricle and told her about his unproductive day at the solicitor's, on the way to the park. She refused to worry, though. Galen had said he would help get her brother away from Uncle Manfred, and so he would, with or without the cooperation of the legal system. Unfortunately, there was no way for her to go off to Sussex herself to see about Ansel's condition. The management of the theater was in alt over the increase in ticket sales, far ahead of the previous week and excellent for these waning days of the social Season. Mr. Ryder would not hear of his latest star taking off for Sussex, not for an ailing brother, not for an impatient bridegroom. The mobs would tear down his walls, he swore. There would be a riot, an uprising, the government could topple, people could be injured. And he'd strangle her dog.

They could wait the fortnight of her engagement before leaving London, Margot reflected, but then there was the party Galen was still planning to hold, despite having neither chef nor housekeeper. How could she worry about a dinner when her brother was ill or simply ill-treated?

"Then I suppose I shall have to go without you," Galen offered. "Perhaps it's for the best anyway, as your uncle seems the type to cut up ugly when he is thwarted. And if I do have to sneak the lad away in the middle of the night, you cannot be accused." The more Galen thought of the plan, the better he liked it. Not that he liked leaving Margot alone in London, of course, but she'd be well protected, even if he had to hire the entire roster of Bow Street Runners. But he could travel faster without her, and he could deal more harshly with the uncle if the need arose. Besides, if he was out of Town for two or three days, those were two or three nights he did not have to watch her on stage, where everyone else could watch her, too. And those were two or three nights where he might get some rest, not thinking of her one door away. Possessive jealousy and unbridled lust were uncomfortable companions, so he'd leave them behind and hope to be cured by his return.

"I cannot ask you to go alone. You don't even know my brother."

"You are not asking. I am offering. Are you afraid I'll fetch home the wrong boy? You'll give me a note for that housekeeper you said was looking out for Ansel, and I'll bring him back to you. Easy as porridge."

She was still uncertain. "Do you know anything whatsoever of little boys?"

"I daresay I was one, once. Besides, I'll take my valet along. Handy chap, knows all kinds of potions and powders, does old Clegg. He'll have the boy right as a trivet in jig time."

Especially if the little baron were suffering from an overindulgence of drink.

Margot decided she would visit the apothecary's shop herself before she let Galen leave. She'd make sure he had fever reducers and restoratives, blankets, beef broth, books to read if Ansel grew bored in the carriage, books to read if

Galen grew bored in the carriage. She'd make a list later. Right now her more immediate concern was neither Ansel nor the dinner party, not even the pressure of Galen's thigh alongside hers on the narrow driving bench. She was not even anxious about her upcoming performance, for once. No, they were entering the park, and Margot had to worry about entering Galen's world.

He did not stop the curricle or rein in his matched chestnuts, not when some mounted officers tried to start a conversation, not when an old lady in a lozenged landau, with a lorgnette and a lapdog, beckoned them over. He drove past a gaggle of giggling girls, surrounded by a parcel of pimply youths, and he barely slowed their pace for a cavalcade of crested carriages. The viscount did nod his head, tip his hat, and smile at the other park visitors, but he did not stop.

"But I thought you wanted me to meet these people?" Margot asked.

"No, I wanted you to see that they wanted to meet you, my dear. Did any one of the dowagers turn her back?"

"No."

"Did any of the chaperones pull their charges in another direction?"

"No."

"Did every man bow and wave and try to catch your eye?"

"Yes."

"That, my dear, is why we did not stop. If I have to leave you shortly, and won't even have your company this evening, I did not choose to share you this afternoon."

He did make one unavoidable introduction, however, as they were completing their circuit of the park. An immensely obese, overdressed man was gesturing to them from an open carriage. Galen groaned. "The worst rake in town." But he did head his curricle in that direction, off the path, to present his bride. "Too bad he's our future king."

*　　*　　*

The new émigré French chef Fenning had found was *au anges* to be interviewed by Lady Woodbridge in his native tongue. Only the French, Pierre swore, had the proper reverence for a well-cooked meal. Only another *artiste* could appreciate his genius. Only the most beautiful woman deserved his highest efforts.

Margot had only one question for him before she left for the theater: "What about the dog?"

"*Le chien? Oui.* Pierre can cook dog, but not even I thought the English such barbarians."

They still had no chef.

That night Margot sang an unrehearsed patriotic ballad in honor of Prinny, who had come to the theater especially to hear her, he told everyone. She curtseyed to his box as the Prince stood and applauded. Next Margot performed the new Italian opera piece that she had practiced—another dying heroine—followed by a French lullaby. Then, as the night before, she stepped toward Galen's box and reached up, as if to touch his fingertips as they lowered another red rose to her. She sang "My Love is Like a Ne'er Ending Joy," and no one watching her doubted the words.

She *was* happy, Margot realized. Galen was in the audience, and she no longer dreaded the hoardes of gawkers or feared that she'd forget the words. She sang for the viscount, and the words were always there. She was not thinking about the Prince himself in the audience, or being accepted by the *ton,* or performing while her husband was away, or finding a new chef. She was not even thinking about Ansel, for once. No, Margot Montclaire Penrose Woodrow was thinking, as every patron in the pit tossed a single red rose at her feet, that she hoped Galen would kiss her good night again.

Chapter Ten

Whoever said he who hesitates is lost could have had a lovely chat with whoever said patience is a virtue. They'd both be wasting their breaths, as Galen was already packing for the trip to Penrosc Hall, Rossington, Sussex.

Galen was packing, his valet was packing, Margot was packing, and the new chef, Eduard, was packing. The first three were readying for Galen's journey. The cook was ready for a new position. He'd declared, with a raised carving knife, that no dogs were permitted in his domain. The dog had declared his opinion with a raised leg.

At least Eduard had made breakfast before tendering his resignation. Margot had the rest of the kitchen staff pack up the fresh bread, some cheese, sliced ham, boiled eggs. What was left after Ruff finished, she put in a hamper for the viscount's carriage ride, since he intended to make as few stops as necessary.

Fenning directed her to the old nursery, where she found books and a box of toy soldiers. Galen did not mind her borrowing them for Ansel; they'd been his sister's, anyway. He did not mind the extra trunk of blankets and sheets and sickroom supplies she packed, nor the box of charcoal and block of paper she unearthed from his study, even though he'd need an extra pair of horses to pull the carriage if she found one more thing to stuff inside. He did, however, take offense at the pages of instructions Margot was trying to press upon him.

"Dash it, woman, you'd think I was evacuating one of the

Peninsular field hospitals. He's just a small boy with, what? Weak lungs? An uncertain stomach? Headaches?"

"He gets nightmares," was all Margot said.

Nightmares? All youngsters got nightmares. Why, Galen had told his sister more than one ghost story at bedtime, just to hear her shriek in the middle of the night. Of course he'd been punished when the brat cried rope on him, but nightmares were no big problem. "I can deal with bad dreams, Margot. Don't fret. I am more concerned with leaving you here alone."

Alone? He'd hired extra footmen, extra night watchmen, and extra security guards for the theater. Margot wouldn't be surprised if a Bow Street Runner were sleeping in front of her door at night. "I cannot imagine why you are so concerned about leaving me. Ella and I managed on our own for almost two years, you know."

"Yes, but you were not my wife then. I guard what is mine. If your admirers find you without protection, heaven knows what they might think."

"That I would welcome their advances?" Margot put down the child-sized nightshirt she was folding into yet another valise. She looked at him through clouded eyes. "You do not trust me, do you?"

Galen stopped tossing books and agricultural pamphlets into a satchel. "Well, I do not think you'd run away while I am gone, not with your brother due back here." Of course, that was precisely what he did fear, that she'd find some handsome devil whom she could love, not feel indebted to. "I trust you," he insisted. "It's the dashed rakes and libertines I don't trust. Lud knows the city is teeming with loose screws. You will make sure not to accept any invitations to Carlton House, won't you?"

She nodded. "I will not accept any invitations whatsoever until you return. I will have Fenning deny me to any callers except your friend Skippy Skidmore. I will not visit Hyde Park," she recited from memory. "I'll be too busy for any of those things anyway, what with refurbishing the nursery and hiring staff and ordering invitations and such for the dinner party, in addition to my time at the theater."

"Remember Madame Duavalier is calling tomorrow about your wardrobe. Ella won't have time to sew you all the gowns you need."

"Yes, my lord, I remember," Margot snapped back. "How could I forget when you keep reminding me that I should wear blue, not too low cut, that will match the family sapphires you swear your father will bring from Cheshire."

Margot was still hurt at what she saw as Galen's lack of faith. After all, she was not warning him against willing tavern wenches and saucy serving girls. She knew how a certain type of female fawned over a gentleman with looks and polish and full pockets, bachelor or not. All the girls at the theater were that type, all the girls except Margot. She raised her chin. "I am not a strumpet, Galen. I will not embarrass you with dampened skirts or nearly invisible bodices. I will not flirt with the flea-wits who proposition married women, and I will not get up an affair three days after our marriage! Why, if you were not leaving this afternoon, I wouldn't be on speaking terms with you right now, I am so insulted by your suspicions."

The viscount gathered her into his arms, stroking the long blond hair out of the ribbon Ella had just fussed over. "Lud, I am sorry, my dear. I never gave a groat over Fl— That is, I suppose I am just too new at this caring business. Can you forgive me?"

Surrounded by his strength and his lemony scent, secure in his embrace and, she hoped, his affections, Margot could forgive him anything. Caring was good, for now. She held him as close as she could and raised her lips to his. Trust would come.

And the servants would come, finding them like that an hour later, only more disordered. The viscount decided to wait until the following morning to set out on his journey.

* * *

Galen's instructions to his friend Skippy were more explicit that night as they waited in the viscount's box for Margot's appearance on stage. He repeated everything twice, in fact, hoping to make some impression in the blockhead's brainbox. Skippy was to escort Margot to the theater, and directly home. He was supposed to sit in the box and remember the rose. No, Fenning would remember the rose. Skippy was to tell everyone that Galen was gone to ask his baronial brother-in-law's belated blessings on the union. Most important of all, Skippy was to keep a list of anyone who approached Margot with anything less than reverence; Galen would have their heads when he got back.

"Give over with your worrying, old man," Skippy told him, using his borrowed opera glasses to look down the décolletage of a demi-rep in the pit. "No one is going to insult your lady, not with you hovering over her like a hen with one chick, and not with Prinny singing her praises. The Beau gave her the nod, too, you know. Said Lady Woodbridge was a rose in the desert or some such. I never could understand that chap. Everyone knows flowers don't grow in the desert. Still, his approval means no one will give Lady W. the cut direct."

Galen had to stop himself from pulling the petals off the rose he held. Dash it, now he was getting stage fright for her. Or was he just anxious about leaving Margot? Lud, if she were a Covent Garden convenient, he'd have had her this afternoon in his library. Did he say six months? The few days he'd be gone seemed an eternity, and he hadn't even left yet. He turned back to Skippy without hearing a word of the drama on the stage. "You're sure no one is blackening her reputation?"

Skippy tossed the flower he held down to the Cyprian. "Thunderation, Galen, the gel never had a reputation, except for being standoffish. Now everyone's saying that was because of you, so that's aces, too. A few of the muslin trade are disappointed you got hitched, but the only person trying to keep the scandal broth about your marriage stirred up is Earl Cleary, and no one's listening to him anyway."

"Florrie's father? Why the devil is he cutting up stiff about *my* marriage? I wasn't the one who eloped from the church steps. Besides, I thought he went to Scotland after the she-devil."

"He did, but his carriage broke an axle. He knew he'd never catch up to them by nightfall by the time it was fixed, so he turned back. He did send his groom on ahead cross-country to try to head them off, but the rider ain't back yet."

"Well, that's not my fault either."

"No, but he's saying if you'd treated the chit better, she wouldn't have run off with that Lytell chap. No one believes a word of it, a'course, at least no one who knows what a widgeon she is. The earl's just mad as hornets that you stepped into parson's mousetrap without her. Seems he was counting on you to wed the gel when his groom dragged her back."

"Why the deuce would he think such a thing? I told him I wouldn't have her to save my soul."

"But he thought you'd have her to save the chit's reputation. She'll be ruined otherwise, don't you know. Cleary was banking on appealing to that streak of chivalry you wear like a suit of armor. Sir Galahad and all that." Skippy bit into a piece of fruit he'd had from a pretty little orange seller. He spit the seeds over the railing, into the pit. "You would have done it."

Shaken, Galen admitted to himself that he might have. He would have hated her, but he'd most likely have married Florrie.

"Lucky escape, what?" Skippy echoed his sentiments exactly. "Have I mentioned that?"

"Innumerably."

"And then marrying Mademoiselle Margot. It was like . . . like finding a flower in the desert."

"Why, Skippy, I never knew you had such a poetical bent."

Skippy sat up taller. "Got good posture. Even the bishop says so. Think she'd know any others?"

Galen had trouble following his friend's train of thought, a not uncommon occurrence with the Reverend Mr. Skidmore. "Margot? Know any other bishops? Flowers?"

"Ladies, man, ladies. Only not the kind what titter. Can't stand a female what titters. Your lady's got a nice laugh."

She did at that, the few times Galen had heard it. When he got back, he'd see about making her laugh more often. Then he realized what Skippy had been trying to say. "What, are you thinking of taking on leg shackles?"

"Why not? Seems to suit you. You're as fidgety as a flea, but at least you're not bored. Can't wait to get back—said so yourself. And you're going to fetch a tadpole from a muddy ditch for her. If that don't spell devotion, nothing does."

Skippy never could spell. What this journey proved was that he was a moonstruck moron, that's all, Galen thought. He frowned. "And you'd like to find a woman to turn your life upside down?"

"Don't seem so awful anymore, with you turning Benedict. Been thinking I'd look for a widow, don't you know. I've got no title, of course, no property, not much in the way of brains, but I like children."

"You've been thinking?" Galen frowned back at the disapproving matron in the box next door. He did lower his voice a shade. "I mean, you like children? I didn't know you knew any."

"I've got nieces and nevvies by the score. Cute little buggers."

"Dash it, I should have stayed here and sent you after the boy."

"Here's a secret, since you're trusting me with your lady: I'm not really cut out for the Church."

"No! I would never have guessed. So you think a young widow with a tidy jointure, perhaps a bit of property, would suit you, eh? It just might. If you help Margot draw up a list of whom to invite to the dinner we are holding, I'm sure she'll include anyone you want. Now hush, it's almost her turn to sing."

Margot had to wait a long time for the applause to die down before she could start her first selection. She sang a popular ditty that had the audience singing the hey-nonny-nonny chorus with her, a French rondel, and yet another Italian aria. This time the heroine killed her lover before turning the knife on herself. Then, while everyone waited, she walked to Galen's box and reached for her rose. She held it to her nose, inhaling the sweet perfume, and then she tossed him the pasteboard knife she'd used to inflict the mortal wound.

"A hit, a palpable hit!" Skippy exclaimed. "You see, I knew you'd been heart-pierced."

She sang "My Lover Goes A-Roving" to him: "Alas, I am left here all forlorn, And I shall weep one hundred tears, for every day he's gone."

Chapter Eleven

Whoever said that money is the root of all evil must have seen Manfred Penrose grubbing around the roots of his family tree. He even looked like something that would crawl out of a hollow log: sharp-nosed, beady-eyed, bucktoothed, with gray hair and grayish complexion. He had dirt under his fingernails, coffee stains on his cravat, and ink on his hands from the newspaper he was clutching when an equally slovenly butler showed Galen into the musty book room.

Galen hated him on sight. Of course he was predisposed to loathe the man for Margot's sake, and the long drive into Sussex had not tempered his opinion. The viscount had taken his turns driving the carriage so they could make better time without waiting for Jem Coachman to rest, but he still felt queasy half the time, long rides over bumpy roads being too similar to sailing on the sea. He was tired, the inns they'd passed had indifferent service and worse cattle for hire, and Clegg, his valet, snored.

The nearer he got to Penrose Hall, the less Galen liked Margot's uncle. The surrounding fields were green with crops and recently shorn sheep grazed on the hills, yet the cottage of his tenants had sagging roofs, sewage in the yards, and missing windows. The meanest, most useless residents of Woburton lived better than these Rossington villagers. The hogs of Woburton lived better than this.

Penrose Hall itself was a modest brick edifice, but the drive was unkempt, roof tiles were missing, and no one came to take the horses or show the viscount's driver the way to the stables. Galen wouldn't have let his cattle suffer that dilapidated structure anyway, not even these woeful nags hired at the last change.

"Walk them," he directed the coachman. "I won't be long."

Clegg decided to get down and stroll around to the kitchen entrance, to stretch his legs after the journey and to gather what information he could. A fellow could learn a lot about conditions by the mood of the servants, the quality of the food, and the welcome a stranger got.

Galen got short shrift at the front door. A greasy-haired butler with an unbuttoned coat took his card and said, "Wait here." "Here" was an empty hall, with bare spots on the wall where paintings must have hung, and dust motes kicked up from the carpet by Galen's pacing. This was not the profitable estate Margot had described. Either Penrose Hall had fallen on hard times due to mismanagement, or it was being bled dry by that same manager. Galen wagered on the last.

Penrose had a diamond in his dirty linen, and another on his dirty fingers. The cognac he grudgingly offered was some of the finest Galen had tasted, and boasted no excise labels. This close to the coast, the viscount was not surprised to find smuggled goods. This close to Margot's uncle, he was not surprised to smell a rat who betrayed his country and its fighting army with every shipment. He set the glass aside and waited while Penrose swallowed his drink and poured another.

The older man's hands never stilled, shifting from the glass to the decanter to his penknife to the newspaper to the diamond at his throat. Penrose did not look Galen in the eye, either, as if he had something to hide. He could not hide his nervousness, nor his dislike for his missing niece.

He stabbed the newspaper with the penknife, right through the notice, no doubt, of Margot's marriage to Viscount Woodbridge. "If you've come for the chit's dowry, you've wasted your time."

Galen raised his eyebrows. "I didn't know she had a dowry."

"She didn't, not once she ran off to disoblige me. I checked with m'solicitor soon as I read this claptrap. I don't have to give any dowry if I didn't approve the marriage."

"Of course you wouldn't be looking for any settlements either, in that case," Galen put in smoothly. "But I do not need Penrose money, you know."

Manfred did know, and it infuriated him even more. This nob could wed a penniless female of dicey repute, while he, Manfred Penrose, had to wed some Cit's pasty-faced daughter, just for her portion. The bitch had turned out cold and barren, before she hied back to her papa's shipyard six years ago. Manfred hadn't seen her since, nor a shilling more of her father's money, either. She'd come back, he had no doubt, when he was baron.

"If it ain't the money, why are you here?" he demanded now.

Galen wiped a speck of dust off his superfine sleeve. "I don't suppose you'd believe I came for your blessing on the match, would you?"

Manfred just snorted. "I doubt you'd care one way or t'other, marrying the jade out of hand to spite those other swells. I might have been a fool to think she'd take old Grinsted to please her uncle, but you're twice the fool, Woodbridge, for taking on a common actress who's no better'n she should be, when you could have had her for the price of a bauble or two."

Galen made the other man's shifty eyes meet his by rapping on the desk. "Because you are Margot's family, I will forgive your insults to my wife. Once. The next time you shall swallow those words, along with your rabbity teeth. Do you understand?"

"No insult, heh-heh. Teasing, is all." Beads of sweat were forming on Manfred's back-sloping brow, though. Changing the subject, he poked at the newspaper article. "I see Maggie's still singing for her supper. Can't need to, with your blunt."

"It was Margot's choice to honor her commitments." He emphasized the correct pronunciation of his bride's name. "I respect her for not disappointing her friends at the theater. And her admirers, like Prince George." Galen might hate that Margot had taken the notice of the First Gentleman of Europe, who was also the foremost womanizer, but he was also more than a little proud.

"Headstrong, that's what she always was. That's got to rankle some, eh, Woodbridge, having a wife tie her garters in public, or as near as makes no difference?"

Galen swore he'd never know how much. "Her voice is too lovely to stifle."

Manfred poured yet another glass. "Got to be firm with the doxies, teach 'em who's in charge." He raised his fist to show Galen the method he'd use. The viscount almost drew the dastard's claret then and there. He promised himself he'd pay this knave back in his own coin for every misery he'd caused, as soon as he had the boy safely out of the cur's clutches. Galen sipped at his cognac, smuggled or not, to get the taste of Penrose's filth out of his mouth.

"So what did you say was your reason for coming here?"

"Actually, I didn't say. I had some business nearby, though, and Margot asked me to undertake a few commissions for her."

Manfred snickered. "She's got you under the cat's paw already. Can't imagine you liked leaving such a cozy armful behind. Couldn't be sick of her yet." He stared into the dregs of his glass. "Less'n she's as cold as the codfish I married. Glad to see the back of that one, I was."

Holding his temper by the slenderest of threads, Galen decided he had to get on with the business at hand, else he'd be laying his hands on the dirt-encrusted dirty dish. "One of the requests my lady wife made was that I look up her old housekeeper. Mrs. Hapgood, is it? She had an infusion for the gout Margot wishes to prepare for my father. She said it worked like a charm for the late baron."

"Well, your father will just have to give up his port. That's what the sawbones told me, at any rate. Hapgood's gone."

"Margot will be disappointed, but she feared the woman might have retired by now. Perhaps you could give me the woman's direction so she could write?"

"How the devil should I know her address? Think I keep track of every servant who passes through? And she didn't retire; I threw her out, I did. Blasted woman was cheating me, I swear. Always had money for some trifle or other I didn't order. Disobeyed me, too. Be damned if I was paying any pension to such a sneaksby."

The dastard was already damned as far as Galen was concerned. The unconscionable act of dismissing a loyal old retainer after years of service, without compensation, only earned Penrose a hotter corner of Hell. "Maybe they'd know in the village if she had any relations to go to," he casually offered.

"I think there was a sister in Maidstone. Maggie would know."

Manfred picked at his fingernails with the penknife, then he picked at his teeth. If the long carriage ride hadn't turned Galen's stomach, his host certainly did. The viscount stood to leave. "I'll tell Margot. Oh, before I forget, the other favor she asked was that I look in on her brother. I'm sure the boy is fine, but you know how women get."

Manfred nodded. "Especially that one, gets a bee in her bonnet and won't let go. Well, the brat ain't fine, and that's a fact. Never been fine, and now he's worse."

"Worse? How much worse? I'd hate to tell her bad news for nothing."

"Can't get much worse. Surgeon says the affliction in his head has migrated to the rest of his body. A wasting sickness. He says all we can do is keep him from suffering too badly."

"My word, I had no idea things were so bad with the youngster. Have you consulted another physician?"

"A'course I did. My only nevvy, don't you know. The first quack half bled him to death, and the next one near killed him with purges. Cost me a pretty penny, I can tell you. Even had to hire a man to play nursemaid. Boy's too old for petticoat coddling, don't you know."

The viscount was shaking his head. "This can't be. My wife said the boy got nightmares. I assumed he had headaches or something."

"Nightmares, eh? The boy used to scream the house down, that's what, like he was possessed or something. Couldn't keep servants in the place. Other times he took to sleepwalking. Near burned the west wing to cinders. I'd have had him locked in a Bedlam years ago if not for Maggie. She wouldn't hear of it, and look where it's got the poor little devil now. At least he's too weak to try climbing out the windows again, or head up to the roof. We don't have to tie him to the bed anymore."

Galen did not have to pretend his dismay. "I don't know what to say. And how am I going to tell Margot? She seems somewhat attached to the boy, you see. Perhaps I'd better send for her to come see him for herself."

Manfred did not want his niece anywhere near the house or the tenant farmers or the villagers. "Mightn't be time. Brat's only got days, I'd guess."

"Lud, she'll be heartbroken. As I am sure you will be, too. How terrible this must be for you, to face such a tragedy. And how deuced awkward, having your ward pass away with no one home but you."

"Awkward? What's awkward about it? The boy's been touched in the upper works ever since his father fell off that cliff. Everyone knows it. Can't hide a thing like that from the locals, not when the servants go running in terror."

"Yes, but now he has a wasting illness. Some people might want to question your care of the boy, you being next in line for the title and all. You know how people will talk.

They might even suggest the solicitors take a look at the estate books."

Manfred turned even grayer, his shaking hand reaching for the bottle. "Nothing wrong with the books. Everything's aboveboard."

Galen went on as though the older man hadn't spoken. "No, it won't look good, the boy passing away in your arms, so to speak. My wife won't be happy with me for not standing by the both of you, either. I know, why don't I take the lad back to London with me? I can make the trip in no time, and that way you'll have the responsibility for young Penrose off your hands. He'll be gone, one way or the other, and so will all those niggling questions."

"I suppose it's only right that his sister gets to make her farewells."

"Yes, but now I think on it, I am not sure I want to deal with a sick child. You say he screams?"

"Oh, not so much anymore. You just give him the laudanum regular like. He'll be no trouble, I swear."

"I don't know. Margot and I are just recently married, after all. I don't want her spending her nights at the boy's bedside, if you know what I mean."

"No need. You'll take the keeper, ah, the manservant I have watching Ansel, of course. I wouldn't think of sending you off with the brat otherwise. Renshaw has all the sawbones's instructions and knows all the right doses, and the estate will bear the expense of his salary, naturally. No, the boy can be your headache for whatever time he has left. You've got to learn the pitfalls of married life, as well as the pleasures. You marry a girl, you get her family."

Galen took one last look at Margot's uncle and swore to himself. Heaven forbid.

Chapter Twelve

Whoever said that the meek shall inherit the earth couldn't have meant this poor little lamb. Galen doubted Ansel Penrose would last long enough to inherit his own barony.

For the first time, the viscount doubted his own judgment. He'd been a good officer and a competent manager of estate matters, knowing his decisions were sound and well-reasoned. Now he had no idea if he was doing the right thing for the boy, or for Margot, bringing her this heartbreak. Galen was no expert when it came to the sickroom, and rarely trusted those who said they were, for he'd seen more instances of incompetence or ignorance than he'd seen cures. Broken bones were easy, like bullet wounds and gashes needing stitches. Broken spirits were quite another affair, and he had yet to hear of a remedy. Now all he had to trust was his instinct, which was shouting at him that the boy would never survive another week at Penrose Hall. The question was whether Ansel would survive the carriage ride to London.

Galen had seen livelier figures in a wax museum. The child's cheeks were sunken in, his color was paler than the sheets he was lying upon, and his wrists were barely wider around than Lord Woodbridge's cane. His hair might have been the gold of Margot's, but it was so damp, dirty, and matted to his head that the viscount could not tell. Ansel's mouth hung open, drooling on a stained nightshirt. Galen had to lean over the bed to make sure the boy's chest was moving, thinking that if he were forced to inhale the noxious odors of this sickroom, he'd stop breathing, too. The young-

ster did not seem to be in pain, but that was the only posi-
tive thing Galen could discern in his condition.

Damn it, he'd seen death: soldiers in battle, old people at
Three Woods, pitiful wretches in the streets of London, even
his own beloved mother. But not a child. Children were supposed to run and laugh and play in the sunshine, not die
unloved in some foul cubby, watched by a ham-fisted
hireling. No one should die like that.

Ansel was certainly going to, though, unless Galen did
something, and soon. A quick look around showed him two
bottles on the nightstand, no lemonade, no bowl of broth, no
barley water, no pastilles, no tea. He'd never seen a sickroom without tea. Then again, he'd never seen a sickroom
presided over by a retired pugilist, either. The flattened ear
and broken nose proclaimed Renshaw's profession; the fact
that he was working for the nipcheese Manfred proved he
hadn't been much of a success at it. He was big enough to
wrestle an elephant, though, so one small boy would be no
match for him. His hands were larger than Ansel's head, and
no cleaner than his master's.

That master did not deign to go up to the attic nursery
with Galen, sending the surly butler instead with instructions for Renshaw to get the boy ready for the journey first,
then himself.

"I'd best be givin' 'im 'is potion early in that case, I
s'pose," the hulking servant said. "Wouldn't want no trouble
in the coach."

Galen watched Renshaw pour a thick, foul-smelling yel-
lowish liquid onto a spoon. He didn't mix it with water or
lemonade to hide the taste, and he did not lift the boy to a
sitting position. He just poured the dose down Ansel's
throat, causing the boy to gag and thrash.

" 'Ere now, none o' that, Anthill." Not my lord, not Lord
Penrose, not even Master Ansel, Galen noted, swallowing
his anger. Then Renshaw clamped his huge hand over the
child's face, squeezing until the boy swallowed. When he

stepped back, Galen could see bruises on his brother-in-law's neck and jaw, from the attendant's past ministrations.

"Why don't you go pack your things now?" the viscount managed to say through clenched teeth. "I'll look after his lordship while you are gone."

"I needs to get 'is medicines an' stuff."

"We don't need much on the way, and we'll worry about his clothes and such in London." Galen doubted the boy had anything worth keeping. There was not a toy in sight, nor a book. "Just pack a satchel for him if you have one."

As soon as Renshaw left to gather his own belongings, Galen found a basin with water that might not have been changed in a week, but it would have to do. Using his own handkerchief, he started to bathe the boy's face.

Ansel jerked his face away, and Galen took that for a good sign, that the nipper still had some fight in him. He kept washing, but as gently as he could without holding the frail shoulders down. Ansel struggled to open his eyes, and then fought to get them to focus. His eyes were all dark pupil, Galen noted, with the slightest rim of blue showing.

"It's all right, lad. My name is Galen."

Ansel did not know anyone named Galen. His hands twitched, trying to bat this new tormentor away. His mouth worked, but no sound came out.

"Would you like a drink?" There wasn't even a blasted glass in the room. Galen dribbled some of the wash water off his handkerchief onto the boy's cracked and parched lips.

The little baron bared his teeth and growled, "No."

It was barely a whisper, but reminded Galen forcefully of Margot's dog. He set the handkerchief aside, then picked it up again to wipe at his own damp brow. "We'll get you some lemonade in a minute then, all right?"

"Go . . . away."

The boy was holding himself so rigid Galen feared he'd break a matchstick bone, but he was even more upset when he realized Ansel was afraid of him. Deuce take it, the nipper thought he was trying to poison him! "Shush, Ansel. I am not going to hurt you. Your sister asked me to help."

"No. . . . Lies. All lies."

"I realize you have no call to trust anyone, but I am Viscount Woodbridge, and I do not lie. On my mother's grave, I swear that Margot sent me for you."

"Margot?"

For an instant Galen thought the child tried to smile. His lips twitched, at least, before falling slack again as the purplish eyelids drifted closed. The viscount grabbed for his pocket watch, holding it near the lad's mouth to make sure his breath was still fogging the glass. Galen's hand was shaking so hard when he put the timepiece back in his pocket that he feared his own heart was threatening to give notice in panic. Lud, it was bad enough her brother might stick his spoon in the wall, without Galen leaving Margot a widow. He hadn't yet signed the marriage contracts, confound it. They had to leave.

Lifting the youngster, blankets and all, Galen decided he'd held cider jugs that weighed more. He kicked the door open, relieved to find the air in the hallway slightly less fetid than that in the sickroom, and carefully, cautiously made his way down the dimly lighted stairs. He did not stop until he reached his own carriage. He did not make his farewells to Manfred or gather his hat and gloves from the dour major-domo.

Clegg went back for his master's possessions, and extra pillows so they could prop the little lad in the corner of the carriage without fear of his bumping his head when they hit a rut. "Poor little blighter looks to be in queer stirrups," Clegg declared. "And no wonder, if half what I heard in the kitchens is true."

The butler ran a tight ship, it seemed, but as soon as his back was turned, the cook and the scullery maid and the pot boy were all too eager to open their budgets. Underpaid, housed worse than the dogs in the kennels, and abused by the master, the staff owed their employer no loyalty and would have left ages ago, they swore, if there were other positions available.

"I asked what happened to bring the estate so low, like you told me to. Asked if it was hard times and poor crops or the Corn Laws or what. They all laughed. The farms were doing just fine, the cook said, but all the blunt was going to line Penrose's pockets, and his wine cellar. No new equipment, no repairs."

"That's what it looked like to me, too. Either my solicitor demands an accounting, or I'll steal the estate books myself. Did the kitchen help say anything about the boy?"

"I asked, casual like you said," Clegg reported, "and no one wanted to talk about him at first, looking over their shoulders, I swear, for that butler or the boy's guard, Renshaw. Quick with his fists, that one is. The pot boy has a black eye to prove it."

Galen tucked another blanket around Ansel while they waited for Renshaw. It was all he could think to do, for now. "The villain will pay, don't worry. What else did the staff say?"

"The cook finally took me aside and whispered that the household ordered enough laudanum to put a horse to sleep, permanent like. It all got delivered to the sickroom. She was afraid to say anything to anyone, for fear of her job and Renshaw. Didn't figure anyone would believe her anyway, but she doesn't want to be blamed if the sprout cocks up his toes. She says she brewed up every recipe in her book of simples for the little baron, but they all came back untouched."

Galen nodded. "Go back and get her name and a different address we could write to, in case we need her testimony, or if Lady Woodbridge hasn't hired a cook yet. And ask if she knows the direction of Mrs. Hapgood while you are there." The viscount tossed his valet a coin. "Give her this, for trying to help the boy, but don't let anyone else see you do it."

Clegg knew his employer was frazzled, by his saying what didn't need mentioning. He cast a worried look on the too-still boy before nodding and backing out of the coach. He thought he'd see if the cook had another bottle of the excellent ale she'd served him. Manfred Penrose did not stint on certain things.

While Renshaw was carrying out his bags and the groom was helping him stow the parcels in the boot, Galen conferred again with Clegg, who was repacking the hamper of food and drinks under the seat.

"The first thing we are going to do is get rid of the ogre who manhandles children," Galen told his man, noticing the two bottles wrapped in wet towels. The cook must have been grateful for the coin. "It can't be here, I am sorry to say, and it has to appear an accident. I don't want the uncle's suspicions aroused, lest he change his mind and come after us. The law would be on his side, dash it, and the local magistrate would send Ansel back with Manfred."

Clegg jerked his head in the former boxer's direction. "Want I should tell Jem Coachman to have a problem with the ribbons on some empty stretch of the road so we can take care of him?"

"No, leaving Renshaw on the side of the highway would not precisely be the act of innocent men. We'll drive on for an hour or two, till it's almost dark, then find a small, uncrowded inn to change the horses. I'll get him aside one way or the other, and we'll leave him there. I'll ride up with Jem to find the right place. You keep an eye on him inside."

For ninety minutes Clegg pretended to sleep, keeping a watch on the boy and Renshaw. He need not have, for Master Ansel never moved, and the attendant never looked at him after patting the laudanum bottle that protruded from his coat pocket, stating the brat would stay quiet as a mouse for a few hours, at least.

When they finally stopped, Clegg volunteered to sit with the boy so Renshaw could fetch himself an ale—Clegg was not offering the fine brew from Penrose Hall—and use the privy. "For his lordship means to drive through the night, you know. He won't be stopping for the comforts."

Somehow Renshaw tripped on the way to the convenience out back. Jem Coachman, on his way back from the same errand, offered him a hand up, but a loose board from the roof of the rundown inn somehow managed to fly off in the slight breeze and strike Renshaw on the back of the head.

His lordship was there in an instant, all full of concern when he saw the fallen man was only stunned. "No, don't get up, Renshaw, you might be concussed. Don't worry, my valet can see to the boy, and I'll make arrangements with the innkeep for you to stay overnight and get a ride back to Penrose Hall when you recover. It's the least he can do, with this hovel in such disrepair a chap gets coshed trying to relieve himself."

Relieving himself of some of his fury, Galen hit the thick-headed thug on the back of the head again. This time he used the butt end of his pistol, to make sure Renshaw stayed down and unconscious, concussed into confusion for sure. "I never hit a man from behind, before," the viscount ground out as he replaced the pistol in his waistband. "But you, sirrah, don't count, being less than human."

As soon as the hostler was fetched and Renshaw was disposed of, Galen jumped back into the carriage, shouting to his driver, "Spring 'em, Jem. Don't stop till you get to the next town of any size where they might have a doctor. Drive as if a life depended on you. It might."

Chapter Thirteen

Whoever said it was better to light a candle than curse the darkness never realized that viscounts could do both. By the carriage lanterns, Galen emptied the contents of the sack containing Ansel's medicines onto the seat next to him. He opened the bottles, sniffed at them or dipped a finger in to taste. Using every swear word he knew in English, Spanish, and French, with a few choice phrases he'd learned from the Prussian army officers, Lord Woodbridge tossed all of the potions out the carriage window. The rain that was starting to fall would dilute the drugs enough that a passing fox or straying cow would not be poisoned, which was more than Manfred and Renshaw had done for the boy.

"Faster, Jen," Galen shouted, damning the night that forced caution on his driver. Bringing his head back inside the coach and fixing the window back in place, he vowed to kill the bastard.

Since Lord Woodbridge had already broken open Renshaw's head, Clegg assumed his lordship meant the nipper's guardian, not poor Jem. "Amen," was all he said, holding out a bottle of ale.

When they finally reached a likely town, the landlord of the Spotted Dog, the only inn in sight, did not want to host an ailing infant. Not even the color of Galen's gold was enough to convince Lemuel Browne that housing a sickly lad was good for his business, or his health.

"What's wrong with the bantling, anyway?" he wanted to know. "The smallpox'd have me shut down for quarantine, and the influenza would scare off my other business, by George, if I didn't catch it myself."

"He ate something that disagreed with him." Holding the featherweight took no effort, but Galen was anxious to see the boy in bed and cared for. Impatiently, he said, "Here, look at him for yourself. No spots, no fever, no catarrh. He has nothing you can contract, unless your relatives want to inherit this sorry place sooner."

At the man's blank look, Galen cursed. "I swear to you my brother is not carrying a contagion. I also swear that your business will indeed suffer if you keep me standing here, after I tell everyone how unaccommodating you were. I can guarantee you'll never see another crested carriage in your stable yard."

The innkeep took up a candle to lead Galen and his burden to a suite of two bedrooms with a sitting room between. "Don't expect my girls to be waiting on the cub," Lemuel muttered. "They ain't nursemaids, and my wife is off visiting her da."

Since the landlord's girls were currently sitting on drovers' laps in the common room, Galen could do without their skills. "My man and I will see to him. We will need hot water, however, a meal for myself and my servants, and whatever else your kitchen can provide that is nourishing for the boy. My groom can help fetch and carry when he gets back with the doctor." He carefully laid Ansel on the bed in the smaller room, after Clegg rushed to turn the sheets down. They pulled aside the dingy blankets from Penrose Hall and straightened Ansel's stick-like limbs before covering him again. He did not move, not even by a flicker of his eye.

The doctor was not happy to see Ansel, either. Having finally reached his home after a birth, a broken arm, three bad coughs, and a bull calf with bee stings, he was not eager to leave. Galen's groom did not give him much choice, for which Mr. Graham blamed the viscount.

"I don't care if you are the King of Persia, my lord, I resent having a pistol waved in my face."

All Galen could do was apologize for the gun, not his man's insistence on the doctor's immediate attendance. "It is an emergency."

"Lemuel says he ate something," Mr. Graham said as he followed Galen toward the smaller bedroom. "I can tell you're not a father. Boys do that all the time. Nothing to worry— Oh, dear."

Graham was a simple country sawbones, but he seemed as competent to the viscount as any Harley Street physician. He pulled the boy's nightshirt off—Galen winced to see Ansel's ribs sticking out, worse than Margot's dog's—and put his ear to Ansel's chest.

"Heart's regular, but too slow. No fluid in the lungs, though. Yet." He pushed down on one of Ansel's fingernails and watched the color change. "Blood's flowing sluggishly, but not pooling. Yet." Then he pinched and prodded at the child's abdomen, lifted his eyelids, looked in his ears and down his throat. Finally, the surgeon turned to Galen. In a voice dripping disdain, he asked, "Did you do this to him, my lord?"

"Hell, no. I just got to him this morning and took the boy away before his uncle killed him with an excess of laudanum. He has been poisoned, hasn't he?"

"It is hard to say without knowing if the child is in pain, but I can find no physical cause for his lethargy or gauntness. He might have been slowly, systematically poisoned. On the other hand, if someone kept dosing him with laudanum, it might have the same effect. I saw an opium eater waste away like this once. The drug depresses the appetite, you know. One way or the other, the poor little mite is starving and doesn't know it."

The viscount tried to remember when he was injured in the war and dosed against the pain. He could not recall being hungry, only the bad dreams. "Could the laudanum give a child nightmares?"

"Nightmares, mirages, irrational horrors, who can say what goes through a mind in such a condition?"

"His uncle said they kept Ansel drugged because he was so prone to nervous tremors, but I'd wager that dastard caused the boy's fears."

"Which came first, the chicken or the egg? The boy has bad dreams, so the loving uncle mixes a soporific, which causes more nightmares, so they give him more laudanum. Could that have been the way of it, my lord?"

"If there were a loving uncle. This one is as affectionate as a cobra. I think he set out to kill his nephew, whose estate he was robbing and whose title he would inherit. He just did not want it to look like murder."

"I doubt you'll be able to prove anything. I am sorry, my lord." The doctor packed his bag and turned to leave.

"But where are you going? You haven't done anything!"

"I thought you understood, there is nothing to do. Except pray, of course. Not that I have had much experience with such an advanced case, but I'd say you do not have time to wean the lad off the drug, if such a thing is possible. He'll starve to death first. If you stop giving him the laudanum, however, his body will suffer too great a shock for this enervated condition."

"You are saying he will die either way, that there is no hope at all?"

"There is always hope, my lord. But if I knew how to get food into a comatose body, I would be famous. If I could cure an enslavement to spirits or opiates, I'd be wealthy. Instead I am a plain country doctor who has to make the occasional poultice for a horse's leg, just to make ends meet. You can try spooning restoratives into the boy, for what that's worth, or try piping liquids down his throat, but he'll likely choke to death that way. If not, you might merely be prolonging his suffering. You'll want to think about it."

Clegg saw the doctor out, while Galen stood by Ansel's bedside. Think about letting Margot's brother fade away, all hollow-eyed and in terror? The viscount had been away from his wife for two days already, nearly as long as he'd been with her, and an emptiness dwelled deep within him. He should be by her side, seeing her established in polite society, helping her take over the reins of Woburton House, making sure she was safe at the theater. He should be building his marriage, by Jupiter, bringing her roses and rubies, not this wretched rag of a brother, not Ansel's lifeless body. Galen pictured Margot, so alive and brave, willing to sacrifice herself for this baby baron. He knew she'd never have married him otherwise, so the boy was part of the marriage contract. He could not let him die. He would not. If his brother-in-law wanted to give up, Ansel would have to tell Galen himself. First he had to awaken.

While Galen tried spooning barley water, broth, hot tea, and lemonade past Ansel's unresponsive lips, Clegg cut the matted hair and washed him. They took turns stroking his throat, encouraging him to swallow. Most of the stuff came out, so they left off his nightshirt, wrapping the little baron in warmed towels instead. Galen kept talking to him, telling about the marriage, about the grand London town house Ansel would be calling home till they moved to the country. He described the music room, promising Ansel could spend as much time there as he wished. He even offered the boy the use of his own hitherto private painting studio in the attic, with its skylight. Thinking that perhaps Margot had exaggerated the boy's artistic nature, Galen starting listing other lures for a young boy: a pony of his own, a tree fort at Three Woods, a swimming pond, a dog.

"No, no dog. Forget I mentioned a dog," he told Ansel, in case the boy should be listening somewhere in his befogged mind. Galen would be damned if that monstrosity of Margot's would get near Ansel, after he'd ruined another pair of breeches trying to keep the halfling fed and alive.

At last, close to morning, Ansel started to stir. The movement was more a twitch, although soon his legs were shaking, as if he were trying to run, and his hands were flapping at his side. His mouth opened to scream, but no words came out. Galen tried to hold him, to stop the wild thrashing, but the child tried, piteously, to throw his hands off.

"Ansel, listen to me," Galen pleaded, trying to keep the desperation from his voice. "I know you are frightened. You do not remember me from this afternoon, do you? My name is Galen Woodrow, Lord Woodbridge, and Margot sent me for you, Ansel. Your sister Margot."

Those soulless eyes widened, searching the dark corners of the room for his beloved sister.

"No, she is not here." Galen felt like the lowest maw-worm in creation having to kill that faint spark of hope. "She sent me to bring you to her. To London. And I will, I swear, as soon as you are well enough to travel."

The boy's eyes closed, but his breath was coming faster and faster.

"No, Ansel, don't go back to sleep. Try to pay attention. You have been ill. Trying to help you, your uncle gave you laudanum." Galen saw no reason to frighten the child worse. Ansel had enough in his dish already without thinking someone was trying to kill him. "But the medicine gave you nightmares, so they gave you more, instead of less."

"Tried . . . to get away. Caught me . . . tied to . . . bed."

Lud, the boy knew. "That will never happen again, word of a Woodrow."

Ansel turned his head to the wall. He'd heard sworn oaths before. The word of a Penrose had not been worth much, it seemed.

"On my mother's grave then, Ansel, and I loved my mother as much as you must have loved yours." Dash it, he didn't want the child thinking about his mother, or joining her in the hereafter! "It's a solemn vow, is all. I will not hurt you. Do you understand?"

The shorn head moved a tiny fraction, to Galen's relief. "Good, you are starting to improve already then." And his mind was not so damaged he could never recover. "But now you have to think even harder. I can give you another dose of the medicine, not as much as before, but you will go back to sleep. And you might never see Margot again."

A tear trailed down Ansel's sunken cheek, but he nodded.

"Or I can not give you any at all. It will be hard on you— I will not lie about that, either—perhaps the hardest thing you have ever done. But then the bad dreams would be gone, Ansel, and you can go home to Margot."

"No . . . nightmares?"

"No." Galen prayed not, at any rate. He did believe the laudanum or whatever else Manfred had been feeding the boy was responsible. "You can dream about music if you want."

"I . . . can stay . . . Margot?"

"Until you reach your majority, at least. I doubt she'd part with you any sooner, but if you wish to attend school when you are stronger, I'll try to convince her to let you go, so long as you promise to come home for holidays."

"Papa went . . . to Eton."

"So did I. You'll do better at it than I did, I'm sure. Margot swears you are the brightest boy in the British Empire."

"Sister."

"Yes, I know. Ansel, will you try to do without the laudanum, then?"

"Yes. No. It's too cold."

Galen tucked another blanket around him. "We'll stoke up the fire."

Ansel started to shake his head from side to side. "Don't know. Don't know. Don't know. Too hard. Can't do it."

"You can! You are Baron Penrose of Rossington, and you can do anything. I'll help."

"Margot sent you?"

Chapter Fourteen

Whoever said out of the mouths of babes . . . did not intend what landed on the viscount's shirt and boots and breeches.

Galen and Clegg kept pouring fluids into the boy, hoping something would stay down long enough to do him some good. When Ansel shivered, they added wood to the fire until they were suffocating, and when he became drenched in perspiration, they opened the windows and sponged his body. They cushioned him with more pillows when the shaking was so bad Galen feared for his bones. Finally, the viscount gathered the boy in his arms and held him, rocking, pacing, whispering to him, reminding Ansel that Margot was waiting for both of them.

Clegg just shook his head.

The doctor came after luncheon, and shook his head. He did recommend they try coffee, for themselves as well as the boy, so Galen ordered a pot, and a lot of sugar to sweeten it. Lemuel Browne brought the coffee, and shook his head.

Galen was not giving up. Neither was he getting back to London this day or the next, it appeared. He could not tend to the child in a moving carriage or control the temperature or keep coffee hot enough or lemonade cool enough. Tomorrow was Sunday anyway, so Margot would not be performing. He need not worry about the rowdy patrons or fire at the theater or Margot forgetting the words to her songs.

She must be worried, though, expecting him back the previous day, or this one at the latest. He thought about sending for her, contract at the theater or not, but that would be admitting that Ansel was dying, that she needed to come share her brother's last moments. He was no worse, Galen told himself. If the boy was fighting off the stranglehold of the drug, he did not need his sister watching, a sister who was so tenderhearted she'd likely give in to Ansel's begging for another dose. Then he'd be bonded to the laudanum bottle for the rest of his short, unhealthy life.

Galen decided to send his wife a message saying that he had Ansel, but they needed to travel slowly, due to some complications. He did not give the name of the inn or the town, fearing that she would rush to Ansel's bedside anyway. Better she stay in London, a goal for the boy.

He took a brief nap before dinner, when Clegg returned from the posting house and other errands. The valet had purchased additional nightshirts for Ansel, and whatever he could find of a suitable quality to replace his master's irretrievably damaged wardrobe. Clegg was more horrified to be dressing his master in ready-made goods than he was to be emptying slops and heating soup.

When Galen woke up, Ansel was screaming so loudly the inn patrons in the next rooms were pounding on the walls. The viscount rushed to his brother-in-law's bedside, where Clegg was frantically trying to keep the boy from throwing himself off the mattress.

"Ansel," Galen shouted over the boy's cries, "I am here, do not be afraid."

Ansel sobbed, holding onto Galen's hand so tightly his fingernails drew blood. "Papa?"

"No, lad, I am Galen, Margot's husband. Margot sent me to bring you to her, remember?"

Ansel did not remember, but the mention of his sister's name calmed him for a time while Galen dabbed at the bloodstains on his wrist. Lud, if the child's memory did not return, if he could not keep a fact in his head for more than an hour, there was no hope of keeping the barony from Manfred Penrose. He'd have Ansel declared incompetent faster than the judge could bang his gavel, and he'd be right.

Galen spooned some thin gruel into him, reminding Ansel of his name.

"Papa? Papa? No!" He started shrieking again, trying to get off the bed.

The landlord came to complain that he was losing business; patrons were leaving, even if they had to drive through the dark to the next inn. Galen tossed him enough blunt to leave the rooms vacant.

"What happened to your father, Ansel?" Galen asked, figuring that if he could get the boy to speak rationally, perhaps the nightmare would let go of Ansel's mind. "Were you trying to warn him he was too close to the cliff edge?"

"It was the gunshot that frightened his horse. I couldn't turn my pony in time. I couldn't stop him from falling, and rolling and rolling and . . ."

Galen shook him. "But you tried, Ansel. I'm sure he knew how you tried, and was proud to have such a brave son, just as any father would be proud to know how hard you fought when they tried to feed you the poisons."

"I tried to run away. I did try."

"I know you did. There were just too many of them, and they were too big, or you'd have done it. Now you have to keep being brave, when grown men would have given up. Swallow now."

The gruel went flying across the room. "I can't do this! I can't. It hurts!"

"You can! You are Baron Penrose of Rossington. The blood of generations of soldiers and statesmen runs in your veins, fighting the poisons. Your father was brave enough to wed against his family's wishes and go live in a foreign country. Your sister is brave enough to face huge crowds of cloth-heads every night, even though it terrifies her. She was trying to make enough money to buy a cottage where you two could live. Did you know that?"

"Uncle wouldn't let her stay with me. He knew that if he told her to marry Lord Grinsted or leave, she'd have to go. I heard them talking."

"He wanted her where she could not interfere. Think, Ansel—Margot went all the way to London by herself and found a position and a place to stay, and she's only a girl. If she could be that strong-willed, you can do this. Now eat. Clegg made the cook put in extra molasses."

Galen thought he'd never get that sticky stuff out of his hair. The night was about a week long, and daybreak brought no end to the round of weeping, shouting, shaking, and shivering, followed by brief, exhausted dream-ridden catnaps. Galen had no idea if any of the food or fluid reached past Ansel's tongue, or if any of his words of reassurance reached past the nightmares.

He sent Clegg off to church when they heard the bells, deciding they needed all the prayers they could garner.

"Too bad the nipper can't just go to sleep for a bit and wake up when the worst of this is over," Clegg offered when he brought the viscount some breakfast before he left.

It seemed the worst was still to come. Ansel's body started convulsing, and his skin felt cold and clammy, his breath coming in gasps. He was terrified, and so was Galen. Ansel begged and begged for the drugs, for an end to the torture.

Galen could not take much more himself. He looked at the bottle the doctor had left with them, the one that could end this innocent child's suffering, for now, and he did the hardest thing he had ever done in his life. He hit the boy.

All his years of practice at Gentleman Jackson's Boxing Parlor had not taught the viscount the best way to level an eleven-year-old. He held the punch as best he could, trying not to break Ansel's jaw, yet knowing that if he failed, he'd not have the stomach for a second blow. The boy's screams stopped in mid-note, and his eyes widened in shock, before rolling back in his head. Considering the lad's faulty memory, Galen could only hope he'd forget this, too.

When Clegg returned, Ansel was sleeping, real sleep, not a restless doze nor a barely breathing stupor. "I guess the good Lord does answer prayers," the manservant commented, ignoring the huge purplish bruise on the boy's chin.

Ansel did not awaken until suppertime that night. His arms and legs still moved awkwardly, without his volition, it seemed, and his eyes still had trouble focusing, but his face seemed to have better color, aside from the contusion. Most encouraging of all, he swallowed what the viscount put in his mouth, without urging.

While Galen gently wiped Ansel's chin, fearing to feed the boy too much all at once, the youngster stared at him and asked, "Who are you?"

The viscount's heart sank, that the lad could have been saved, and still end in an asylum. "I am Galen Woodrow, Viscount Woodbridge, at your service, Lord Penrose. This is my man, Clegg."

Ansel ignored the servant. "But who *are* you? Why are you here?"

"Didn't I say? Your sister sent me. Margot."

"You might have, I cannot recall. Why?"

"Why can you not recall? You have been ill and—"

"Why did Margot send you, sir?"

"Oh, because I am her husband, of course."

"No, you are not. She would have told me. Mrs. Hapgood would have known."

"I'm afraid it was too sudden to ask your permission for your sister's hand, Baron, but we are, indeed, married."

Ansel was not convinced. "How do I know you are not lying to me like everyone else? You might not even know my sister."

So Galen pulled out the pad of drawing paper he'd been working on while Ansel slept. He showed the boy the pastel sketches he'd done of Margot, studies for the oil painting he hoped to begin soon. On one page she had her hand upraised, holding a rose. In another she was wearing the ivory gown she'd donned for their wedding, flowers twined in her hair. Galen's favorite, though, was the portrait of Margot he'd conjured from his imagination, her blue eyes staring straight at him, her lips turned up in a smile, and her glorious flaxen hair trailing down her half-bared shoulders.

Tears rolling down his cheeks, Ansel stared longest at the picture of the sister he thought lost to him forever. Then he said, "You've used too much ochre for her hair. If you lay the yellow over the burnt umber, you'll get better contrast."

Galen dropped the box of colored charcoals, but Ansel was already back asleep.

The next time he woke, just a few hours later, Galen fed him some beef broth and helped him sit up. Ansel was like a rag doll, but he was not raving. An even better sign was that he seemed to recognize Galen. At least he was no longer afraid of him.

"You might try calling me by my first name, Ansel," the viscount offered, in case Lord Woodbridge was too much for the boy's weak wits to remember. "After all, we are related now, you know."

"You really are married to Margot then, my lord, ah, Galen?"

"I really am, to my great pleasure." Galen found the words came easily.

"Does that mean we are brothers?"

"Brothers-in-law, the next best thing."

"I always wanted a brother."

"Me, too. Now go to sleep so we can go home soon," Galen got past the lump in his throat.

Ansel was a bit stronger every time he awakened. Galen even helped him stand once to use the chamber pot, to everyone's relief. He was still weak, though, and weepy. Sometimes he just sobbed from the agony of his body's recovery. Now that he was more aware, Ansel would be embarrassed to be held like an infant, so Galen just sat by the bedside, feeling less than helpless. He tried telling Ansel about the music room and the painting studio again, in case he hadn't remembered, as well as the pony and the swimming pond. Finally, out of desperation, Galen began singing, every lullaby he ever heard, every love tune, and a few lusty barroom songs. He could not carry a tune in a basket, but he soldiered on, switching to hymns and Christmas carols when he ran out of ballads. The viscount was midway through "Adeste Fidelis" when Ansel stopped crying.

"Do you swear you and Margot are married?" he asked.

"I swear."

"I guess she didn't choose you for your voice."

Galen was eager to leave by Tuesday, to get back to Margot. Ansel was anxious to leave, worrying that Uncle Manfred would find him and take him back, despite Galen's reassurances. Clegg was looking forward to seeing his lordship dressed as a viscount should be, and the innkeeper was looking forward to seeing the last of these well-paying but worrisome guests.

The doctor, however, would not hear of it. "What, take the boy out in the damp?" he demanded. "Can you not see it is pouring rain? The slightest chill will carry him off, in his state. What was the point of curing him of the noxious influence, if you are going to let him die of an influenza?"

So they waited until Wednesday, a beautifully sunny day. But the road was rutted, and traffic was heavy, since it was market day. A shepherd was taking his entire flock to the next town, slowly. Two young girls were leading a flock of geese, their webbed feet coated with tar. Wagons loaded down with vegetables were barely traveling faster than Galen could have walked. Ansel turned out to be as poor a traveler as Galen, but the young baron could not ride on top with the driver and groom, not where he might fall off or chance a cool breeze in his face. The detour one peddler recommended took them miles out of the way, and the lead horse came up lame. Then it began to rain again. Galen began to worry if they'd get to London in time for Margot's final performance on Saturday.

Chapter Fifteen

Whoever said out of sight, out of mind, was absolutely correct. Galen was out of sight, and Margot was going out of her mind. How could she miss what she'd never known? Besides, everywhere she went, scores of people were wanting to see what the viscount found so attractive, wanting to ask questions for which the new viscountess had no answers. Margot should have taken the knocker off the Grosvenor Square house door, or moved back to Mrs. McGuirk's until Galen returned, she realized, for she was not going to find a moment's peace here, or a decent meal. People were constantly at the door to leave cards, pay morning calls, ask her to sponsor this or that charity, invite her to attend some house party or other, where she'd be welcome to sing, of course. Fenning handled the door, at least, keeping track of the cards with corners turned down to show who had called in person, as opposed to those who had sent wedding gifts, invitations, or congratulations via their servants. The mail he simply stacked in the butler's pantry when the viscount's desk became invisible under the blizzard of white vellum.

The Oriental Parlor was given over to the wedding presents. One more silver epergne, Margot counted, and they could open a shop. She didn't know what to do with ten tea sets or thirty silver candelabra, or how to thank perfect strangers. Why, one of the hideous centerpieces might be an heirloom from Galen's godmother, whoever that might be, requiring a more personal acknowledgment. Besides, she had rehearsals, and a room to prepare for Ansel. Fenning suggested she hire a secretary.

How could she hire a secretary when she couldn't even find a housekeeper or a chef? Margot had asked Galen to see if Mrs. Hapgood would come, so she only wanted to hire an interim housekeeper anyway, which the agency guaranteed her was no difficulty, with so many people eager for positions. Not this one. Half the women the agency sent over for the housekeeping position looked around as if this were a house of ill repute. That was the half not sent screaming by Ruff. Too many of them eyed those silver candlesticks with a calculating glance, calculating how much they could get from the fences, Margot made no doubt. Meanwhile, she was overseeing the maids and the menus, striving to earn Fenning's approval of her house-holding skills with as much effort as she put into pleasing her audience. Hiring a chef was all too easy; keeping one was harder. Philippe broke out in splotches from dog hair. Jacques refused to cook for a dog. Georges wanted the kitchen refurbished before he could create culinary marvels. Jean-Claude hated the English and tried to burn the kitchen down around their ears, so they had to redecorate anyway. And Antoine ate garlic, a great deal of garlic. Margot decided to let Ruff do the interviewing from then on. Any chef who did not run, was to be hired.

They were not starving. Margot had her mother's recipe for crepes, Fenning could make toast, Ella was a dab hand at frying eggs, and the scullery maid knew how to slice vegetables and beef for soup, although she could not read the labels on the sacks and jars of spices. They had lovely teas, at any rate. Fenning had contracted with Gunther's to deliver.

Margot's standing at the theater was troublesome, too, with Lord Woodbridge absent from Town. On the day Galen left, she was delivered to the side door in style, escorted by no less a dignified personage than the Duke of Woburton's own London butler, Fenning . . . and the dog, the maid, and the two footmen Galen had insisted she have as guards. No actress had ever been accorded such respect. She sang her selections as usual, and the audience accorded her resounding but dignified appreciation. When she faced the family box, everyone held their breath until a single rose was tossed down by a dark-clad arm, then roses fell to Margot's feet from all sides, until she was standing in a bower.

On the second night, however, Skippy got too excited about his part in the drama, or else he forgot his instructions altogether, but he stepped to the railing of the box and waved to her and to the audience.

Whispers rose as people recognized the lanky reverend.

One wag in the pit called out, "What's the matter, sweetings, Woodbridge left you already? Don't worry, I'll keep you company."

A woman with hennaed hair stood up and shouted that it took a real woman to keep 'is lordship from wanderin', not a china doll. "Send 'im my way, love," she shouted, "iffen you know where to find 'im."

"Mayhaps he shabbed off to Scotland after the other bride," another would-be wit added to the rumors and speculation.

"I know right where *mon cher* is," Margot said, trying to banter with the groundlings sitting close to the stage. "My own Sir Galahad is off slaying dragons for me, to bring back the richest jewel I know."

Disappointed, angry they'd been duped, cheated of the romantic happily ever after, the crowd now seemed to consider Margot's marriage a hole-in-corner affair that Woodbridge already regretted. Suddenly, this was no great love match; it was a sordid liaison. The flowers were thrown *at* her instead of *to* her, almost pelting Margot as she ran off the stage without singing her last selection.

The manager was furious she had not finished the set, for now the lower-price-paying patrons would grow more raucous, with minutes still to go before the stage and the actors were ready to open the next act. "You be here tomorrow ready to sing, missy," he insisted, forgetting she was now my lady, "and get that husband of yours back here."

As if Margot wasn't praying for Galen's return hard enough. She was almost sick with worry. He should have been back; she should have resigned and gone with him. Now she'd made micefeet of all their machinations. Galen had married her to salvage his pride; now he would hate her for this new mortification. Worst of all, she was afraid to go back on stage Saturday night if he was not there.

The message from Woodbridge waiting at the house was no help. He had Ansel, but they had some matters to attend before reaching London. What, she fretted, was his lordship having a new suit of clothes made while she was being undressed by all those hungry eyes in the audience? How dare he dither when she was so distraught! She was too upset to mind the meager meal set out for her.

Galen had enclosed Mrs. Hapgood's address, however. Concerned that their old housekeeper was not looking after Ansel, Margot wrote to her immediately, and to the cook at Penrose Hall Galen thought might be available. Mrs. Shircastle was a solid country cook, not a fancy French chef, and Margot would welcome her with open arms, even if her cooking was not what the *ton* preferred. Let them eat at someone else's table, Margot thought defiantly, for she would not welcome such fickle, unfriendly people to hers. Three invitations had already been rescinded. Too bad no one wanted their epergnes returned.

Rather than trusting her notes to the post, Margot ordered Fenning to send a carriage for the women. She might as well get some benefit from being a viscountess, she told the butler, for as long as she was one.

Despite Fenning's reassurances that she would suffer no insults that evening, Margot left for the theater Saturday with a whole flock of butterflies practicing acrobatics in her stomach. She could not concentrate on her music, and did not care which gown Ella laid out for her. Instead of reciting her lyrics, Margot kept repeating to herself that Fenning said it would be all right, and Galen said she could trust Fenning about everything.

When she peeked out from the side of the stage during the drama, trying to gauge the mood of the crowd, she could see the butler's handiwork: every footman and groom from Woburton House was dressed in Woburton livery and scattered around the pit. Fenning himself was going to sit in the family box, beside Skippy Skidmore.

The crowds were noisy during the intermission, not paying attention to Margot. At least no one would notice if she forgot a stanza or two. Those in the tiers went visiting or gossiped loudly between the boxes, plainly showing their disdain. She was sure the beturbaned matrons would have turned their backs on her or pulled their skirts aside if she passed their way in the park. She'd warned the viscount that she'd never be accepted, that going on stage had blotted her copybook for all time, but Galen had not listened, the clunch. Now he was going to be so disappointed, if he ever returned, the bounder, after leaving her here like this.

Margot sang, her voice wavering a little in the beginning, but smoothing as she realized no one was going to start booing or hissing or throwing rotten fruit. The Woburton House servants quickly surrounded the first young man castaway enough to consider their mistress open to suggestive remarks. They changed the drunkard's mind, and any other would-be troublemakers'.

When the time came for her last song, Margot did not step closer to the family box. She was not going to place herself nearer to the men in the pit whose hands reached out to touch her ankles or her skirt, despite her menservants' frowns and fisted hands. Before she could begin the last selection, though, a gentleman in the viscount's box stepped forward into the light. Margot could not see very well, with the flambeau between them, but he was elegantly dressed, with a large pearl at his cravat. He was tall like Galen, inches taller than Fenning, and broad-shouldered, not chicken-chested like Skippy. Her husband had come home.

Smiling radiantly, Margot stepped toward the lights, toward the box, as the crowd craned their necks to get a better look. The gentleman threw an orchid down to her—a beautiful rare orchid, with purple throat and pink-tinged petals. Margot cradled the flower in her hands, realizing this was not Galen's token; this was not her husband. The gentleman resembled him, but with silver at his temples and a more prominent nose. Someone gasped, "His Grace," just as she was reaching the same conclusion.

Margot dipped into a curtsey and silently thanked Fenning, who must have sent for the Duke of Woburton. Most likely her father-in-law had left his gardens and come to Town to ring a peal over Galen's head for marrying so recklessly. Perhaps he'd try to dissolve the marriage. Perhaps he'd throw Margot out of the house. For now, though, he was lending her countenance, bless him. With the duke so obviously showing his approval, no one even whispered during her last song.

Margot hoped Fenning had asked His Grace to bring along his cook.

His Grace invited Margot to dine with him that evening at the Pulteney. He wanted to show off his new daughter-in-law, he told everyone who stopped by their table.

"Knew her father, I did," he told a few old cronies who were sure to pass on his words. "Sound as houses, Marcus Penrose. Married for love, same as I did. Same as my son did. Good show, what?"

When they were alone back at Woburton House, Margot had to confess that the marriage was not truly a love match. She could not lie to this gruff, courtly gentleman.

"Think I don't know that?" He patted her hand as Fenning brought in the tea cart, laden with delicacies to surpass Gunther's, for the duke had, indeed, brought his own cook. While Margot poured, His Grace went on: "I know the name of every opera dancer, every actress, every high-priced Bird of Paradise my son has ever tumbled."

Sipping at her tea, Margot decided she'd think about every one of those mistresses later.

"I know you aren't one of them, either," His Grace continued, "which pleases me. Forgive my plain speaking, my dear, but I wouldn't trust any marriage based on a passing fancy or a moment's lust. No, this may not be a love match, but it will be soon, I'd wager, as soon as that gudgeon gets back to Town. Woodbridge is a likeable enough chap, if I say so myself, and you'll suit him to a cow's thumb. Why, I'm halfway jealous of him myself, simply hearing you sing. Now that I have met you, I have no worries. In fact, I have great hopes of bouncing my grandson on my knee within the year."

That was not in the marital agreement, but Margot could not say so, of course. Feeling her cheeks grow warm, she said, "Thank you, Your Grace."

"No, thank you, my dear. Now I think one more day of my company ought to put paid to any lingering gossip. We'll attend church together in the morning, then I'll make sure the bow-window babblers know your marriage has my approval, and the gabble-grinders at the Botanical Gardens at Kew. The gossipers will find another juicy morsel soon enough, even if that nodcock son of mine does not return soon. I've got to get back to my grounds and greenhouses—it's the growing season, don't you know—but I promise to return for the party Fenning tells me you are planning. I claim the first dance, and that jackanapes you married can have the second."

"You won't stay until then?"

"No, I hate the City. Nothing grows here but mildew."

"I don't suppose you'd leave your chef? Monsieur Claveau had a racing hound of his own as a child in France, and he adores Rufus."

"I am willing to sacrifice almost anything for my children, my dear. I do have to draw the line somewhere, however." Woburton had already lost a pair of slippers to the cur. He was not going to lose his cook.

His Grace and his chef left on Monday morning. His daughter arrived Monday afternoon.

Chapter Sixteen

Whoever said spare the rod and spoil the child was most likely itching to lay a birch to the backside of Lady Harriet Woodrow. Margot was certainly itching to put her in a coach and send her back to Cheshire.

No one had ever denied the duke's daughter anything. If some poor governess had tried in all the ten and seven years, the chit had gone to her doting papa and wheedled her way to the village fair or wept her way to a new bonnet better suited to Cyprian than a schoolgirl. The string of governesses gave up. The academy for young ladies she briefly attended surrendered after two months. The proprietress was afraid of losing His Grace's patronage if they reprimanded the chit for sneaking out after hours, or applying lip rouge or waving to the soldiers at a military parade. The headmistress sent Lady Harriet home, declaring, quite correctly, that the school had taught her all they could.

Harriet's latest companion, hired to take her about London while they were in Town to attend Galen's wedding, gave her notice as soon as they had left the metropolis. Lady Harriet, excited and eager, was difficult enough. Disappointed, dragged away from the delights of Town, denied her chance to dance at her first adult party, she was downright impossible. Who knew what trouble she'd get up to? The governess left before she got blamed.

The duke had dried Harriet's tears on the way home with visits to every shop along the way. His Grace could do nothing about his son's appalling loss of a bride, but he could console his daughter for the curtailed visit. With no companion to restrain her, Harriet had chosen a wardrobe for a wanton, all diaphanous fabrics in bold colors. Her new frocks would have to be delivered to their home, however, where she had no place to wear them, which brought on another bout of weeping. From where he rode alongside the carriage, the duke tut-tutted her misery. Her aunt Mathilda could see to Harriet's come-out next fall, he promised. In fact, the more he thought about it, and a summer full of tantrums and tears, the duke decided Harriet ought to spend the summer in Bath, getting reacquainted with her aunt and cousin, polishing her social skills on the matrons and retired military gentlemen who gathered there.

What, thought Harriet, molder amongst a bunch of dodderers who spent their days discussing their digestive systems? Worse, being seen with Cousin Harold would quite sink her chances of making a stir when she finally got to London. No, Lady Harriet wished to be in Town, where all the interesting gentlemen were, and she wished to be there now.

As soon as her father left on some foolish errand, likely to do with his fusty old flowers, Harriet followed in a hired chaise with a girl from the posting house to serve as attendant, less for respectability's sake than because Harriet had no idea how to do up her own hair or iron her own gowns. Her sense of adventure did not extend to fetching bathwater. Money was no problem, for she directed all the bills to her father.

Harriet was far behind the duke in arriving at the London town house because she insisted on stopping at each of the village modistes to gather her new wardrobe. She also detoured for a horse fair, purchasing a darling mare, the exact chestnut color of Harriet's hair. She'd be the Toast of the Town on such a mount, and show her brother she knew something about horses, too.

Of course the chestnut color washed off the mare's gray muzzle with the first rain, and the horse stopped prancing as soon as the pebble worked its way out of her shoe, and she bit the groom at the last inn before Town. Harriet traded the mare for a pocket watch, thinking to turn her brother up sweet so he would let her stay in Town. The poor dear needed consoling, after all, and who better to do it than a loving sister? When the watch stopped ticking, she tossed it out the carriage window.

Now here she was, on Margot's doorstep. Harriet would not believe her older brother had married such a dasher, nor that her father approved, until she heard it from Fenning himself, and then Skippy Skidmore, whom she'd known her entire life. Then she was delighted. Having married a notorious performer, her brother could not possibly fault Harriet's own behavior.

Declaring that her hired chaise and hired maid had already left, Harriet ordered her boxes and trunks moved upstairs. She was not leaving until her brother returned, and that was that. Margot hated to say it of her new sister-in-law, but Galen's sister was a spoiled brat. And she could not cook, either.

When applied to, Skippy, spiritual guide that he was, suggested locking the chit in the wine cellar for a year or two; perhaps she'd mellow with age. She'd been a pest as a child, he declared, and still was. Fenning advised Margot to ship the female to her aunt in Bath in a carriage with armed guards, the guards' weapons being less for protecting Lady Harriet than for self-defense. Margot couldn't send Galen's sister away, though, not knowing the pitfalls waiting for a young woman on her own. Lady Harriet seemed younger than the dawn to Margot, already exhausted from the duke's visit and worrying over Galen and Ansel.

"Very well," she told the minx, "you can stay until your brother returns to decide what to do with you, but with conditions."

"Anything," Harriet promised, having no compunctions about lying to an opera singer. The maids who'd done her unpacking were chattering about a party to be held at Woburton House in a few weeks. The dinner party had now escalated to a ball, at the duke's insistence, they said. Harriet vowed she would not leave before what promised to be a grand affair, even if she had to perjure her soul.

"First, you shall write to your father so he knows where you are." Margot and Fenning had both already written while Harriet was overseeing the unpacking of her clothes, but the chit ought to learn some sense of responsibility. "Second, you will stay in the house or on the grounds while I am at the theater. I'll not have you traipsing about London on your own, destroying your reputation. We are not accepting callers or making visits, so you'll find things quite dull. If you wish to reconsider and travel to your aunt in Bath, I can send Fenning with you to ensure your safe arrival."

Even Harriet was intimidated by Fenning. "Please, not Aunt Matty! I'll do anything if you don't send me to Bath. She'll make me take the waters and stroll the Pump Room with Cousin Harold. Why, your dog would be a better escort than Cousin Harold." Since Harriet was feeding Ruff one of the last strawberry tarts the duke's chef had baked, Margot did not think much of either of them. She did feel sorry for the girl, though, having her activities thus curtailed, so she offered to take Harriet to some of the shops tomorrow morning. Margot had to see about expanding her own wardrobe, and she had not yet decided on a gown for the party.

Harriet clapped her hands and declared Margot the best of sisters-in-law. Lady Floria had never invited Harriet anywhere, not since the time Harriet set her horse to a mad gallop in the park so that handsome lieutenant could come to her rescue.

Margot could do no more that afternoon, since she was already late for rehearsal. She went off to the theater with Ella and Skippy and Ruff, confident the young woman would be content with the latest novel, the daily papers, the finely tuned pianoforte. Margot even suggested Harriet might make an early night of it, after her tiring journey.

Harriet went upstairs and cut off all her hair. Her brown locks were never going to be as stunning as her sister-in-law's gold ones anyway, so she might as well have a style that was all the crack. Then she unpacked her gowns again, trying to decide which to wear to the theater that night.

Margot's performance went well that evening, until she looked toward Galen's box and spotted a bright pink gown, surrounded by scarlet regimental jackets. She thought she might have the wrong box, but there was Skippy Skidmore with her sister-in-law, tossing her roses.

"How could you have let her attend the theater?" Margot demanded of the irreverent reverend as soon as they were all in the carriage for the ride home from Drury Lane. "And wearing such an ensemble! Everyone in the audience must have noticed her. I suppose most of them would have recognized her as Galen's sister and not your fancy piece." Ignoring Lady Harriet's gasp, Margot angrily told Skippy that he, at least, ought to have known better.

Skippy tugged at his cravat. "I knew I had no choice. The brat sent a note saying she'd go on her own if I didn't escort her."

"Without a maid? Were you trying to ruin her before she made her come-out?"

The neckcloth and Skippy's conscience hung in limp disarray. "There was one, I swear, only the girl went off with one of the soldiers. Said she wouldn't put up with Harry's niffy-naffy nonsense. 'Sides, with so many men in the box, no one would have noticed whether there was a maid or not. People thought His Grace was still in Town, in the box, too, so her reputation ain't totally destroyed."

Lower lip trembling, one tear glistening on her eyelashes, Harriet whimpered, "I just wanted to hear you sing. I thought no one could criticize my presence with such an escort as the bishop's own assistant."

Skip the ceremony and get on with the toasts Skidmore? Margot decided her sister-in-law was either attics-to-let or a great actress. "Can't you see that you will ruin your chances of making a decent match? You know my social standing is too shaky to lend you countenance."

Lady Harriet's solitary tear disappeared as she stepped down from the carriage at Woburton House, without even thanking Skippy for his escort. The girl looked back at Margot and said, "I am supposed to be the innocent, not you. Do you really think the *ton* is going to turn its back on the Duke of Woburton's daughter?" She waved a hand at the imposing edifice, the servants waiting to take their wraps. "Not with my connections and my dowry, they won't."

Margot followed her sister-in-law to the parlor, still trying to make the peagoose see the dangers of her prideful actions. "Certain doors will close even to you, if you continue to tie your garters in public. Don't you care?"

The conversation was concluded, as far as Harriet was concerned. "Are you going to eat that slice of poppyseed cake, Margot? You really have to do something about getting a cook, you know. Why, I had to make Skippy stop at a chop house on the way to the theater, I was that famished. Did you know, Skippy tried to tell me women rarely eat in such places? I swear, he hasn't the wits of a widgeon. There were at least two females. One was wearing a gown almost as fine as mine."

If the female's frock was anything like Harriet's, the woman was a whore. Margot prayed Galen came home soon, so she could shoot him.

A message did arrive from the viscount the next morning, saying that Ansel was better, they were on their way. The brief note relieved Margot mightily, since Mrs. Hapgood and Mrs. Shircastle had also arrived, with dire tales of Ansel's circumstances at Penrose Hall. If Galen had not approached her with his ridiculous offer, Margot realized, she would have been too late to save her brother.

The two older women settled into Woburton House as if they'd been born there. Cook's father was a kennel-master, so she threw her arms around Ruff, promising she knew just

SAVED BY SCANDAL   117

what to feed such a handsome creature, and now she had a fine kitchen in which to do it. Mrs. Hapgood started counting linen, thrilled to be working for Miss Margot again, and in the same household as her best friend. The two women were best friends, that is, until they began to vie for Fenning's approbation, but Margot was going to pretend she did not notice.

If she had started the day being tired from another evening of performing and another night of wakefulness over her brother, her husband, and her future, she was even more exhausted after a morning of shopping with Lady Harriet. The child refused to consider white or pastels or sprigged muslins. She had her own funds to finance her outrageous purchases, and enough boldness to ignore Margot, the modistes, the milliners, and the current mode for young misses.

Every purchase turned into a debate until Margot developed a headache—and a great deal of sympathy for her father-in-law. Rather than argue with the impossible chit, she simply informed each shopkeeper that if her unfledged sister-in-law was permitted to purchase goods more suitable for a bird of paradise, Margot would take her own business elsewhere. Forced to choose between a duke's daughter or a viscount's wife, the dressmakers wisely opted for the level-headed, and wealthier, Lady Woodbridge.

Harriet was not speaking to her when they returned to the house, for which Margot would say an extra prayer. She decided to forgo luncheon, even if Mrs. Shircastle was cooking, in favor of a nap.

Fenning himself knocked on her door as soon as her head hit the pillow, it seemed. A caller had arrived. "But I am not at home to visitors. You know that."

The butler extended a silver platter on which reposed a single card, one corner turned down. "I think madam had better make an exception."

Chapter Seventeen

Whoever said the grass is always greener on the other side of the fence had never seen the gray gorse and the purple heather of Scotland. Neither had Lady Floria Cleary.

The Earl of Cleary's groom had caught up with the eloping couple not much past where the earl's carriage had come a-cropper. Floria and Sir Henry Lytell had not outdistanced the earl or his rider because of the frequent stops necessitated by the lady's headaches, hunger, need to use the necessary, and outright boredom. Sir Henry was wishing he'd been able to afford to bring his horse along, so he did not have to ride inside the cramped coach with his inamorata, who had brought her entire trousseau.

The groom dutifully passed on the earl's message: Unless Floria detoured to her grandmother's in Wales, without Sir Henry, she would never see a groat of her dowry, or the inside of her father's house again.

Suddenly, Lady Floria did not appear quite so fetching to the below-hatches baronet. Perhaps Lytell's change of heart was not so sudden, because he'd been fetching the demanding female's shawl, a glass of lemonade, a bouquet of wildflowers from alongside the highway, for days, it seemed. Nothing he did was good enough for the lady, and nothing, he found out, was going to convince her to anticipate their wedding vows. He, in turn, had not anticipated the cost of hiring two bedrooms whenever they stopped. Without Floria's bride's portion, it was bellows-to-mend with him. Floria's assurance that she'd be able to talk her father around, in a few years, was not going to pay his creditors now.

Clutching his heart in regret—and her jewel case in repayment of his expenses—Sir Henry stepped down from the hired—and unpaid for—coach.

Good riddance, thought the lady. Since leaving London, Sir Henry had not written one poem to her beauty, nor bought her one pretty trinket, quite unlike his previous courtly devotion. Furthermore, he had wanted a great deal more than to kiss her hand. Lady Floria might have flirted—didn't all women?—but she did not go beyond the line, not even with her betrothed. Woodbridge never wrote poems or showered her with gifts, but at least he never slobbered on her.

Going to her grandmother's, where the servants barely spoke the King's English, was out of the question. Why, rusticating in Wales would be as boring as marrying Woodbridge, with his plans to take up estate management or some tedious rural activity. Of course Floria never intended to let the viscount bury himself in the country, not with the elegant town house right in the center of the social world. No, they'd have to be in London to see about all the renovations she was planning, in the Egyptian style. Woodbridge would understand that they had to stay *au courant,* of course. The more Florrie thought about her options, the better Galen looked. Looking at the depleted contents of her reticule, she decided to marry him after all.

The groom reminded Lady Floria that her father was not going to welcome her with open arms. With the door slammed in her face was more like it, was his opinion.

"La, he always comes down from the boughs in a week or so." Nevertheless, Floria decided to give her father a fortnight to get over her latest escapade. Besides, he'd open the purse strings that much sooner if she could present him with a *fait accompli,* in the form of his favored son-in-law. Woodbridge would just have to get a special license.

"No, Woodbridge would not have married you," Lady Floria insisted. "He's much too concerned for the conventions." He was dry as dust, but Floria would not belittle her betrothed in front of this . . . this mushroom.

Fenning had placed the unexpected, unwanted, and entirely unwelcome guest in the library, away from prying eyes and listening ears. He had not been able to do much about Harriet.

"Well, he *did* marry her!" Lady Harriet was all too happy to dash the hopes of the woman who'd jilted her brother. Worse, Lady Floria had made the viscount's sister wear a frumpish frock to the wedding, most likely so the bride wouldn't be overshadowed by the groom's young sister, Harriet told herself. "She's prettier than you and nicer, too, I swear."

"Harriet, go upstairs," Margot ordered. "This discussion does not concern you."

To no one's surprise, Harriet didn't budge. "Of course it does. The most interesting scandal of the Season, and in my own family! Isn't it smashing?"

Margot felt like smashing something, for sure, especially when Lady Floria declared the marriage was not legal, since Woodbridge had been previously promised and the banns were read. Margot eyed the bust of Plato on Galen's desk, but reminded herself that she was a lady, even if the other two women had been born with the title. "I am sorry to say . . ." she began. "No, I am not sorry at all. I am pleased to say that Lord Woodbridge and I are indeed wed, and His Grace has given his blessing to the match. Notices were in all the papers, and an announcement was made at the Drury Lane theater. I understand your father himself publicly released my lord from any prior commitment, in light of *your* reneging on your promise. In fact, I believe Lord Cleary ceded your dowry to Lord Woodbridge to satisfy his sense of honor."

"He gave *my* portion away to satisfy *his* honor? Damnation!" Poor Plato hit the carpet.

"Harriet, go upstairs." Margot stepped in front of the desk before the inkwell and the stacks of invitations could join the philosopher. "Don't you think Lord Woodbridge was entitled to something for the embarrassment you caused him?"

"Something besides an opera singer, you mean?"

When Margot gasped at such a blatant insult, Harriet tossed back, "Something like a baron's daughter, you must mean, Lady Floria. Dear Margot is the daughter of the late Baron Penrose of Rossington, you know."

Floria did not know, of course. She did not apologize, either. "La, Woodbridge's pride was hurt, that was all. But you do not understand." Her tone seemed to imply that Margot was incapable of such a feat. "If I have no dowry, who will marry me?"

"No one with any sense," Harriet put in, causing both of the older women to frown at her.

Floria was tapping her foot, thinking. "Woodbridge will simply have to give it back, that's all. When did you say he's returning?"

"My lord should be in Town before the end of the week. I am certain he will be willing to discuss the matter with your father then."

"My father? He'd only give it to some other fool. It is my money. With such a sum I can set up an establishment of my own, an elegant salon for aspiring poets. Yes, and then I can marry one of them if I choose."

Margot stepped toward the door, indicating the visit was, mercifully, over. "I'll tell Lord Woodbridge that you called and you are eager to speak with him."

"No, I'm not leaving, not without the dowry."

"Of course you are. You cannot stay here."

Floria crossed her arms over her chest and narrowed her eyes. "I was nearly mistress of this pile, and I know to the inch how many bedchambers are in it. Surely one of them is empty."

Margot countered: "Surely, you would not wish to stay here, with another woman in charge."

"My father is not pleased with me, and I cannot very well put up at a hotel, can I? Without funds and without Woodbridge's protection, I cannot call on my friends, either. You married my fiancé, so you can deuced well give me lodging until he gives me my money."

"Good grief, people will think . . . will think that . . ."

"That we are conducting a *ménage à trois*?" Floria laughed. "So what? If you were at all familiar with the Polite World, you'd know it happens all the time. There's the Melbourne House arrangement and—"

"Harriet, go upstairs! Lady Floria, I do not wish to hear any more. It will not do, and that's all. As you can see, my young sister-in-law is residing with us. I would not have her tarred with the brush of scandal."

"La, that one is bound to blot her copybook sooner or later." Floria took the time to notice Harriet's low-cut, emerald green gown. "Sooner rather than later, I'd wager."

For the first time, Margot had to agree with Galen's former fiancée. "Nevertheless, I shall not permit my home to be an *on dit,* not with my innocent little brother coming to stay."

"Very well, then, I shall have to remain incognito."

Margot shook her head. The green-eyed, auburn-haired beauty with her voluptuous curves and aristocratic airs would be as easy to hide as Harriet in her bright gowns.

Seeing Margot's doubts, Floria hurried on. "I could wear a disguise. La, I have always loved a masquerade, don't you? But I forget, actresses are always in costume, aren't they? Why, I could dress as one of your maids. No one ever notices the servants, you know."

No one except all the other servants, who would spread the tale through every pub and pantry in Town, Margot knew. "Somehow I cannot quite see you dusting the parlor or scrubbing the fireplace tiles."

"No, of course not. I know, I can be your cousin from France, your widowed cousin, with a black veil to hide my face."

"I have no French cousins."

"*Allors, chérie,* you do now. Madame, ah . . . Millefleur.

Just think, I will be able to accompany you on your rounds, and no one will know the difference. Do you think I should have a title?"

Comtesse Cork-brain ought to do the trick, Margot thought, but Harriet squealed. "Capital! Now I can have a chaperone while you are at the theater, Margot, so I don't have to stay at home."

"I thought I told you to go upstairs, Harriet." Margot sighed, feeling as if she'd been run over by a carriage. "And neither one of you is to leave the house, is that quite clear?"

They were both at the theater that night, naturally.

Chapter Eighteen

Whoever said neither a borrower nor a lender be, could not have meant sisters, sisters-in-law, or superior house guests. Lady Floria was wearing Margot's black lace mantilla, from when she sang Spanish love songs, and Lady Harriet was wearing some of Margot's stage makeup.

Not all the young gentlemen visiting the box were wearing uniforms this evening, Margot noted from the wings. She did not know if that was better or worse, and supposed there was safety in the numbers of nodcocks swarming around Harriet. She could not imagine His Grace handing his daughter, and her dowry, to any impecunious second son or pockets-to-let lieutenant. The older flirts and fortune hunters were, thankfully, less interested in the infantry than in preserving their own skin, not daring to dally with such a well-connected chit. Lady Floria was a horse of another color, though: the black of a widow, experienced, available, alluring in her veil. If she kept fluttering her black lace fan—Margot's black lace fan—in so seductive a manner, she'd have every libertine in London in that box.

Reverend Skidmore did not escort the ladies home, skipping the lecture he was sure would be coming. "The brat just arrived at the theater on her own, so you cannot blame me. At least she had her duenna along tonight," was all he said as he handed them into their carriage. "So she's halfway respectable."

If he only knew! Margot thanked him and sank back against the cushions, drained from her performance on stage, and from watching Lady Floria's in the box. She was too tired to remonstrate with Harriet, which would have been a waste of her breath in any case, and too angry with Floria for jeopardizing an innocent's reputation, flirting with another scandal. Margot did not even stay in the parlor for tea when they got home, unwilling to converse with either of her aggravating house guests. Let them eat all of Mrs. Shircastle's macaroons, she told herself, unworthily hoping that Harriet would break out in spots and Floria would get fat as a flawn.

Ruff ate the whole plate, though, so Margot's hopes were dashed. Then the dog's stomach kept rumbling all night until she had to get up and put him out in the back garden. Now she had to hope her father-in-law was not particularly fond of that ornamental shrub. Sitting on the stone bench, Margot pulled her robe closer around her and looked up at the moon and the stars. Was this really the same sky that hung over-head at Mrs. McGuirk's house? she mused. How could it be, when she was such a different person? Margot was living in luxury, but that was not even the biggest change, and being married felt the same as being single. What was so different was that she was no longer alone in her thoughts. So used to relying on herself, now she kept wondering what Galen would do about his sister, about his former fiancée. Was he looking at the same sky, and did he ever think about her?

Lud, Galen thought, he could walk home faster than this blasted journey was taking. He'd have driven through the night; Zeus, he'd have driven through the rain, through the sheep, through that overflowing stream, to get back to Town, but not with Ansel in the coach. The boy was still too fragile. He was so delicate that the least draft sent him to shivering, his digestion so uncertain that he could only bear an hour of the rattling carriage at a time. He never com-plained, though, or grew peevish. Galen had to order him, in fact, to stop apologizing for all the fuss and bother he was causing.

No, if Galen did decide to get down and walk, or hire a

horse to ride ahead, he'd have to carry Ansel along with him to London. Having come this far, he was not abandoning his brother-in-law to Clegg's care, as devoted as the valet was to the nipper. Galen wanted to be there when Margot caught the first sight of her little brother, now that he was cleaned up, with a bit of flesh on his bones, and the light of understanding back in his blue eyes.

Adding to the length of the journey was the stop they had to make to purchase Ansel a trunkful of clothes. Thinking to be in London within a day or two of leaving Penrose Hall, Galen had left the boy's things behind, but Ansel could not walk into inns in his nightshirt or step behind a bush to relieve himself, and he refused to be carried. The lad was pluck to the backbone, just like his sister.

They had to stop for more drawing paper and crayons, also, for Galen had used up an entire pad, drawing Ansel while he was peacefully asleep, or when he marveled at the wonders of his first horse fair. The cattle market was not much of a detour, Galen convinced himself, and he'd promised the boy a pony, hadn't he? Besides, they'd only stayed long enough to sketch the new acquisition, arguing over the proper mix of colors, so Ansel could have something to keep before the pony was delivered to London. The other horses Galen had bought for his breeding stock were to go directly to Three Woods in Cheshire.

Galen thought Margot would like best the last picture he'd done, showing Ansel with a wide grin, his short blond hair gleaming in the sunshine. The more recent drawings he'd done of Margot were not as pleasing to the viscount, since they were more copies of his previous sketches than new compositions. Her eyes could not be that blue, and where did that faint band of freckles begin, anyway? Damn, he'd been gone too long.

One more night, Galen promised himself, willing the night sky to stay clear so they could travel on the morrow, unless the bantling's cough worsened. That was why the viscount was blowing a cloud in the inn's backyard now, not wanting to breathe smoke on the sleeping boy in the chamber they shared. Even with Clegg keeping watch in case Ansel got another nightmare or a fever, Galen decided he would not stay outside for many more minutes. He also decided that they would not keep Ansel in the soot-laden City for long, just long enough to hold that blasted party.

Despite his assurances to Margot, what had seemed an excellent idea a week ago was looking more and more of a disaster. The entertainment was only supposed to be a small gathering for dinner, to introduce Margot to his closest friends in the comfort of her own home. But what if no one came, not even Galen's father? Without Galen's guidance, an inexperienced chit like Margot could have blundered into another scandal while he was away, putting her beyond the pale of polite society. Damn, he'd been gone too long.

Galen told himself that he wouldn't care for himself if his wife was given the cut direct. He'd married her knowing just such a thing could happen, hadn't he? They could retire to the country all that sooner, and stay there. Margot would care, though, and Ansel would care if his beloved sister was slighted. For that matter, Galen would not wish his sons to be taunted, or his daughters unwelcome at Almack's. Deuce take it, having a family was the devil of a thing.

Sons and daughters? Just the thought of begetting that family with Margot raised Galen's heart rate, and his temperature. Damn, he'd been gone far too long.

Margot saw neither her sister-in-law nor her "cousin" the next morning. They were either sleeping till noon or avoiding her, which suited Margot just fine. Another message had arrived from Viscount Woodbridge, stating that he hoped to be home within a day or two, and to warn the stables of a new addition. The infuriating man was dawdling at horse breeders along the way, drat him, not caring that Margot would be on tenterhooks. She doubted Lord Woodbridge gave her feelings the slightest consideration, no more than Lady Harriet did, or Lady Floria. After all, she was only

Ansel's sister, and she was only the mistress of this establishment.

So she declared that breakfasts would not be served in the bedrooms. If the two ladyships wanted more than chocolate and rolls, they could deuced well come downstairs.

Feeling a great deal better, Margot consulted with Fenning about his lordship's favorite meals so she and Mrs. Shircastle could plan the menus, and she and Mrs. Hapgood directed a squad of maids in turning out the viscount's rooms, so all would be in readiness for his return. The bedroom on the nursery floor was scrubbed again, and fresh linens put on the bed. Margot arranged flowers for the public rooms, and sent back the bouquets delivered for Harriet. She penned thank-yous to Harriet's admirers herself, hinting that her sister-in-law was not old enough to receive either floral tributes or gentleman callers. Fenning might not be able to keep that hoydenish female in the house, but he could certainly keep her beaux on the other side of the door.

The nosegay that arrived for Madame Millefleur was from a gentleman who had sent similar ones to Margot many times. A married gentleman, he was, which ought to suggest to Lady Floria that her behavior had been suggestive, to say the least. Margot couldn't toss the flowers on the dust heap, since Floria was not a schoolgirl relation, but she could relegate them to the library, which, containing only books, had little interest for Lady Floria.

For good measure, Margot took the carriage with her and Ella to the theater for rehearsals, and left Rufus home. Unless her houseguests' swains brought bonbons instead of bouquets, they'd get a far different welcome than they expected.

Having waited as long as she could before leaving, in case Galen arrived, Margot had to suffer a reprimand from the theater director. No, she did not think she was better than anyone else just because she had fallen in clover, and no, she would not be late for the three days remaining of her contract.

She suffered worse that evening when she scanned the tiers, for her husband was not among the gentlemen in the viscount's box. There would be no room for him, anyway. If Margot's singing was somewhat lackluster that night, no one noticed. The novelty of a performing peeress was wearing off, and no juicy tidbits of gossip were to be had until Woodbridge returned from whatever mission he'd undertaken. With most of the menservants from Woburton House scattered among the audience, the groundlings had lost interest in badgering her, turning for entertainment to the painted pretties in their midst.

Thursday and Friday were much the same. Galen did not come home, Harriet did not stay home, Floria made herself at home, Margot made her home ready, and Ruff protected it.

Surely Galen would come back by Saturday, for her last performance, Margot prayed. Talk was that the Prince would attend again, along with a party of foreign dignitaries. Margot thought she was developing a weak upper register. She was certainly developing weak knees. Perhaps her carriage would overturn, or the theater would be closed by some legal writ. Dear Heaven, she could barely remember all of Galen's names and honorary titles; how could she remember the words to her songs? She'd miss her high notes, miss her cues, or mistake the Prince for the actor playing Falstaff. Oh, how she missed Galen's calming presence.

He did not come all day. Despondent, she left late for the theater, but the manager did not bother to scold her for her tardiness, seeing how sad Margot was and how full his theater was. Everyone wanted to see the Magnificent Margot's final performance before she took up her duties as Lady Woodbridge, and everyone waited to see if her wayward groom would bother to come. He did not.

The box was filled, Margot noted from the wings. As usual, her sister-in-law was only visible among the scarlet uniforms and the dark jackets because her gown was such a vivid color, magenta this evening. As usual, the veiled lady sitting beside Harriet was flirting with an older, married man and, as usual, Mr. Skidmore was nervously pulling at his cravat.

The stage manager had to push Margot out in front of the curtains when her turn to sing came, and her accompanist had to start the introduction to the aria twice. Margot had to keep telling herself that this was the last night, the last time she had to do this. Before, she'd told herself she could do it for Ansel; tonight she was doing it for Galen, to make him proud of the woman he'd married. So she did it.

Midway through the aria, she glanced at the viscount's box to see if her sister-in-law was even bothering to listen. The box was nearly empty except for Skippy and another gentleman in dark evening clothes; the little vixen was most likely promenading in the halls with more unsuitable suitors.

Margot completed her second selection, a German anthem in honor of the visiting allies. Next she sang a medley of sprightly country tunes, encouraging the pit-sitters to sing the choruses with her to drown out the loud scene-changing behind her. At last she was ready for her last song, her very last public performance, for Margot vowed to become a milkmaid if her marriage failed, rather than face this terrifying ordeal again.

Since everyone expected it, Margot turned to direct her final love song toward the viscount's box—and Galen was there, standing by the rail, ready to hand her a red rose. She flew toward the edge of the stage, nearer the box, all but tripping on the lights when she saw another figure next to him, a much smaller figure leaning over the railing with a white rose in his hand. Only Galen's grip on the back of the boy's coat kept him from tumbling onto the stage.

"Mon ange!" Margot cried out. "My angel."

Two doxies in the front row started weeping at the tender scene, unaware Margot was calling to Ansel by her pet name for him, not to her husband. But Galen was an angel too, tonight, Margot's hero, her own knight in dark blue superfine, so she sang "Sweet, O My Sir Stoutheart," about a knight and his fair maiden. She sang as if her heart would burst with joy if she did not let some of the love within her tumble forth.

The applause was thunderous when she finished, demanding an encore, begging her not to retire, but Margot heard none of it, only Galen's "*Brava,* my darling."

Chapter Nineteen

Whoever said time heals all wounds forgot to mention the scars.

Margot rushed to her dressing room as soon as she finished her curtsey to the Prince and hurriedly scrubbed at her stage makeup. Then she almost floated to the rear door of the theater, clutching her two roses, shouting farewells to the friends she'd made. Only one lamppost illuminated the back exit, but it cast enough light for Margot to spot Galen, standing by the carriage, just as she knew he'd be, Ansel at his side. She ran to hug and kiss her brother until he protested, at which she hugged and kissed Galen, who did not. Then she remembered the others who might be watching, all the footmen, Floria, Galen's sister. Dear heavens, where was his sister?

When he saw her glance toward the coach, Galen said he'd sent the others home in the town carriage and hired vehicles. "I wanted you to myself. And Ansel, of course."

So she hugged him again, then Ansel again, and then she started weeping. Galen wrapped her in his arms, even though his new silk waistcoat would be quite ruined by her tears. Looking over her head, he told Ansel, who was looking worried, "Isn't that just like a woman, to cry when she's happy. I know it makes no sense, my boy, but get used to it. Women's reasoning is as logical as a fish in a tree." For some equally as illogical a reason, Galen's arms refused to release her, even when Margot stopped sniffling. He kept an arm around his wife as he guided her to the carriage, and then he squeezed her hand the whole way home while Ansel chattered.

Between yawns, the little baron enthused about all the sights he'd seen and his new pony, the horse fair, the inns, some jugglers, and his new pony. He told her how Galen was going to teach him to swim in the pond at Three Woods, and let him paint in the attic in Grosvenor Square. He seemed so happy, so normal, so like other little boys, that Margot could not keep the tears from flowing all over again. When her handkerchief became a sodden lump, Galen quietly placed his in her hand.

At their arrival home, Fenning opened the front door and bowed to his employers. Then, with great ceremony, he bowed to Ansel. "Welcome to Woodrow House, Lord Penrose. We are pleased and honored to have you."

Margot asked Fenning to find a vase for her roses to be placed in her bedroom, before she turned to her brother. "I know it is long past your bedtime, angel, and your room has been ready for you this age, but let me take a good look at my little brother, now that there is light enough to see you properly." Enough candles lit the entry at Woburton House to rival daylight.

"My, how you have grown," Margot told him, disguising her dismay at Ansel's thinness. She'd seen beggar children in London look better nourished. "You'll grow even faster here, I swear. Mrs. Shircastle has been baking gingerbread all week, for your coming."

Margot knelt down to Ansel's level so she could finally look into those eyes so much like hers, finally study the dearly memorized face she had not seen in almost a year. Ansel's complexion held a healthy color, likely from standing in the sun at that horse fair for hours. He had a few freckles dotting his cheeks . . . and a huge yellow-and-purple bruise on his jaw.

"Goodness, angel, whatever happened to you? Did you fall off the coach?"

"Oh, no. Galen hit me, but—"

*   *   *

Now the nipper's memory worked fine? Galen cursed as he watched Margot drag the child up the stairs so fast Ansel's feet barely touched the treads. When she reached the first landing, she halted long enough to demand that Fenning send for the doctor, the magistrate, the Watch, the militia.

Fenning raised his eyebrows.

Galen said, "She'll feel better if she has a physician look at him." Then he shouted loudly enough to be heard on the third floor, before Margot disappeared from sight, "Whatever you do, don't let any quack give him laudanum. In fact," he told the butler, "I don't want a single drop of laudanum in the house. Is that clear?"

"Quite, my lord. I am certain the doctor heard you in his house on Half Moon Street." Anticipating the need, as any good butler would, Fenning had already sent a footman to fetch the progressive young physician Lady Woodbridge had previously selected. Anticipating Galen's need, Fenning directed him to the Crimson Parlor, where tea was being served, along with a bottle of cognac.

Only one thing stood between Galen and the parlor, the same thing that stood between him and the stairs—a very large, very ugly, fang-flashing, rib-showing canine who'd been told to guard against strange men.

"Thunderation, don't tell me the mutt's memory is gone missing now! I live here, you misbegotten mongrel. Shoo."

"Grr."

"Fenning, either fetch me a slice of something from the tea cart to bribe the fleahound, or get me my pistol. I don't much care which you bring."

"Yes, my lord."

"Grr."

This was not the welcome Galen had been anticipating for a sennight. He'd been envisioning Margot showering him with kisses, before they went upstairs to renegotiate the terms of their marriage contract. He'd pictured all that glorious golden hair spread across his pillow, and that luscious, sultry voice singing his name, not calling him a black-hearted bully. He'd saved her brother from certain death, brought him to her safe and sound and sane, and what did he get? Her back, and a belligerent bag of bones keeping him boxed in his own entry hall.

Fenning eventually returned with some slices of ham on a platter. "Sweets are not good for a dog, my lord."

"Neither is a pistol. Here, let me feed the beast. If he does not recall me as the one who pays for his supper, you coax him out the door, then bolt it behind him. He's too stupid to remember his way back in."

Ruff wasn't too stupid to follow Galen to the parlor, where good food often resided on low tables.

Denied a warm welcome, obviously denied his wife's trust, much less her bed, Galen was in no mood to be pleasant. He stalked into the drawing room, not seeking refreshment as much as an argument. After he'd cleared the theater box of all the raff and scaff, Lord Woodbridge had sent his sister home with Skippy and the black-draped female. Galen guessed the supposed widow was a school chum of Harry's, masquerading as a chaperone to make the appearance at the theater of a chit not out yet, sans family, more *convenable*. Like hell it did. He'd see them all later, the viscount had declared, meaning he'd have a piece of their hides when he returned home. All three were in the parlor, enjoying a comfortable coze and Mrs. Shircastle's cherry tarts.

They would not be enjoying his hospitality for long.

"You, sir," he began, poking his finger at Skippy's puce-and-purple waistcoat, "were supposed to guard my wife. You were supposed to stay in the background, shielding her from gossip. What did you do? You dragged my sister into an indiscretion that could cost her reputation. I have a good mind to call you out over this, you chawbacon."

"Well, you can't challenge a man of the cloth." Skippy was praying—a rare occurrence indeed—that his statement was true. "Asides, you've never been able to break the brat to bridle yourself." When the brat kicked him, Skippy amended, "I mean, Harry, ah, Lady Harriet."

"You mean my sap-skulled sister. And I dashed well can challenge you to meet me at Gentleman Jackson's in the morning to continue this discussion of a gentleman's responsibilities."

"Deuce take it, can't we skip the fisticuffs? Last time we had that kind of discussion I ended up with my daylights darkened. The bishop wasn't happy, said I was a bad example."

"Well, you are."

Galen turned toward the women, but before he could say anything, the still-veiled widow stood to leave. "This is a family matter, *non? Pardonnez-moi.* I excuse myself, *s'il vous plaît.*"

Galen bowed slightly and faced his sister, who was feeding a cherry tart to the mongrel, pretending to be rapt in the chore of breaking off tiny pieces. Rufus was half across her knees, pretending to be a fluffy lapdog.

"I do not know what you were thinking of, by coming to London on your own, or what you hoped to accomplish by making your name a byword in polite circles, but I won't have it in my house."

Harriet raised her chin. "It's Papa's house."

"And when he is not here, I am master. Or were you thinking to wrap me around your little finger the way you do His Grace? Well, you won't, by George, not even if you turn into a watering pot, which usually turns the trick with our father."

The tears getting ready to fall from Harriet's eyes dried up on the instant. "I have done nothing wrong."

"Nothing except show the world what a hoyden you are! I know Papa intended to send you to Aunt Matty in Bath, and that's where you are going, tomorrow morning."

"No, I am staying for the party. Papa is coming, and I can go home with him."

"That party is too far off. By then you could ruin your

chances of making a respectable match, and I could be left with you on my hands for the rest of my life! No, thank you, Harry. Besides, you have not been presented, so you cannot attend an adult entertainment."

"Pooh, what do I care about the silly old rules? Those are for plain girls of undistinguished backgrounds and no dowry to speak of. 'Prettily behaved' is the best that can be said for those unfortunate females, so they have to toe the mark if they hope to be accepted."

"What, you think your forty thousand pounds will make up for a blackened name? It will not."

By now, Skippy was trying to edge his way out of the room, but Madame Millefleur was blocking the door, unabashedly eavesdropping. The chit had forty thousand pounds? Floria had only twenty, if she could wrest it away from Woodbridge.

Galen helped himself to the last cherry tart. "You are leaving tomorrow, and that's that."

"No, I won't!" Harriet stamped her foot, then she came and stamped on his toes. When he jumped, the pastry flew out of Galen's hand, right into the dog's always-open mouth.

Galen raised one eyebrow. "After that charming example of your maturity and manners, I rest my case. You are not ready for London."

"I am, too! And I am staying!"

The viscount had to settle for a slice of seed cake. "You are leaving if I have to carry you out over my shoulder. And don't bother holding your breath until you turn purple, brat. I've seen you do it too often."

"You are mean and hateful and . . . and stiff-rumped," Harriet shouted. Then she started to reach for a knick-knack to toss at Galen. Unfortunately, she did not see the dog in her way, wolfing down the last tart, until it was too late. Harriet tripped, fell, and hit her head on the corner of the low table. Her screaming increased in volume, more so when her fingers touched her temple and came away bloody.

Galen grabbed for a napkin and was on the floor in an instant, Skippy on Harriet's other side. "It's just a scratch, Harry. Tell her, Skippy." But the reverend was turning green at sight of the blood, so Galen had to push his friend's head down between his knees. Meanwhile, Harriet kept shrieking.

"Dash it, woman, don't you have a vinaigrette or something?" Galen shouted to the widow, who hadn't moved from the door.

The chit had forty thousand pounds, Floria was thinking; she could get her own vinaigrette.

Then the room started filling with servants who thought the house was under attack. Fenning had a blunderbuss, and Mrs. Hapgood and Mrs. Shircastle had pots. Margot rushed past them, to see her sister-in-law on the floor, bleeding. White-faced and wide-eyed, Margot looked at her husband.

"Damn it to hell, wife, don't look at me like that. I didn't hit her, too!"

The doctor had followed Margot, and now he knelt at Harriet's side, examining the wound. "Hush, my lady, 'tis a mere scratch. You won't even have a scar on your pretty face."

That stopped Harriet's screaming—not the words as much as the handsome young gentleman gazing at her so attentively, holding her hand.

"Is she truly all right?" Margot asked Dr. Hill, the physician.

"Of course she is," Galen answered before the doctor could make a pronouncement. "She is perfectly well to get in a coach in the morning and go to Bath. Maybe there her forty thousand pounds can buy her a respectable husband."

The young lady had forty thousand pounds? The young doctor had ambitions. Besides, females with fortunes were notoriously fragile. Dr. Hill patted her hand. "I think you might be too hasty, my lord. One never knows about injuries to the head, of course. Why, the young lady might be concussed. No, I think she needs to stay in her bed for a few days of rest, to make sure. I can leave some powders in case she develops a headache, or perhaps a drop of lau—"

"No laudanum. I will not have it in the house."

"But if the young lady is in pain, my lord . . . ?"

"Then she will suffer, the way the rest of us have suffered over her horrid behavior for years."

At least four people in the room silently said amen.

Chapter Twenty

Whoever said to err is human, to forgive divine, should have considered a compromise.

The doctor and Mrs. Hapgood helped Lady Harriet upstairs, while Mrs. Shircastle hurried to concoct a posset. Madame Millefleur decided this was not the ideal time to ask Woodbridge for the return of her dowry, paltry though it was, and played least in sight.

Reverend Skidmore skipped the rest of his tea, hoping Galen would forget their engagement at Gentleman Jackson's. Skippy surely intended to forget it. He also intended to do some thinking about how well a fellow could get by on forty thousand pounds, if he invested it wisely, lived at his in-laws' expense, and cut back on his gambling a bit, now that his wager on Woodbridge and Mademoiselle Montclaire had paid his debts. Why, he wouldn't need to see the inside of a church again until the day he died. Skippy decided he really had to look around him for an heiress. He wondered if that cousin of Lady Woodbridge's had any blunt, although he doubted it, since she was acting as Harry's chaperone. She didn't act like any poor relation he'd ever known, though, disappearing when she was most needed. Mayhaps she didn't like the sight of blood, either. Skippy decided to ask the viscount, if Galen ever spoke to him again.

Galen wasn't speaking to anyone, not until he had his wife alone. Fenning glanced from his master to his mistress, then ordered all of the remaining servants gone. He took the empty pastry plate, then he came back and removed the priceless Ming vase from the mantel. He closed the door quite firmly behind him, leaving Galen and Margot alone.

Galen had his arms crossed in front of his chest. "Well, madam, are you prepared to apologize?"

"I did not accuse you of striking your sister."

"No, but you thought it for a minute. I could see it in your eyes."

"What you saw in my eyes was terror that your sister might be too injured to go home."

"Very well, you do not believe I am so lost to honor that I would hit a woman. Am I supposed to be proud that my own wife thinks that is the limit to my restraint? That beating small, defenseless children is more in keeping with my character?"

"You struck my brother. Ansel seems to believe your actions were justified. He also believes you can walk on water, however, since you bought him a pony, so I do not credit his impartiality. You struck a sick little boy to end his crying."

"I hit him to end his suffering. They did it in the Army all the time, when they ran out of drugs or spirits. You, however, let my sister attend the theater to end her whining."

"I didn't *let* her do anything. You are changing the subject."

"So are you. The subject is neither your brother, Margot, nor my sister. The fact is that you do not trust me."

Margot put down the blue jasperware teapot when she realized her hands were shaking. The tea would be cold by now anyway. "You do not trust me, either."

"I left you, my new bride, a virtual stranger, alone in my house with a fortune in art on the walls, and I left you a *carte blanche* at my bank. What do you mean, I don't trust you?" Galen was pacing in front of the fireplace, but now he came to stand over her, where she sat on the sofa.

"You didn't tell me you painted, or that you had an attic studio. I thought those were all storage rooms or bedchambers for the servants. I had to learn otherwise from my brother."

The viscount's cheeks were red, and not from the fire. "I do not make my hobby public knowledge. I would have mentioned it to you, of course, when I got around to it. There was no time before I left."

Margot was not finished. "Furthermore, you do not trust me to know proper behavior if you think I encouraged your impossible sister to cut off her hair and half the fabric of her gowns. To you I am still Margot Montclaire, the singer."

"To you I am just another wealthy care-for-naught if you don't trust me not to beat a child." He pounded on the mantel, making the ormolu clock there lose an hour. The Ming vase would have lost more.

Margot folded her hands in her lap, vowing that one of them, at least, would not resort to childish behavior. "I trust you enough to know that you must have had good reason for what you did."

"The reason I hit Ansel was that I had to choose between giving him more laudanum or letting him die in agony. I'd shoot a horse in such pain; I could do no less for your brother."

Ansel was that close to death? She had not realized. "I . . . I forgive you, and I do apologize for doubting your honor."

"And I apologize for not telling you about the studio. It has always been a private type of thing, and we hadn't been married long enough for me to get used to sharing confidences."

She sniffed. He hadn't promised to change his ways, either, she thought, but at least it was an apology. "What about your sister?"

He sat beside her on the sofa and reached for her hand. Stroking it, he apologized again. "I am sorry for thinking you might have invited my sister to Town to make a public spectacle of herself; no one in their right mind would invite the brat anywhere. Harry's been a hellion from the day she could walk. No, when she was crawling, she toppled our mother's dressing table and smelled like a bordello for weeks. We should have known then, and drowned her.

There, I apologized again, and the moon did not fall out of the sky in shock. You must be a good influence, my dear. Am I forgiven?"

"I suppose so." With him flashing that dimple, she'd likely forgive him much worse.

"Here, then, let us kiss and make up, shall we? That's what all the scribes say married folk are supposed to do."

Margot leaned over and placed a chaste kiss on his cheek.

"That is all the forgiveness you can spare? I can do much better." Galen kissed her lips, briefly. "I forgive you for doubting me." He kissed her again, for a much longer, breath-stealing time. "And I apologize for doubting you." Now he played over her lips with his tongue. "And for inflicting my sister on you in the first place."

"Hmm. I forgive you for not mentioning the studio. Do you paint as well as you kiss?"

"I'll show you tomorrow. You can decide." He proceeded to give her a lot more samples to compare, samples of kisses, not paintings.

When his lips moved to her neck and her ear and the hollow between her collarbones, Margot whispered, "I forgive you for being gone so long." Which was, of course, the real reason for her anger.

"And I forgive you for being so deuced beautiful." Which was the reason for his frustration. "Did you miss me?"

"Too much."

"Me, too." By now Margot was on his lap. Her slippers were on the floor, next to Galen's cravat. He was pulling the pins out of her hair, letting it fall past her shoulders. "It really is as smooth as silk. I wondered, the whole time I was gone."

"I wondered if you thought of me at all."

"Endlessly. You know, this apologizing bit can be quite, ah, good for the soul."

Margot's soul was humming, along with the rest of her. "Indeed. Um, was there anything else you wish to argue about so we can kiss and make up some more?"

"No, but that's no reason we cannot continue." So he did. "I still need to make amends for my sister landing on your doorstep. I owe you a debt of gratitude for making sure she had that widowed French cousin of yours as chaperone, at least, so her standing is not sunk altogether."

Margot was kissing the side of his mouth, running her tongue over the rougher skin where his beard was beginning to bristle. "She's not really French."

Galen was unfastening the buttons on the back of her gown under her hair. Fumbling, he told himself he'd have to remember next time, buttons first, hair second. "Hmm. I guessed as much from that atrocious accent."

Margot touched her lips to his chest at the collar of his shirt while she was opening his waistcoat. "She's not really a widow."

"No, I didn't think she was, but the blacks do give her a bit more respectability, so you and your cousin showed great ingenuity."

"She's not really my cousin."

He laughed, now that the buttons were undone and he could slip his hand into the bodice of her gown and feel the soft fullness of her breast. He bent to kiss what he had uncovered. "I never supposed so. You'd have had her at the wedding if you had a cousin. Who is she, an actress from the theater or one of Harriet's schoolmates?"

"Actually, she's Lady Floria, your former fiancée."

Galen jumped up so fast Margot's posterior hit the floor before the first curse left his lips. "That she-witch is here in my house? Companioning my sister? And you just now thought to tell me?"

"Well, I forgot." If his lovemaking hadn't swept every wisp of wit out of her head, she'd never have told him. "Your kisses made me forget."

"Oh, so now it's my fault? Am I supposed to beg your forgiveness for that?"

Margot got to her feet and tried to recapture the warmth they'd been sharing. "Well, you could kiss me again. Floria's been here for days, and no one knows but Fenning and Harriet. She had no money and nowhere else to go."

"That feckless female can go straight to hell, for all I care. Good gods, if the gossips get wind of this, I'll never be able to visit my clubs again." He was pouring out a glass of wine. Recalling his manners, he poured another for Margot.

"I did try to tell her you wouldn't like it."

"Now that, madam, is the understatement of the ages." He drank her wine, too. "I don't suppose I can toss her out in the middle of the night, can I?"

Margot shook her head, sending wheaten waves cascading across the back of the sofa. The viscount was annoyed that he was almost distracted from his indignation, so he told her: "No, don't throw out your lures, I have seen them all. Harry's tears and tantrums won't work, and your come-hither looks either."

"I never come-hithered in my life!"

"No? Then how come your gown is around your waist and your lips are swollen from my kisses?"

She gasped. "Is that my fault? You did those things!"

"Aha! You see, I am always in the wrong. I knew how it would be, putting on leg shackles. Let a woman put a ring on her finger, and she thinks you have a ring through your nose."

"Is that what we are arguing about now? Your loss of freedom? You asked me to marry you, my lord lackwit, if you would bother to remember. I did not entrap you into offering."

Galen ran his fingers through his already disordered hair. "Lud, I have no idea what we are arguing about. Yes, I do. It's that woman." No, it was frustrated desire. "She is determined to ruin my life."

"But *I* am not. I did not invite her here, any more than I invited your sister, and Lady Floria is not a comfortable guest for me, either. I could very well blame you for cluttering the countryside with former attachments. For all I know, your prior mistresses will be knocking on the door next."

"If any do, *then* you may ring a peal over my head. Devil take it, are you sure I have to wait for morning to toss her out?"

"Unless you want the entire household awakened. Besides, she does not rise before noon, which is all to the good. You promised to show Ansel, and me, your studio in the morning, and the mews where his pony will be stabled."

"He'll be too tired from the trip. Lud, I forgot about Ansel. Is someone staying with him? He shouldn't be alone!" Galen leaned on the mantel, resetting the clock from his pocket watch.

"I didn't think he should be by himself, either, so I put him to sleep in my bed. Ella is there keeping watch until I come, but after all the excitement, one glass of warm milk sent him right to sleep."

Ansel was sleeping in Margot's room, in her bed? Galen wished he'd left the sprig in Sussex. "What did the doctor say? I should have asked before."

"He said that Ansel appeared to have been ill, and was now recovering. He did not even suggest he stay in bed."

What a competent physician she'd found. Galen liked the fellow already.

"He did say Ansel should avoid strenuous activities."

Galen had to force his mind away from a certain strenuous activity once Ansel would be in the nursery where he belonged. "He still gets nightmares, though nothing as bad as those about your father. Did you know about them?"

"No, he never spoke about his dreams to me. He always said he could not remember the nightmares, or my father's accident."

"I don't think it was an accident. I intend to send a man back to Penrose to dig around."

"You mean you think someone tried to kill my father? That he did not die in a freakish riding misfortune?"

"Ansel heard a gunshot. That's why he's been kept drugged, so it became part of his bad dreams. And the someone is your uncle. We might never be able to prove it, since the event occurred so long ago, but I aim to try. I'll stop in at Bow Street in the morning to start the investigation."

"Could you ask about Ella's husband while you are there? She doesn't even know where he's been taken, only that there are not many more days before he is transported. Ella swears he is innocent."

"Yes, I did promise that, didn't I? Very well, while I am there, I will hire another Runner to locate Mr. Humber, then I'll send my solicitor, Hemmerdinger, to argue an appeal. It is about time that pompous little puffguts earned his keep. If he won't subpoena those Penrose Hall estate books now, on my say-so and Ansel's, Mrs. Hapgood's, and the cook's, then I will get a new solicitor. That dastard uncle of yours is going to pay, one way or another."

"And you are not angry at me any longer?"

"By George, we'd better kiss and make up again." He gathered her back onto his lap. "Here, I forgive you for driving a man to distraction, and for letting Ansel sleep in your bed instead of me."

"And I forgive you for acting like a bear with a sore foot. You are wonderful for taking on the burden of my uncle, and Ella's husband, and for taking such good care of Ansel."

Soon her skirts were over her knees and his coat and waistcoat had joined the cravat and slippers on the carpet. Galen smiled and said, "This marriage business is fairly easy, isn't it? I cannot imagine why so many people make such a muddle of it."

Chapter Twenty-one

W hoever said a picture is worth a thousand words could have written an entire encyclopedia from the works in Viscount Woodbridge's studio. Ansel was awed, Margot was amazed, and Galen stood awkwardly, apprehensively, in the doorway while they surveyed the vast, sky-lighted room, waiting for their verdict.

"Well, ma'am, do I pass muster?"

Margot went from piles to stacks to portfolios, shaking her head. She was finally used to living with the masters downstairs; now she was married to one! Galen had a style of his own, she decided, which was looser than the classical works, but not as amorphous as a Turner. His work was somewhere between, and eminently pleasing. The watercolors were so pure and jewel-like, they might have been stained glass windows. The oils were rich, glowing still lifes, portraits, landscapes. Was there nothing he could not do? For certain there was little he had not tried or material he had not experimented with. One corner table held a wire armature, with clay in a basin waiting to be sculpted over the form. Blocks of stone and chisels were on a shelf above. No wizard's workshop was half so fascinating.

Since he had not received an answer, Galen found the latest sketch pads and tore out the pastel drawing of Ansel at the horse fair. Margot was thrilled, as he'd known she would be, but she wanted to flip through the other pages of the pad.

"Later, my dear. We have much to do this morning."

"They're all of you, Margot, the first ones," Ansel piped up. "That's why he doesn't want you to see." Ansel had not stirred from a collection of small equine paintings. The horses were running and jumping, grazing in meadows, not standing stiff-legged as in so many others of the type.

Ansel was carefully studying each painting, his hand resting on Ruff's head. Ruff had quickly learned that where the small one was, food was sure to appear. Mrs. Hapgood, Ella, Margot, and Clegg were constantly bringing Ansel treats and sweets. Even Fenning kept a dish of sugarplums nearby, and naturally the boy shared with his new best friend, to Galen's chagrin.

"How come Attila the Hungry has not eaten Ansel?" he asked now, trying to distract Margot from her intense scrutiny of his work. No one else had been up here in years, and Galen found he did not like the feeling that his very soul was on display. Devil take it, what if she said something damning like "Very nice" or "How lovely"?

What she said was, "Oh, I told Rufus that Ansel was a friend," without looking up from a stack of pen-and-ink drawings.

"You never told him *I* was a friend," he exclaimed in indignation.

"I wasn't sure you were. Besides, I think Ruff has some herder in him, and he thinks Ansel is one of his lambs."

"If that menace has shepherd in him, it is from eating the poor herdsman. If he saw a lamb, he'd declare lunchtime." Galen, of course, had ordered a plate of sweet rolls brought up from the kitchens, for Ansel, he told Fenning. Rufus barely tolerated the viscount in the room with the Penrose pair; Lud knew what he'd do when the rolls were gone. "We'd better hurry along now, my dear. I told Mr. Hemmerdinger to expect us within the hour."

Margot was still studying the black-and-white sketches. One of them was of her on the stage, in her lace mantilla, playing her guitar. She had not performed that song since long before they were wed, so seeing it warmed her heart, that he'd been interested in her, admired her, months ago. Galen hadn't offered for her merely out of pique with the vanished Lady Floria, then, as the handiest, most unsuitable female he could find. Of course he had also depicted flower-sellers and orange-girls, too, but Margot chose to believe that Galen was drawn to her. She smiled.

Ah, she did not hate his work, Galen thought, surprised at the relief he felt. He knew he was a decent enough dauber, and he'd never cared what anyone else thought since he only painted for his own satisfaction, but Margot's approval mattered a great deal.

He turned to his other critic. "So what do you think, Ansel?"

The boy had not moved from the block of horse paintings. "I still think you don't use the earth colors enough for contrast, and some of the foreshortening seems skewed. And here, these horses' heads are much too small."

"Whoa, bantling. Those horses are my Arabian breeding stock, and they are built differently from what you are used to. After you've seen them for yourself at Three Woods, I'll demand a retraction."

"Can I ride one?"

Embarrassed at her brother's presumption, Margot chided, "Ansel!"

Galen only teased. "What, have you outgrown your pony already? Mrs. Shircastle's cooking is excellent, but I didn't think it was that good." He ruffled Ansel's short hair and added, "Of course you may ride the Arabians, as soon as I am certain you are strong enough. Look, here is Charlemagne, and this one is MacHeath, the two stallions even I have a hard time controlling. There's Peaches and her foal Schemer, who was always finding a way out of the paddock. The Beau hates getting his feet wet, and . . ."

Margot listened to her husband and her brother, seeing their closeness, and felt such a burst of affection that she wanted to embrace both of them at once. Ansel would have been mortified, and Galen— Well, they had a lot to do this morning.

Reminded, Galen tried to lead them out of the room, but

Margot was not leaving without her drawing of Ansel. "This one goes in my bedroom, of course. But why are none of your paintings displayed downstairs? Surely they would not look out of place near the masterpieces you have hanging."

Galen's heart swelled, not that she thought his work fit to be in the same room as a Rembrandt or a Fra Angelico, but that Margot was fond enough of him to say so. "I never paint for anyone else's eyes. I think that would ruin my pleasure in creating, wondering if someone else is going to like it."

Margot tilted her head. "We call that stage fright, my lord. Nevertheless, these florals would look lovely in the morning room, instead of that dreary Zepporini. He might be renowned for his brush strokes, but I cannot admire a gruesome hunt scene while I am having my breakfast. I could embroider cushions to match the paintings, but that would take too long, so we ought to have new floral seat coverings made. Your father asked me to refurbish some of the rooms that have not been touched since your mother's time, you know, so I am not being officious and encroaching. The horses would be perfect for your book room."

"No." Galen realized he'd spoken with unwonted force when Ruff showed his teeth. "No, that is, I do not choose to put myself on public display like a—"

"Like a common performer?" Icicles could have formed on Margot's voice. "A viscount is above such plebeian pursuits, is that it?"

"Dash it, Margot, I meant no such thing. I was going to say, I will not puff up my paintings like a dilettantish dabbler."

"No, you'd hide your light under a bushel instead, where no one can enjoy such beautiful works of art. I think you are merely modest, my lord, or afraid of criticism. We'll see about that. I want at least three of those flower paintings for the morning room, and I mean to have them."

Ansel had one of the horse pictures, the one with the mare and her foal, in his hand. "May I borrow this one for the nursery sitting room, Galen? The only things hanging there now are an ugly, muddy watercolor picture of this house and a sampler that's so ragged I can't make out the words."

"That's Harriet's work. And no, you may not borrow the painting for your sitting room. The resident of the nursery has to fill the walls with his or her own work. That's the rule of Woburton House, and I expect you to start shortly. You may have the painting for your own, though, for your bedroom, if you wish."

"Come on, Ruff, let's go find the right spot for it!"

When Ansel was gone, Margot turned to Galen with a martial glint in her eyes. "Ansel can have one, but I cannot?"

"Well, perhaps we might negotiate, my dear. If I hung them in my bedroom, would you come visit? Just to see the paintings, of course."

After a rather breathtaking round of negotiations, during which Margot's hair became so tangled again that Ella clucked her tongue, they all went to the mews behind the house to see if Ansel's pony had arrived, and to pick out a stall for it. Galen would have left the boy behind then, but Ansel asked if he could go with them to Bow Street, since there would be so much to see along the way. Margot pleaded silently. The house was so big and so new to her brother, and he was so small. Ansel ran back to the house to get a cap when Galen said yes, he could come, and the viscount watched him dash off.

"He'll do," he told Margot.

"He'll do wonderfully." She quickly kissed his cheek while the groom's back was turned. "So will you."

Ansel answered the few brief questions that were all Galen permitted the Bow Street Runner to ask him, then he was sent to watch another officer who was trying to draw a wanted poster of a highwayman from a witness's description. Ella answered more questions about her husband. Margot supplied the names of her housekeeper and cook, and the vicar at Rossington who could vouch for their honesty.

"Sounds shady to me, all right, m'lord. I doubt your man fired the shot what got the nipper's da killed, not by hisself. But mayhaps someone in the neighborhood would be talking now, for a bit of blunt."

Galen placed a heavy leather purse on the battered desk. "Whatever it takes."

When they left, Galen was that much poorer, but Ansel had earned a shilling, doing a better job at the wanted poster than the Runner.

They were late for the appointment with Mr. Hemmerdinger, but Galen remembered sitting on the unpadded bench waiting for the solicitor, so he was not too concerned. This time, they were shown directly into the inner office, and Hemmerdinger's corset creaked when he bowed to Lady Woodbridge. Ansel's eyes grew big, but Galen pinched the back of his neck, so the boy did not say anything.

After Galen explained their mission, the man of affairs harrumphed a few times and said, "Oh, dear. We'll have to look into your charges immediately."

"I do not want you to 'look into' anything. I want the guardianship of Ansel transferred tomorrow, if not this afternoon."

"Does that mean Uncle Manfred couldn't take me away?" Ansel wanted to know.

"It means the magistrate will be taking your uncle away if he so much as speaks your name. Which means you'll be stuck with me for governor, lad, and I mean to be a strict one, too. No gambling, cursing, or womanizing. Understand?"

Ansel laughed, as Galen had planned, so he would not dwell on the past and his repulsive relative. "But what about Penrose Hall?" he asked.

"We'll have to wait for the estate books to be examined, but I'd wager there are enough discrepancies in the accounting that Manfred will give up that trusteeship also, rather than be brought up on charges of embezzlement and mismanagement. We'll hire an honest manager, and visit ourselves to make sure the estate and its people are restored to good condition, the way your father would have wished."

His words relieved another longstanding worry of Margot's, so she thanked her lucky stars once more for sending her the viscount. She could even find it in her heart to thank Lady Floria, the fool, for not marrying this paragon of a *parti*.

Galen was not finished. Before leaving the solicitor's office, he made Margot read the marriage contracts he had ordered drawn up right after their marriage.

"But I trust you," she said, not wanting to take the time, with Ansel growing restless.

"You still need to know what is yours, so there is no question in your mind."

After she'd found her spectacles and Mr. Hemmerdinger pointed out the pertinent passages, tears came to Margot's eyes. "A whole estate?" As if rescuing her brother and looking after Penrose's dependents were not enough, Viscount Woodbridge was deeding an unentailed property to her and her descendants. "It's way too much, my lord. Far too generous."

Galen handed over his handkerchief. He'd have to start carrying two or three if his wife was going to turn into a watering pot, but she seemed pleased, despite the red, puffy eyes and red, splotchy cheeks, so he'd carry five if he had to.

"But we have Penrose," Ansel complained, concerned about his sister's tears. "Margot doesn't need another estate."

"No, Ansel," Galen corrected. "Penrose is yours, for your wife and children someday. Your sister deserves a place of her own, where she will always be mistress, no matter what."

"Where she can hang any pictures she wants?"

"That, too. Of course, I am hoping she'll let me stay there with her, for I cannot see any other way to get you those nieces and nephews to play with."

Mr. Hemmerdinger turned red, too.

Chapter Twenty-two

Whoever said that opportunity knocks but once did not know that Sir Henry Lytell would be at Gentleman Jackson's that morning.

Recalling his appointment with Skippy, Galen stopped at the boxing parlor after introducing Ansel to ices at Gunther's. The boy was full, sticky, and obviously weary, so Margot used bringing an ice home for Ruff as an excuse to end the excursion. Now Galen's carriage was sticky, too. He walked.

Skippy was not at the popular gathering spot, but the man who had run off with Galen's bride on the day of their wedding was. Galen owed Sir Henry a debt of gratitude for his deliverance from the devil's own marriage, but the dastard had not finished the job. Galen had a wife who pleased him far more than Florrie ever had or ever could, but he still had that harridan on his hands. Lytell had taken Floria—and taken her reputation and her innocence too, for all Galen knew, if she'd had it—and then tossed her back, like an inedible species of fish. Galen owed that muckworm a debt, all right.

Sir Henry was joking with his friends when Lord Woodbridge entered, laughing about his own close call with parson's mousetrap. Galen supposed Lytell had to make light of it, since the baronet likely owed all the other cabbage-heads money. For the first time one of life's everyday injustices rankled Galen: Florrie was ruined, an outcast from everything and everybody she knew, but the man who had partnered her in that offense against polite society was back in

Town, enjoying himself with his friends as if nothing unto-ward had transpired. Well, he would not be enjoying himself much longer.

One of the coxcombs in Lytell's circle laughed. "I guess you'll just have to look around for another heiress, eh?" Then he spotted Galen approaching. "I heard your sister is in Town, Woodbridge. Is it true she has forty thousand pounds?"

Galen was removing his coat and cravat. "What she has is a father and a brother who would protect her interests and her reputation with their lives. Would anyone care to banter my sister's name around again?"

He had no takers, only a few nervous chuckles. "Perhaps you thought to turn your attention to my sister, Lytell? Keep your villainy in the family, so to speak."

The baronet was backing away. "Zounds, no. The chit is much too young for me. I already decided to try for a widow next, one with no papas. Or brothers."

"Ah, but I think you need practice, just in case your widow has a cousin or an uncle . . . or a fiancé. Get in the ring before I pick you up and toss you in."

Lytell was nearly Galen's height and weight, but nowhere near his skill or superb condition. He would have run in the other direction, in fact, if he'd had tuppence to hire a hack-ney, and somewhere to go. His friends were already laying bets, though, and whereas they forgave a man who tried to better himself with a wealthy bride, they would not be so charitable to a craven who backed down from a challenge, or one who weaseled on a wager. The baronet stripped and stepped onto the canvas.

Galen knocked him down, too soon for satisfaction, so he helped Lytell back to his feet. Then he knocked him down again. With the crowd urging him on, Sir Henry stood up. Galen let him jab a few times before knocking him out of the square altogether. His friends hauled him upright and pointed him toward Galen, which they would not have done, of course, if they were true friends. If the baronet had any brains, he'd had stayed down, but anyone addled enough to run away with Lady Floria Cleary could not be counted a deep thinker. The fool staggered right into Galen's left.

He would not be sniffing around any wealthy widow in the near future, not with that nose, anyway.

On his way home, Galen stopped off at Rundell and Bridges, Jewelers. He wanted to buy Margot a necklace, since the family heirlooms were all locked in the vault in the country. He'd have to ask His Grace to bring something suitable for the party when he came. Meantime, Lord Woodbridge wished to purchase a pretty trinket for his wife, not because she'd hinted, the way Florrie always had, nor because she expected it, the way a mistress always did. He was not even thinking to use the bauble in hopes of winning Margot's affections—taking Ansel to Astley's Amphitheater that evening would do more than any diamond could—or her favors. That last campaign was coming along very nicely, he fancied, considering the parting kiss she'd bestowed on him, and the way she'd murmured his name this morning in the studio. Galen was not going to rush his bride, although he'd be damned if he was going to wait the full six months of their original agreement to share her bed. As for his own frustrated feelings, he believed he'd perish in a fortnight if he could not consummate the marriage.

No, Galen wanted to give his wife a gift simply to bring her pleasure. He'd say it was in recompense for the uninvited female guests in the house, but to see her smile was his only real excuse. If a man could not buy a present for his wife, what was the point of having money, or a wife?

He liked everything in the store. Margot would likely flood the floor with tears if he presented half what he wished to purchase for her, though, so how the deuce was a fellow to decide? A mistress always wanted the most expensive; Florrie always wanted the showiest. Margot would want something fine and delicate, tasteful without being ostentatious. The clerk started to take out tray upon tray of necklaces for his perusal, but Galen had too much to do to spend all day in the jewelry store, under the stares of three dowagers, two dandies, and a demi-rep. The ladybird had just rejected a simple strand of diamonds as too tame, so Galen told the clerk to wrap them.

He left the store whistling, planning the rest of the day and the rest of the week. He wanted to show Margot so many things, the galleries and art dealers, Vauxhall by moonlight, the maze at Richmond, Venice by moonlight. He'd start with the circus tonight. With so much to do, Galen realized he wasn't even in as big a rush to return to the country and his horses. They needed to settle the questions about Ansel, and hold that blasted party that seemed to be growing larger every day, but there was no hurry. He was happy.

Margot was happy. For the first time in so long, she could smile from the inside, too. Ansel was sitting quietly with a book from Galen's library after they'd played duets, he on the pianoforte and she on her guitar. Now Margot was just sitting, without sewing in her lap, without a new score to memorize, without her account book to agonize over. All she had to do was watch her beloved brother, and watch out the window for her husband's return. What joy!

With such a heavy weight off her mind, a tiny spark had been kindled in her heart. Every one of Galen's smiles and touches and bits of tenderness fanned that spark until she felt a warming glow right down to her toes, whenever she thought of him. Whenever he was near, the glow threatened to become a fire, and his kisses could start a conflagration.

In a moment she'd consult with the butler and the housekeeper, because she wanted to make sure his lordship's house was as comfortable and as smooth-running as she could make it. How else was she to show Galen her growing affection? Margot wanted to make certain that he had no regrets, that he would not think of dissolving their marriage or leading separate lives. Margot wanted his children.

*   *   *

Ansel was deliriously happy. He was going to see the trick riding tonight, and tomorrow perhaps his pony would arrive so he could practice all those daring feats Galen described. Music and art and books were all well and good, but a fellow who could stand on the bare back of a galloping horse was something special, no matter what Margot said. He just wouldn't tell her, that's all.

Fenning was happy. Perhaps he was not as enraptured as Master Ansel, nor as dreamy-eyed as Lady Woodbridge, nor as cat-in-the-creampot as his lordship, but he was the butler, after all, and above such undignified passions. The viscount was home to see about the large details; the viscountess was handling the minor ones as if she were to the manor born, which she was, thank goodness. The elite of London were leaving their cards and *douceurs* with Fenning, and the butler had more and more underlings to impress. Fenning's domain was all it should be. Moreover, his linens were being ironed the way he wished, and his favorite dishes were being prepared in the kitchens. He might even smile one of these days.

Lord Woodbridge's sister was not happy. Lady Harriet was ill, suffering grievously. Well, she was suffering illusage at any rate. Her brother hated her; her father thought she was an infant; her sister-in-law was doting on that puny child instead of sitting by Harriet's bedside; and they all wanted to ship her off to Bath, to Aunt Matty and Horrid Harold. Nothing could be worse, except the awful wound on her head. Why, any deeper, the physician said, and she would have required stitches. As it was, she needed a sticking plaster, a tisane, and a doctor's care—a lot of that handsome doctor's care. He didn't think she was too young; Harriet could tell by the way he smoothed her hair back to look at the bruise. That nice Dr. Hill would never let her be sent to Jericho, not when Margot and Galen were entertaining here in Town.

Harriet made sure she was wearing her prettiest dressing gown, and a bit of Margot's face powder to give an interesting pallor, when he called that morning. She practiced draping herself on the chaise longue until she reached what she considered the perfect balance of seventeen-year-old siren and sickly swan. Before the physician could declare her fit as a fiddle, she moaned and begged, "You do not think I should have to sit cooped up in a carriage, do you, sir? My poor head aches just thinking about it." She brought the back of her hand to her forehead for emphasis.

"Definitely not, Lady Harriet. An injury to the head could cause permanent damage if exacerbated by further jostling. Your memory might be affected, for one thing."

"What did you say your name was, doctor? Oh, yes, Dr. Hill."

"There have been cases where a head wound leads to loss of sight."

Harriet squinted at him. "You don't say?"

"Or the wound might turn septic, without constant watching. Furthermore, a young woman of your delicate constitution, having suffered such a trauma, should not be subjected to any untoward upset such as a sudden change of surroundings."

"Or a chawbacon cousin."

Dr. Hill smiled. "Decidedly not a chawbacon cousin. They can be quite detrimental to one's health, as bad as wet feet."

"Why, I might go into a decline if I have to leave London, mightn't I?"

"If I were a gambler, which, I assure you, I am not, having dedicated my life to science and the betterment of mankind, I would definitely wager on your chances of falling into a decline."

"You'll tell my loathsome brother that, won't you?" She clutched his coat sleeve. "You'll tell him I cannot possibly travel until . . . until . . ."

"Until the wound is entirely healed? That should take a fortnight, at least."

Harriet was content with that, for who knew what two weeks could bring? Surely something would happen that would keep her from spending the summer in Bath. The world could not be so unjust, otherwise. Aunt Matty's rheumatics might grow worse. No, Harriet would not consider such a possibility, for her father might think Harriet ought to go keep the querulous old woman company. Cousin Harold might drown in the Roman baths. Yes, that would do. Now Harriet was happy.

The well-born, well-educated, but not well-off doctor was happy, too. In two weeks he could collect a tidy sum in fees from Lord Woodbridge, and who knew what other treasure might fall into his waiting hands?

Lady Floria was not happy, and she was never going to be, especially after Galen told her to leave his house.

Chapter Twenty-three

W hoever said hell hath no fury like a woman scorned
would have known to batten the hatches for the coming storm. Standing firm and tall in his own parlor, Galen
got bombarded with a hurricane of hatefulness, a spate of
spite, a torrent of threats, and the Ming vase Fenning hadn't
thought to remove.

The fact that Lady Floria had scorned him, rejected his
suit in public, not once but twice, meant nothing to the earl's
daughter. No matter that she had made Lord Woodbridge a
laughingstock, a byword for buffoonery, Floria did not like
being told she was dishonorable, disreputable—and dowerless.

"No, I will not return the twenty thousand pounds your
father gave me, Florrie. That sum was signed over to me,
and I fulfilled my part of the contract by showing up at the
church. You did not, so you lose." Galen thought that was
straightforward enough that even his former fiancée would
understand. The conversation would end, she would leave,
and he could get back to seducing his wife.

Lady Floria had other ideas. "If you are entitled to my
dowry, then I am entitled to the marriage settlements," she
insisted, drumming her fingers on the arm of the sofa. The
sound was becoming as annoying as her high-pitched voice.

"Florrie, you are entitled to nothing but contempt. You
could have had a perfectly respectable marriage, the one our
fathers wished for us, but you chose to run off with a fortune
hunter. The fact that he took your jewels—most of which I
paid for anyway—should be a lesson to you."

"It was. I have learned that a woman cannot trust a man!"

"Hah! Coming from you, that is laughable." The viscount turned in his pacing to glare at her. "Your promise means less to you than yesterday's dinner."

"Tomorrow's dinner means more, Woodbridge. That's the one I won't be eating if you turn me out without my twenty thousand pounds."

"I told you I would give you the carriage fare to your father's, or anywhere else you wanted to go. You still have the diamonds you were wearing when you left, and a fortune in clothes. I ought to know, because I am still getting the bills for them. Sell them and you can eat very well for years."

"What, living in a rundown cottage in the wilderness? Don't be absurd, Woodbridge." The finger tapping grew louder and faster. Galen paced farther away. "Besides, you don't need the money, and I do."

"I am sorry, Florrie, but the money has been deposited in Margot's account, as her marriage settlement."

"What? You gave my money to that trollop?"

In a flash, the viscount was in front of the couch, looming over Lady Floria, shaking his fist in the air so he would not shake her. "How dare you sit in my house and insult my wife? That *lady* is not the one who eloped on her wedding day and spent two nights on the road with a known libertine."

Floria waved her fingers dismissively, which was better than discordantly. "La, nothing happened."

"La," he echoed in jeering tones, "it does not matter if anything happened or not. People may have wondered if we anticipated our wedding vows after such a long engagement, but they will absolutely assume that you and your baronet did."

She arched her plucked eyebrows. "Well, they would be wrong. Sir Henry was importunate and unpleasant about it, but I knew what was due an earl's daughter."

But not a duke's son? Galen asked himself. Gads, he'd

had a luckier escape than he'd thought. So had Lytell, broken nose notwithstanding. The viscount decided he could be magnanimous, in light of her leaving. "Very well, Florrie, I will make you an offer. I will give you half of the dowry, ten thousand pounds, if you go to Bath and marry my cousin. It's a perfect solution, for no one else would have either one of you. I'll pay you the other half if you bear him a child." That half of the blunt ought to be safe on two counts: Floria wouldn't go near Harold's bed, and Harold wouldn't want her to.

"Marry Horrid Harold?" Her voice's pitch went up a notch; so did the volume. "I'd rather be a . . . a . . ."

"A rich man's mistress? That's about all your sullied reputation leaves you suitable for."

Her look of distaste answered that question, but not Galen's curiosity to know if she'd ever intended to grant him—or Lytell—his husband's rights. "No, I did not think so. Besides, even a protector demands some degree of loyalty for his money."

"Then what am I supposed to do?"

"I'll spell it out for you, Florrie. No, that would make it too hard for you. I'll just speak slower: I do not give a rap. And if you rap on that arm rest one more time, I will use that black lacy thing to tie your hands together. Dash it, Florrie, you never even said you were sorry!"

"Of course I am sorry, when I see how well appointed this house is, and how well run. I am immensely sorry to miss the end of the Season, sorry to be left without funds, sorry that basket-scrambler made off with my emeralds."

He shook his head. "No, Florrie, you are sorry for yourself, for the coil you've landed in, but you haven't spared one thought for me or the wretched mess you almost made of my life. Well, I am sorry I never cared enough to matter to you, but I was willing to make a go of the marriage. You were not. So go. I want you out of my house, for you are not fit company for my wife."

That's when the names and the knickknacks started flying.

Fenning reached the parlor before Margot, and made a dive for the Oriental vase. He caught the priceless pottery just before it reached the floor, but his white powdered wig went sailing, leaving him with a shiny, bald pate. Ruff, seeing what appeared to be a particularly furry rabbit, or perhaps a cat, flying across the room, gave chase.

Over went the Chippendale chair, the Sheraton table, the Meissen bonbon dish, and Margot, who was trying to get to the hairpiece before the harebrained mutt. As Galen's wife lay sprawled on the carpet, her skirts above her ankles and her hair trailing down her back, Lady Floria smirked behind her veil. "*That's* your lady, Woodbridge?"

The viscount helped Margot to her feet and wrestled the wig away from the dog, who was shaking the hairpiece, making sure the thing was dead before eating it, thus coating the carpet and the viscount with the white powder. When Margot ordered, "Drop it," Ruff spit out the wig and went after the fallen bonbons. Galen handed the hairpiece to Fenning, who held it at arm's length in two white-gloved fingers. He held the Ming vase in the other as he left the room, his back rigid with disapproval.

Margot was attempting to tuck her loose hair back into the topknot, and Galen was brushing down his navy superfine and his satin-striped waistcoat, which were now covered in white dust and dog hair and, no doubt, drool and droves of vermin. Lady Floria was studying her fingernails for nicks.

"What is this about, my lord?" Margot asked, once the furniture was righted and the broken dish was taken away. "Do you wish to cause yet another scandal with such a contretemps? Why, the staff will think you were having a lovers' spat with my cousin, Madame Millefleur, if they do not already suspect the truth. And you, Lady Floria, are you not in enough difficulties without drawing attention to yourself? Any number of servants might recognize your voice, despite the veil over your face, once they start wondering what my cousin is about, brawling with Lord Woodbridge. Ansel and Ella, of course, already know I have no French cousin."

Galen had not listened past "lovers' spat." Did his wife suspect him of dallying with the she-demon? "You know deuced well all I wanted to discuss with the witch was her departure. I met Florrie here alone so that I could throw her out of the house without embarrassing her in front of you or the servants. This is the thanks I get."

"If you had been more accommodating, you might have had more success," Lady Floria snapped at him. Then she turned to Margot. "He refuses to give me back my dowry. Twenty thousand pounds might be a pittance to you, missy, now that you have married Golden Ball, but I want my money and I am not leaving without it." She dabbed at her eyes, as if a tear could form any minute. She even managed a sniffle. "Without the brass I have nowhere to go, no way to live. I'm not nearly as brave as you, to try to earn my way in the cold, cruel world." She was not as talented as Margot, either, but she was a deuced good actress.

Galen's arms were crossed over his chest. He did not so much as glance in Floria's direction. "The money from Earl Cleary became your portion when we married, Margot. I will not renege on that."

Margot looked from one to the other and shook her head. "I thought Ansel and Harriet were the only children in the house. Lady Floria, you know your father will support you if you go home and beg his forgiveness. He'll undoubtedly even restore your dowry in hopes of finding you a husband. I told you *my* husband was not your savior. But you, Lord Woodbridge, did you truly think I would spend another woman's fortune on frills and furbelows? I would not touch tuppence of Lady Floria's *dot*."

"Perhaps she is a lady, at that," Floria said. "At least she shows good sense, unlike you, Woodbridge. La, to prove I am as much a female of refinement, I have decided to travel to Bath after all, as you proposed. My twenty thousand pounds will be a vast sum to an elderly gentleman who has little else to choose from in that benighted place, or a retired military man. I do believe I am weary of callow youths."

The viscount made a rude noise.

Floria pretended not to hear him. "Yes, I shall escort your sister to Bath, saving your having to hire a *duenna* for her, and I'll stay at your aunt's house, as you suggested, to help that lady chaperone Lady Harriet, a headstrong minx if I have to say so myself. She'll bear careful watching if she's to make a decent match, and I doubt your aunt is desirous of attending all the waltz parties and picnics of which young people are so fond. I do believe Mrs. Woodrow has a fashionable place in the Royal Crescent, hasn't she?"

Galen almost shouted, "That wasn't what I suggested, and you know it. You think to save money on the price of a carriage, and you plan to trade on my poor aunt's respectability to reestablish yourself in the quieter Bath society. I don't want you anywhere near my aunt, my sister, or my carriage horses! And I have not agreed to hand back the money I earned by waiting at that church altar in front of a thousand smiling spectators."

Ignoring her husband's intransigence, Margot told Lady Floria, "I am afraid Lady Harriet won't be leaving for a few days. The doctor feels that her skull may have suffered more severe injury than first appeared. He believes that the motion of the carriage will worsen her condition, and a sudden jarring, as from a bad rut or a sharp turn, could actually imperil her life or her reason."

"Gammon," Galen said. "The chit hasn't enough brains to be shaken up, and she is healthy as a horse. I heard her send for enough food for an army, at breakfast time."

Floria ignored him, too. "La, if the poor child is ailing, you'll need me to bear her company. You'll be too busy, Lady Woodbridge, getting ready for your little gathering and trying to learn how to run a household of such distinction. Then there is your brother, taking a great deal of your time,

although you'd do better to hire a tutor for the lad, of course.
I can see to dear Harriet, chat about the people she should
know, play quiet games, peruse the fashion journals with
her, the type of thing I can tell you are not interested in,
Lady Woodbridge." She let her eyes travel from hem to
neckline of Margot's simple lavender round gown, devoid
of ornamentation. "Yes, that is best for everyone. I'll go on
to Bath when Harriet does, me and my twenty thousand
pounds."

She drifted out of the room in a flutter of black lace,
while Galen sent black looks her way.

Chapter Twenty-four

Whoever said reformed rakes make the best husbands had been reading too many purple-covered romance novels.

Margot did not want a rake, reformed or otherwise, for a spouse, no wandering-eyed womanizer, no roaming-affections Romeo. She wanted a husband to rely on, to trust, as her mother had believed in her father. How could she trust Galen's intentions toward his former intended? Margot wanted Lady Floria under her roof as little as Galen seemed to, but his attitude could change; Margot's never would.

Oh, Lord Woodbridge might be angry with Lady Floria now, and no one could blame him, but they'd known each other for so long that Margot had to worry. Galen and Floria shared so much—friends, interests, backgrounds, and experiences—while Margot and the viscount had only a marriage contract in common.

To add to Margot's concerns, Floria was beautiful. She'd been the Toast of London since her very first Season, of which fact she never hesitated to remind Margot and Lady Harriet. Men had swarmed at her feet, writing poems to her eyebrows, which were perfectly arched, of course, and bringing her gifts. How could any warm-blooded man not be attracted to that lush, rounded figure and auburn hair that hinted of hidden fires? She even looked stunning in black, never mind that no respectable widow would wear her mourning so low-cut or clinging.

"Do you think she is pretty?" Margot finally asked, when Galen stopped cursing under his breath.

"Floria?"

"No, your aunt Mathilda. Of course, Lady Floria."

"Do I think Florrie is pretty?" He had to think, which Margot took for a good sign. "Right now I think she is as homely as a hyena's hind end, but I know in my mind's eye that she is exquisite."

"Oh." Exquisite was *not* a good sign.

Galen picked up a green jade horse from a corner table. He held the figurine up to the window, so the light flickered across the carved surfaces. "Florrie is as exquisite as this sculpture, and as cold and heartless. The woman has no soul, no honor, no shame. How could she possibly consider staying here, otherwise?"

He was looking so angry again that Margot hurried to take the jade horse away from him. "Did you love her?" she asked, having to know, no matter how painful the truth might be.

"Good grief, what's that got to do with anything?" Then Galen noticed how upset Margot was, the way she was clutching the carved horse in white-knuckled hands. He took the figurine and carefully placed it back on the table, then held her hands in his. "Could it be that you are jealous, my dear? Don't be, sweetheart, for Florrie means nothing to me, nothing but a parasite to exterminate, like Ruff's fleas."

"Rufus does not have fleas. Did you love her?" she repeated.

"I might have, in a casual, brotherly sort of way. I could not have loved her so deeply if I fell out of love so quickly, could I? Besides, if I loved Florrie to distraction, I couldn't lo— That is, I couldn't have grown so fond of you in such a short time."

"And you are quite sure you won't change your mind again, and fall back in love with her?"

Now she was grasping his hands as desperately as she'd held the horse, but his fingers were not carved of stone, so Galen pried them loose before her fingernails drew blood. "Silly goose, worrying over such an impossibility. Why would I ever think of that bloodless beauty when I have you? Florrie is like a cold porcelain fashion doll; while you are a warm, loving woman."

"Truly?"

He kissed her, raising that warmth a few degrees hotter. "Truly. Besides, a man does not easily get over such a blow to his pride. No, Florrie will be an old hag, living in Bath, I pray, long before my feelings for her soften."

As usual when Galen kissed her, Margot's wits went begging. All she could do was sigh in relief and contentment and pleasure at being in his arms again. The morning in his studio seemed days away. Lady Floria could be miles away.

Galen misinterpreted that sigh as one of reluctant acceptance of his attitude toward Florrie. "What can I do to convince you that it's you I admire, your beauty that takes my breath away, your sweetness that gladdens my heart? I am delighted that I married you, sweetings, instead of an ice maiden from the *beau monde*, and you will just have to believe me."

Of course Galen intended to prove his delight every night—and a few afternoons. If it took a year of lovemaking for Margot to stop doubting his sincerity, well, a fellow owed his wife peace of mind. Meantime, he recalled the necklace from Rundell and Bridges. "Here, I know what will persuade you." He took the velvet box out of his pocket and put it in her hands. "I bought this for you today. Not for Florrie last month, not for some courtesan last year."

Margot was raising the lid of the box. "But why? You have done so much for me al— Oh, how magnificent!" She lifted out the shimmering strand of perfectly matched diamonds, flowing like a crystal waterfall through her fingers.

"Why? Because I want to please you, my dear, because your happiness is my happiness."

Luckily Clegg had provided Galen with two handkerchiefs that afternoon.

After drying her eyes, Margot fretted that she could not wear the necklace to Astley's Amphitheater that evening. "I cannot imagine diamonds being quite the fashion at the circus."

"No, but they will be perfect for Vauxhall Gardens tomorrow night. There is to be a concert, dancing under the stars, and fireworks. Some of my friends and their wives invited us to share a box. Should you like to go?"

"It sounds heavenly, but what about Ansel? I hate to leave him alone."

"Alone, with all the servants tripping over each other to cater to him, and the dog standing watch like Cerberus guarding the gates of Hades? He'll be fine. You cannot keep the boy wrapped in cotton wool forever, you know." And she could not keep the boy sleeping in her bed forever either! "In fact, I have been thinking that we will need to hire Ansel a tutor one of these days, to start preparing him for school if he wishes to attend. He's so bright he can catch up to the others his age in no time, I am sure, if he isn't already ahead of his years."

"I don't know that he's had any lessons at all since I have been gone. He told me he read a great many books in Papa's library, though, which had an eclectic collection. I have not wanted to question him too closely yet."

"Formal schooling can wait till we get settled in the country, I suppose. Meantime, I thought to send for my old nanny. She's been living with her brother since Harriet outgrew her, but she's always complaining that she has no babies to cuddle, which is her way of urging me to marry. I know Ansel doesn't need a nursemaid, but I thought you'd feel better having Nanny sleep in the nursery with him. You'll like her; she plays the fiddle. And she will be thrilled to have you in the family."

"You think of everything! Your nanny sounds perfect. When can she come?"

Not soon enough, for Galen's sake.

"If I know Nanny, she will be here within the week. Between Clegg and Ella, Ansel should do fine until then. So may I tell my friends we will attend Vauxhall with them?"

"What about your sister and Lady Floria?"

"If my sister is too ill to travel to Bath, her health is certainly too precarious to jeopardize with a boat ride in the night air. As for Florrie, we've had enough fireworks with her. Come, let us see how the necklace looks."

Galen leaned closer and reached behind her to fasten the clasp. Somehow his arms stayed wrapped around her, and the necklace was forgotten. Everything was forgotten for that matter, including the six months of celibacy, until the viscount's reaching fingers encountered a thrice-folded page where he'd expected soft, warm flesh in the bodice of her gown.

Margot sat up—goodness, how had she come to be lying down, anyway?—and took the paper from him. "I forgot all about the letter from your father. Fenning was just handing it to me when we heard all the shouting, and I did not have a pocket, so I stuffed it there."

"Whatever His Grace had to say, I am sure it can wait." Galen was sure *he* would expire if he had to wait much longer.

Margot was already putting her finger under the seal to open the letter. "I wrote to him as soon as your sister arrived here, you know, so he would not worry."

"He was most likely relieved that she was gone." Galen would be.

"Gammon. His Grace is a devoted father. You'll be just like him."

"If I ever get the chance," he muttered, while she read.

"Oh, dear. His *Epidendrum cochleatum* is in bud."

"He'll get over it, whatever that is."

"It is a cockleshell orchid, which has never set a bud at Three Woods before."

"Ah, then the governor should be in alt. We'll send congratulations back with Harriet. First, though, let me admire the necklace a bit more before we have to get ready for Astley's." In Galen's mind, Margot was reclining on the sofa in his studio, wearing the diamonds and nothing else. Regrettably, he would not be painting that portrait any time soon, not with Ansel wandering through his studio. Then again, if Margot was posing nude, Galen doubted he'd get much painting done.

His reverie was rudely interrupted. "You don't understand. Because his orchid is about to flower, he cannot come to London to fetch Lady Harriet."

"Fine, we'll send her in the coach."

"But he is asking us to keep her here until he arrives for our fete."

"What? Let me see that!"

Galen snatched the paper out of her hands and started reading. "Bloody hell!"

"He does apologize for the inconvenience, with us so newly wed."

"Inconvenience? This is a catastrophe. He says he has decided that Bath won't do for Harry. What he means is Bath won't survive Harry."

"He is wise enough to realize that she won't stay there, not after she showed up here. Your sister would depart your aunt's house without a by-your-leave as soon as she could hire a coach."

Galen kept reading, and kept cursing. "So His Grace has decided to take her with him on a garden tour this summer. You think he is wise? Of all the bacon-brained notions! Harriet has as much interest in flowers as she does in philosophy."

"Yes, but she might enjoy visiting various summer houses, where the hosts might have sons or other, younger guests."

"Yes, and their travels will give us some time alone in the country, when we get there, so I suppose that is a blessing. Oh, no, His Grace writes that the neighbors are already planning receptions in our honor. Harry won't want to miss them, so she'll talk my father into leaving her behind with us. Botheration." He tossed the letter aside, in aggravation.

"We'll face that when the time comes. But what shall we do with her now, here in London?"

"Well, you are not to fret, for one thing. Harry is not your responsibility, and I don't mean to make her one. I was hoping you'd help with her come-out in the fall, since we'll have to see about your presentation anyway, but I never meant for you to have charge of the brat."

"Your sister is my sister, remember?"

"You didn't know what you were getting when we made the bargain."

Margot was reading the rest of the duke's letter. "Your father says that if we don't have dancing at the party, Harriet can attend." She looked to Galen for his opinion.

"Just what we need, a rag-mannered schoolgirl ruining our first entertainment. Why don't we cancel the whole thing, so His Grace does not have to leave his orchids at all, and we can send Harry home tomorrow?"

"You were the one who wanted to host a party, you know. The invitations have been printed and the food ordered and the orchestra hired. Fenning is looking forward to showing off the house again."

"And I live to please my butler. Blast. When is the wretched event, anyway?"

"In two weeks."

"We'll have Harriet on our hands for another fortnight? Devil take it."

"Worse, I suppose we'll have Lady Floria, too."

"Not on your life. Remember what I said about never striking a woman? I take it back. If she is here, I cannot guarantee my actions. Harriet is horror enough, but Florrie is far more than a man can bear. Besides, we won't need her to chaperon my sister, for I intend to lock Harry in her room and throw away her shoes. And the sheets, so she cannot climb down the window. And her money, so she cannot bribe the servants, and . . ."

Margot returned to the unfinished letter. "Your father

thinks we should have a musical evening with a late supper, instead of a ball."

"Good. I was not looking forward to seeing my wife in the arms of every other gentleman in London."

"While I was afraid not enough people would come. But His Grace suggests that I should be among the professional entertainers."

The Town beaux would all be ogling his wife, but from a distance, so Galen liked the idea better. "That would be splendid, my dear."

Margot creased the letter. "But I thought you wanted the *ton* to forget I was on the stage, so they could pretend I am one of them."

"You are one of them: Viscountess Woodbridge. I want them all to see you for what else you are: a marvelously talented woman. But don't perform if you do not wish to, Margot. You can play and sing for my father this summer, so he will be content."

"Very well, then I can tell His Grace to send my regrets to His Highness."

"His Highness? Here, let me see that." Galen took up the letter again, reading all the way to the end this time. "My father was not merely suggesting you sing, my dear, he was passing along Prinny's request."

"Yes, I read that, but I already sang for the Prince once."

"I am sorry, pet, but I fear a royal request is as good as a command. You'll have to sing for your supper—our supper—and pray Prinny does not invite you to Brighton for the summer."

Margot raised her chin. "If I have to sing, then your paintings go on exhibit in the library."

Galen dropped the letter as if it were on fire. "However did you come to that conclusion? You are a consummate professional, trained by Italian and French masters."

"Do you expect me to believe you never studied with the finest artists you could find?"

"That's different. I merely dabble. I'd never think of

showing my work to the *beau monde,* where everyone is a critic, especially those in the Prince's entourage. Brummell is a connoisseur, and Prinny fancies himself a collector."

"Good, then we will both be anxious about trying to please them."

Chapter Twenty-five

Whoever said eavesdroppers never hear good of themselves would have said, "Aha!" But whoever said pretty is as pretty does would have said, "Uh-oh."

Floria would not have been listening at the keyhole if Fenning had been on duty, but the stately, bald-patey butler was trying to refurbish his wig in time to serve a proper dinner. Mrs. Hapgood and Mrs. Shircastle were outdoing each other in offering assistance, soaps, or sustenance, as their talents directed, so the wig restoration was taking twice as long. The footman assigned to guard the parlor door had been hurriedly delegated to escort Ruff to the side yard, the ingested bonbons having a predictable effect on the animal's innards.

Floria did not like what she was hearing. Throw her out, would he? Lay hands on her person? Never. No one had ever so abused Lady Floria Cleary, and no one would now, certainly not her faithless former fiancé. Besides, she had nowhere to go. If the brat Harriet was not going to Bath, then Floria could not very well go visit at the aunt's house by herself. Without the old lady's sponsorship, Floria would be in worse case than she was here, pretending to be Woodbridge's wife's cousin. Why, horrible, heavyweight Harold might be the only escort she could command. No, Bath was no longer an option. The chances of her being invited, or permitted, to join the family at the viscount's country estate were less than negligible.

Floria could go to her grandmother's in Wales, after all, she considered; Woodbridge would be pleased to send her in his carriage. She would not give him the satisfaction, though, the traitor. As a last resort, Floria supposed she could go grovel to her father. He'd be a bear about it, but if she pleaded hard enough, the earl would take her in and find someone to marry her, whatever it cost. But an earl's daughter did not beg. She got even.

This whole mess was entirely Woodbridge's fault, after all. If he had not betrayed their betrothal by marrying someone else, Floria and he would be wed by now. A gentleman would have waited, to know his promised bride was safe and sound and solemnly, solidly hitched. Why, if Woodbridge had been more interesting and attentive in the first place, Floria would never have been forced into seeking excitement elsewhere. Now he planned on tossing her out like yesterday's slops? He'd regret so much as thinking of it, much less telling that syrup-sweet songbird of his.

She would not go until she was good and ready, Floria decided. Woodbridge might threaten to throw her out bodily, but she could simply threaten to tell the servants her name, and that the viscount had invited her to share his home and his marriage bed. In fact, she'd tell that tale anyway when she was gone, twenty thousand pounds in hand, but she wouldn't bother with the servants. She'd go straight to the reporters who wrote the *on dits* sections for the news sheets. See how the high and mighty Lord Woodbridge liked that scandal on his doorstep.

Another go-round in the gossip columns might not be enough to ruin his marriage, though. Judging by the sounds she was no longer hearing from the parlor, Floria knew she'd need heavier artillery to breach the wall of wicked lust being built on the sofa. Rutting men disregarded rumormongers.

Floria vowed to use every weapon in her arsenal to bring down Woodbridge and his wife. Timing was everything, of course, for she had to be on her way before Woodbridge realized who to blame, and she had to wrest her wealth away from the clunch's clutches before leaving. He should have handed her the blunt with a smile, the simpleton. No, he should have doubled the amount, for all the trouble his miserable misalliance was causing her.

Rubbing her back that was aching from bending over so long, Floria promised herself that Woodbridge and the wench he wed would be sorry. She'd ruin their party, for a start, making them look no-how for the Prince and the Polite World. She'd ruin those perishing paintings of his. He'd forced her into looking at them some years ago, all horses and houses, and he'd even suggested painting her portrait himself, rather than paying one of the famous, fashionable artists. She'd put paid to that idea on the instant. First of all, however, Floria swore, she'd ruin his sister.

"They are going to lock you in your room until the party," Floria told Harriet that night while Galen and Margot and Ansel were at Astley's. Harriet was painting her toenails with some of Galen's paints she'd stolen from his studio. Floria was poking at the crumbs on the dinner tray they'd shared, since Harriet was supposedly too ill to dress for dinner, and Floria was too ill-liked to invite. She'd have her revenge for that slight, too.

"I heard your brother say those very words. And he's going to take away your clothes and bedding."

Harriet's brows furrowed. "My blankets? Whatever for?"

"Why, to make you miserable so you will never think of coming back, I suppose. How should I know how such a devious mind works? I merely happened to hear that scoundrel tell Lady Woodbridge he was going to keep you prisoner until your father came. Oh, he also said that Bath was too good for you, that your father has decided to drag you to a series of horticultural lectures as punishment for disobeying him. They agreed to tell you His Grace was attending various house parties so you'd be more amenable to the journey, but you know your father. He'll be staying with dry-as-dust old men who never leave their greenhouses."

"Galen said that?"

"In my very presence. Oh, and they are not holding a ball after all, just another tedious musical evening, so you do not have to regret missing the entertainment."

"Missing it?"

"Of course. Your brother has decided you are not to be seen in public until your presentation next fall, but do not count on that, either, my dear. The viscountess is likely to be breeding by then, the way those two are pawing at each other, so you'll be kept in the country to bear her company."

"Dash it, I won't!"

Floria waved her hand around. "What can a woman do? You know the men hold the purse strings and the power. Marriage would be your only escape from such tyranny, but how can you find a proper gentleman when you are so confined?"

"There has to be a way!" Turning red with rage, Harriet tossed the jar of paint at the wall.

"I don't see how. Of course, if they took you with them on their social rounds before your father arrived, you might meet an eligible *parti*. They attend Astley's Amphitheater tonight, for instance, where crowds of young gentlemen go to leer at the female riders in their scanty spangled outfits. You could have encountered any number of beaux there, but Galen is too busy impressing that sickly child to bother with you."

"I'll have his liver and lights!"

Floria shuddered. "Much too bloodthirsty, Harriet. You'll have to do better if you wish to attend a ball before your twentieth birthday."

"Well, I can get the doctor to declare me well enough for an outing, so they have to take me along tomorrow night."

"Oh, tomorrow they are attending Vauxhall Gardens with some friends. You'd never be invited along, even if you could convince your brother to let you out of the house. You must have heard of the Dark Walks? Why, Vauxhall is no place for innocents at the best of times, not with scores of gentlemen always strolling the grounds."

"Scores of them?"

Floria nodded. "Most of them are well to pass, though. You would not like that, all the singing and joking. Have you ever tasted the arrack punch served at Vauxhall? No? What a shame. Perhaps you'll get to go eventually, if your aunt and cousin come from Bath to chaperon you. I am sure Harold would escort you, if the night was not damp, if no one sneezed on him, and if he could find a waistcoat to match your gown, one that was large enough to fit him. Oh, but I forgot. Didn't Harold get seasick in the rowboat that time we all went on the lake at Three Woods? He'd never take the boat ride there, which is the most romantic part of Vauxhall. Woodbridge and his wife are going by water, naturally. La, it really is too, too bad you cannot go with them."

Whoever said one good turn deserves another might have been taking a turn in Lord Woodbridge's garden the night the viscount and his wife went to Vauxhall.

Jake Humber was enjoying the evening, after spending nearly a year in the depths of one hellish prison or another, with barely a breath of fresh air. Now he couldn't get enough of the stuff, or supper, or his wife's welcome home. By some miracle, home was now upstairs in Viscount Woodbridge's town house, instead of the dismal one-room flat Jake and Ella had shared. Damn, freedom was some sweet stuff! So was the cigar he was smoking, one of his lordship's finest. Even the old jacket he was wearing was a castoff of Lord Woodbridge's, since Jake's own clothes had to be burned before they brought vermin or prison fever into the grand residence. Jake would sooner put his own hand in the fire than queer his chances with his nibs.

Two days ago a solicitor had come to the prison, asking for Jake. Viscount Woodbridge had sent him, that Hemmerdinger bloke announced. Jake didn't know any viscounts, and he couldn't afford a lawyer. If he could, he wouldn't have been in this fix in the first place. The old man had coughed—he couldn't have contracted the fever yet—

and asked Jake if he had stolen that blasted pistol from the gunsmith.

"Hell, no," Jake had answered, truthfully. He'd twigged many a bauble in his days—a chap had to eat, didn't he?—but he wasn't gudgeon enough to rob anyone who could shoot back. Besides, he told the solicitor, he already had a pistol of his own.

"Not if you wish to get out of here, you don't."

Just like that, Jake was a free man, with an offer of honest work at Viscount Woodbridge's, where Ella was looking after the gentry mort's silks and laces, at twice the wages she'd been earning at the theater. They'd be able to purchase that little shop of their own someday, at that rate. Of course, Jake wasn't niffy-naffy enough to serve the swells. Hell, that starched-up butler near had conniptions just thinking about Jake handling the family silver.

Old Fenning might be top-lofty, but Jake's cockloft had a full head of hair, and something in it besides a disregard for the law. He'd turn his hand to anything his nibs wanted, Jake swore, from carpentry to carrying bathwater. If it needed doing, Jake would do it, rather than go back to prison. What the viscount wanted, though, was someone to look after the nipper, make sure no one made off with the tyke or tipped him any drugs. Jake thought he must have died and gone to heaven while he wasn't looking.

While he wasn't looking tonight, right now, b'gad, someone was slinking around the side of the blasted house. Jake snubbed out his cigar and faded back into the shadows, watching. Two figures, there were, with dark capes and hoods, making for the rear of the building. They must have found the library doors locked, from the direction they came, so decided to try the service entrance. That rear door was indeed open, for Jake had gone out it himself. Damn, he wished he had his pistol.

Unarmed or not, Jake was not about to let anyone rob the viscount's house, not after all Lord Woodbridge had done for him and Ella. Besides, Jake knew he'd get blamed if anything went missing. Darting between shrubs and ducking behind benches, he followed the two inept cracksmen, who didn't even know enough to keep to the grass, but were making enough racket to raise the Watch as they crept along the gravel paths. Dash it, what if they were here after the boy? Jake took a deep breath, gave forth a banshee wail, and rushed at the two intruders, who started screaming. Before they could run away, he leaped up, grabbed both hoods, and knocked the two heads together. One of the sneak thieves collapsed in a heap, but the other tried to escape, so Jake tackled the dastard.

Needless to say, Lady Harriet wouldn't be going to Vauxhall Gardens and her ruination this night after all, and Lady Floria wouldn't be revenged. Neither of them would be leaving Woburton House soon, either, for Harriet really did have a concussion this time, and Florrie's ankle was swollen to twice its usual size. Galen measured it himself when he got home, to make sure she was not pretending. Florrie screamed so loudly at his rough touch that the Watch came running back.

Chapter Twenty-six

Whoever warned that the best laid plans of mice and men often go awry, should have mentioned wicked women. And weasels. Manfred Penrose was going to Town.

He'd been expecting a summons to a funeral, confound it, not a hearing about changing custody of the brat. The boy was not dead, by Jupiter, despite that expensive sawbones declaring he wouldn't last a week, no matter what anyone did, or did not. Now some officious prig was coming around, demanding to see the estate books. Well, Manfred wasn't worried about that, at least. The set he was bringing with him to London ought to pass muster.

Manfred was not about to put up with this interference in his plans, not by half, not when he was two-thirds of the way to having it all: the land, the money, the title. He knew whom to blame, and where to go to demand satisfaction. The more he thought about it, getting rid of that plaguey viscount ought to be satisfying indeed. If his niece became a widow, Manfred could set himself up as Maggie's trustee, too. Of course, he couldn't challenge his notably accomplished nevvy-in-law, not if he hoped to live to enjoy the barony. Nor could Penrose simply shoot the man. Renshaw could, though.

Yes, and then maybe he'd move into that vast pile in the center of London, Manfred considered, to console his niece. And he'd slam the door in his Cit wife's face, when she came to Town to lord it over the mushroom class.

Unfortunately, although the door to Woburton House was not precisely slammed in Manfred's face, neither was it opened wide in welcome. The self-consequential butler looked as if he'd just sucked a lemon when Manfred handed him his card, and then he directed Manfred to a narrow side room, likely where tradesmen waited to be interviewed. Treat Manfred Penrose—son, brother, uncle to Baron Penrose of Rossington—like a toadstool, would he? Renshaw's list just got longer by one priggish popinjay in a powdered wig.

Galen was in his library when Fenning brought in the cad's card. Thunderation, that scurvy, sharp-faced scoundrel was not what Galen needed right now. He had enough problems in his dish without Margot's murderous kin. His own relatives were nigh to driving a man to drink, witness the twice-filled glass of wine on the desk.

What the devil had Harry been thinking last night, Galen wondered, sneaking off to Vauxhall without an escort? She hadn't been thinking at all, obviously. The chit had always had more hair than wits and, since she'd barbered her pretty brown curls, her pea-brain had diminished proportionately. Harry was fortunate a broken head was all she suffered after that foiled foray to the Gardens.

Lady Floria, however, must have known what she was about, the witch. She'd been to Vauxhall enough times to understand how rowdy the roving bands of young men could get, how those unlighted paths could lead to unleashed passions. More than once, Florrie had refused to go down them with him, her own fiancé.

A badly twisted ankle was far less than the woman deserved for leading Harry into such danger, and after Galen had ordered her from his house, too. He should have paid Florrie the wretched dowry, just to see the back of the she-demon, but her efforts at blackmail had rankled. Any decent woman would have left when she was not wanted, without resorting to extortion, but not Florrie. The bitch had gone straight from blackmailing Galen to blackening his sister's chances.

Now she was an invalid, and not even Galen could toss her out. He could, however, keep a firm hold on his ban of laudanum in the house. If Florrie begged him sweetly, he might just plant her a facer, to relieve her pain.

Thank heaven for Jake Humber, Galen thought, else he'd be in even deeper waters, trying to explain to His Grace how Harry had come to be tripping down the Primrose Path. Too bad Ella's husband could not keep an eye on Floria, Harriet, and Ansel all at once, but since Harry was seeing double, and Florrie couldn't put her foot down without screaming, Galen thought he'd have some peace and quiet for a while. Ansel was in the studio, the stables, or at his sister's side, so Humber should have no trouble keeping him safe, especially with Nanny on her way, and Ansel's promise not to try any more handstands on a moving pony's back. Was the whole world insane, Galen wondered, or just him, for wishing he had nothing more to think of than his wife's soft skin and blue eyes?

He'd thought to have some time with her today, just the two of them. The viscount's plans for quiet conversation and kisses, to start, after Vauxhall, had come to naught when they returned to find chaos in the house with Fenning brandishing a fireplace poker and three maids in hysterics. By the time the Watch left and the doctor came, and Galen had promoted Jake Humber from man-of-all-work to security guard, and Margot had checked on Ansel, she was yawning in exhaustion, eager for her bed. She was not as eager as Galen was, but he had to leave her at her door.

This morning Margot was at the linen drapers with two of his friends' wives they'd met last evening, seeing about those blasted seatcovers. Galen wanted her to have friends, of course, but deuce take it, he wanted her by his side!

The whole house was at sixes and sevens, what with the overpriced doctor underfoot giving orders, and the servants not at the physician's beck and call starting to get the house ready for the musicale. Galen had escaped to the library, declaring that room off limits to the squads of dusters, sweep-

ers, and carpet-beaters. He'd thought to go over some correspondence until Margot returned, then take her driving in
the park. With Ansel, of course. Or take her to visit the Gre-
cian marbles on exhibit. With Ansel. Blast, when was he
going to get his own wife to himself?

Not soon, not with Manfred Penrose waiting down the
hall.

Before sending for the son-of-a-baron, Galen sent a message to Jake Humber, that he was to get Ansel out of the
house by the back door and keep him away until dinner.
Galen handed Fenning a purse for their use. They could go
to see the new steam locomotive, or the horses at Tatter-
sall's. Galen did not care, as long as the boy was out of Manfred's sight. Later, after the makebait left, Galen might even
get to spend time alone with Margot. Who said you couldn't
kill two birds with one stone?

Galen wished he had another stone. He did not get up
from behind his desk when Margot's rodent-faced relative
edged into the room, beady eyes darting from corner to corner of the library. Galen couldn't tell if Manfred was looking for the boy or pricing the rare books. He wouldn't find
Ansel, and he wouldn't have time to fondle the folios.

"I'm afraid you've caught me at a busy moment," Galen
told the older man without offering him a seat. "How may I
be of service?"

Penrose placed a box of candies on the desk. "Oh, I won't
take more'n a minute, Woodbridge, and it's me who's come
to do you a favor. I've come to see m'nephew, don't you
know." He nodded toward the box of sweetmeats. "I
brought his favorites, see? I found I missed the little bugger,
and decided I ought to come fetch him on home. You must
be wishing to see the last of him, so you can enjoy your honeymoon, eh? Asides, everyone knows city air ain't healthy
for a delicate mite like Ansel."

"Quite right, Penrose. Margot and I had the exact same
notion. That's why we sent Ansel into the country."

Eyes never meeting Galen's, Manfred shifted his weight

from foot to foot and licked his thin lips. "My man didn't—
That is, I didn't think Maggie would let the lad out of her
sight."

"It's only for a short while. Too bad you came all this way
for nothing, but he just left this morning; we'll be following
shortly. Margot was too busy gathering a trousseau and
planning for a small gathering we are having to spend much
time with the boy, at any rate. Ansel was bored." Ansel was
not idle for one minute since his arrival. Galen never knew
a child to have such energy, or so much interest in everything around him. He looked as if he might never have been
so ill, except for his thinness. Penrose was nodding, though,
as if Ansel were a whining, restless sort of boy.

"Aye, you'd want him out from underfoot. A party, is it?
To introduce Maggie to your set, I'd guess. Suppose you'll
want her kin there, to show the family supports the match."

"Oh, Ansel is much too young for a musical evening."

Manfred screwed his face up in what might have been a
smile, if a stoat could smile. "Heh-heh, I meant the gel's
uncle, of course, not the tyke. I suppose I could stay in Town
long enough to show m'face at your do. When did you say
it was?"

Galen hadn't said, and wouldn't. "You won't need to put
yourself out, Penrose. My father and sister will be in attendance, perhaps my aunt and cousin. Their approval will be
sufficient, I am sure. It seems to be enough for the Prince, at
any rate."

"Prinny, eh? It surely would make me proud to see little
Maggie rubbing shoulders with royalty."

Making the muckworm proud did not figure into Galen's
schedule. He did not extend an invitation, not to the party,
not to dinner, not even to share a glass of wine. He did lift
the lid on the box of candies, though, and offered them to
Manfred, who took a step back, refusing. "Oh, I couldn't.
Brought them for the boy, don't you know. Asides, they stick
in m'teeth."

Porridge would stick in those rabbity choppers. Galen

picked up a page of figures from the desk. "I really am quite busy, Penrose."

Manfred pulled at his yellowed shirt collars. "Yes, yes, well, I'll be toddling off, then. Ah, where did you say Ansel was visiting? I might stop by if it's on my way, make certain the boy is well. You did say he was recovering, didn't you?"

"Actually, you never asked. He is in fine health, for a lad who's been overdosed with medications for a year. And Ansel is in Cheshire, with His Grace, my father." He would be soon, at any rate, about the time that Penrose should be back in Town after traveling to Three Woods to discover the lie. "Since His Grace is to be Ansel's guardian in the event of my demise, and Margot's trustee also if she should be widowed, my father thought he'd like to get to know the boy. You wouldn't have any arguments with that, would you?"

"Now that you mention it, I do. I looked after the little devil for years now, and see no reason why I shouldn't stay on as his guardian. M'brother wanted it that way."

"According to the records, your brother's will was never found." Galen used the penknife to sharpen his point. "I wonder why that was? At any rate, you petitioned the court for the trusteeship. Now I am petitioning to replace you. My solicitor advises that there should be no problem, but if you wish to challenge my request, feel free. Of course, I might be inclined, in that case, to see you charged with attempted murder."

"Here now, you can't prove a thing!"

Galen sat up straighter. "Enough of this roundaboutation, Penrose. You will never have the boy in your keep again. If anything untoward should befall him, an accident, say, or another mysterious illness, I will see you clapped in jail so fast you won't have time to hire a barrister. That also includes my wife and myself, in case you were thinking of extending your range of villainy. Oh, and do not suppose you will profit by my demise or Margot's, for every pound, pence, and shilling is protected by the Woburton administrators. Is that clear?"

Penrose pounded on the desk. "What's clear is you mean to use your father's influence to see an honest man choused out of what should be his by rights, his only kin stolen from his care."

Galen tossed the penknife from hand to hand. "Is that all?"

"No, b'gad, it ain't all. I'll let you keep the boy, miserable mewling maggot that he is, but you can damn well keep your nose out of Penrose Hall. I won't have you or that shrew you married snooping in my books again, do you hear? I brought them to Town like your man asked, and they are all right and tight, so you've no call to bother me anymore, confound you."

What Galen heard reminded him to send a man to Sussex to look for another set of estate ledgers while Penrose was chasing around, looking for Ansel. Margot thought she remembered the vault combination, or else Galen could send Humber, who'd had more experience with safes than the viscount wished to think about right now. "No."

"No? What do you mean no?"

"I mean that I intend to see Ansel's patrimony preserved for him. I mean that if the accounts show a profit, I'll still bring charges of mismanagement, if I have to drag every tenant farmer, every sheepherder, every milkmaid, to town to testify that you have run the property into the ground, lining your own pockets. I mean you are finished, Penrose. Now get out. I never want to see your ferret face again. And that goes double for your man Renshaw."

"You'll regret this, I swear!"

"I'll regret spilling your claret on my Aubusson carpet if you don't get out of here soon, Penrose." He could hear barking, which meant Margot was home. Galen would be damned if he let this pond scum upset her, or take one minute of her time, time she could be spending with her husband. He stood and walked to the glass doors leading to the side gardens. "In fact I'd go out this way if I were you. Margot's dog has not had his dinner yet today, and I just might feed him your miserable hide."

Too bad Galen needed the candies for analysis and evidence. Otherwise he'd feed them to the dog, too.

Chapter Twenty-seven

W hoever said that every cloud had a silver lining ought to provide a looking glass to find it. And an umbrella in the meantime.

Margot could not see one bit of benefit to the storm raging outside, nor one advantage to the deluge of disasters she was facing inside. To her thinking, things could not be much worse. Her sister-in-law was still dizzy, and dismayed at the gash on the back of her head and Galen's doubly angry double image. Lady Floria was like a one-legged albatross hanging around their necks, and Ansel was irritated that he could not ride his pony in the rain. Mrs. Shircastle was in a swivet over cooking for the Prince, and Mrs. Hapgood was jealous over Fenning's solicitousness to the dithery, disconcerted cook. The seatcovers would not be ready on time, since the fabric to match Galen's paintings had to be specially ordered, and Ella was finding fault with all of the dressmaker's gowns, so Margot still had nothing suitable to wear for the party. No one had refused the invitations, but Ruff had frightened away four servants delivering replies. Wedding gifts kept arriving, all silver candlesticks, it seemed. Worst of all, Margot's uncle was in Town, and her husband appeared more anxious over hanging his paintings in the library than in protecting Ansel from Uncle Manfred.

"I told you, I sent a groom to follow your uncle," Galen retold her the next, dreary afternoon after her uncle had come. He continued sorting through a stack of landscapes he'd brought down from his studio. "I'd wager Penrose is off to Cheshire to see if he can't winkle Ansel away from my father, as if His Grace would let that gallow's bait get his hands on the lad. We should hear from my man any time now, and Ansel is not playing outside in the rain, anyway. He is safe as houses, listening to Nanny's stories when he is not in the studio or the music room or curled up in here with a book, or being pampered by one servant or another. No one can hurt him, my dear. Now what do you think of this view of Three Woods?"

Nanny was a kindly, competent soul, and Ansel adored her tales of knights and dragons. His latest drawings were all of caparisoned destriers and chain-mailed heroes, and his pony, of course, who had been named Excalibur. Margot felt better, having Nanny to look after Ansel, and Ella's husband to keep an eye on both of them, but Nanny's eyesight was not what it used to be, and Jake's language was not what it ought to be, and her uncle was not where he should be. Distracted, she said, "Very nice."

Galen frowned. "You are looking at it upside down."

"I am sorry, but I cannot help worrying." She reached for a candy on his desk, but Galen pushed her hand away.

"No, don't eat that. The box is from your uncle, for Ansel, and I do not trust it. I locked the box up overnight, but I simply haven't had a chance to deal with the stuff yet today."

Margot looked at the sweetmeats as if bugs were crawling on them. "What are you going to do with them, then?"

"I mean to have them tested. I had thought to offer some to Florrie. If the candies simply contain laudanum or syrup of poppies, she'll stop plaguing the servants for a while. If Manfred used rat poison, she'll stop plaguing me."

"The chemist in Half Moon Street seemed knowledgeable."

"You mean I cannot try them on Florrie?" He smiled. "Very well, the chemist it is. Now, about the landscape. I have to decide soon, in order to get the pieces framed in time. You are certain I have to have three paintings?" His smile turned into a scowl at the painting of his ancestral home, set amid its surrounding forests. "This one is definitely not good enough."

Margot put a different picture on top of the pile. "This one is lovely, and yes, three. If I have to perform three songs for His Highness before the quartet plays, as we agreed, you have to exhibit three paintings."

"The florals in the morning room don't count?"

"No, for the guests won't see them there. More will come here, where we will have card tables set up after the concert."

"What if Prinny asks you for an encore? Am I supposed to run up to the attics to fetch another drawing?"

"Silly. At least you don't have to worry that the Prince will climb all those stairs to inspect your studio, while I have to be concerned that he'll ask me to sing something I don't know."

"We'll merely tell him you are out of practice." He was carrying another picture to the far wall, trying to decide where to hang it. "You're sure this portrait of my mother is suitable?"

Margot came over to admire the painting. "It is perfect, and I am sure your father will be proud and pleased that you chose it. Your mother was a beautiful woman."

"Hm. You are lovelier. I wish I had time to paint your portrait before the confounded gathering."

His words brought a blush to Margot's cheeks, especially when he went on to describe the pose in which he wished to paint her, and the scrap of gauze he'd dress her in.

"Goodness, you would never show that kind of portrait in public."

"I suppose I cannot even paint it, at least not until Ansel goes away to school, not with him ensconced in my studio."

Ansel. Margot was reminded of her little brother, and her uncle. "Do you think we should send Ansel away?"

"Why, because he is taking over my workroom?" Galen had moved to the space between the library windows, holding his mother's portrait there.

Margot tapped her foot impatiently. How could he bother with such inconsequentialities at a time like this? "No, my lord, because he might be in danger."

Looking over his shoulder, Galen asked, "You do not trust me to keep him safe?"

Margot was tempted to ask how she could have confidence in a man who couldn't choose between ten paintings, but she did have faith in her husband. She knew he would do his best to protect Ansel, as he already had, but Galen's best might not be enough. "It's Uncle Manfred I do not trust. I doubt he'll give up his wicked plans when a small boy is all that stands between him and a barony."

Galen put the picture down and put his hands on both her arms. "Ansel is not the only thing in his way, sweetheart. I am there, and the law is, too. As soon as we can prove that he tried to poison Ansel, or that he embezzled the estate funds, or that he contributed to your father's accident, any of those things, we can force Manfred to leave the country and renounce his rights to the succession. Depending on the evidence, we could have him hanged, otherwise, but I would like to avoid that, for Ansel's sake. So off-putting to have a convicted felon in the family, don't you know."

"Until we have that evidence, you do not think Ansel would be safer elsewhere? Perhaps at that estate you deeded to me?"

"Peake Cottage has only a caretaking staff now, not nearly enough protection. Besides, you would fret yourself to flinders if you couldn't keep an eye on him yourself. I know I would not wish to entrust Ansel's safety to anyone else, not even Jake Humber, not even your dog. I am sure Ansel can find enough to do in the house until we all leave for the country."

"Cook said she would teach him to make gingerbread—if she ever recovers from her nervous agitation—and Jake is going to teach him to read a racing form. Did you know they call him 'Numbers' Humber?"

"What a well-rounded education the boy will have. He'll

be the envy of the other lads at school. Now, where do you think the still life should hang?"

"The still life goes between the windows, your mother's portrait hangs over the mantel, and the house, or the horse, or the three houris goes above the desk, when you finally decide. I am going to check on Ansel."

Ansel did better than Margot in the days to come. He was busy polishing silver with Fenning and turning pages for the quartet that came to rehearse. He practiced bareback riding by standing on Jake Humber's shoulders, and taught Ruff to jump through hoops like the trick dogs at Astley's, by throwing Galen's leather gloves through first. Ansel even read to Lady Harriet, although he complained that the books she liked had too many pages where nothing whatsoever happened.

Margot, meanwhile, was being driven to distraction by all the preparations necessary for the formal dinner, the larger concert, the supper afterward. Rooms had to be prepared, gowns had to be fitted, and those wretched thank-you notes had to be written for the wedding presents. She also had to sit with some of her new friends, Galen's friends' wives, when the ladies paid morning calls, lest anyone deem her above herself.

Heaven knew what Galen was doing during all the days before the musicale; Margot did not. He was rarely home during the day, and at night, after escorting her to whatever gathering they were invited to attend in the evening, he left her with a brief good-night kiss.

Margot could not ask where he went, knowing how the viscount would hate a wife who pried or tried to keep him in fetters. They had agreed not to interfere with each other's lives, and she had to accept that he was going his own way. Galen was everything courteous to her in public, the attentive, affectionate husband Margot had always wanted. Even the staunchest doubters now believed theirs was a love match. Unfortunately for Margot, she very much feared it was.

Somehow, she was smitten. Between saving Ansel and seducing her senses, Galen had managed to make Margot fall
in love with him, despite knowing theirs was only an
arrangement of convenience. He must be tired of her already, she mourned, for he never asked her to share a private
glass of wine, nor teased about sharing her bed, not even
when she made sure he knew that Ansel was sleeping in the
nursery, guarded by Jake and Ella on one side, Nanny on the
other. No, Galen did not love her, was not even attracted to
her anymore. As soon as they left London, she supposed
he'd find some excuse to leave her at Peake Cottage, or with
his father, while he returned to the gayer life of a married
bachelor. That was their agreement, after all, no matter how
much Margot might wish otherwise.

How was she to know that Galen was spending his days
looking for evidence against her uncle, or keeping track of
his whereabouts? How was she to know that his nights were
spent taking turns with Jake Humber, patrolling the house or
sitting outside Ansel's door? How was she to know that
Galen had decided to spend less time in her company here
in London, lest he have a permanent, embarrassing bulge in
his breeches? Finally, how was she to know that his public
performance as a doting husband was no act?

Even whoever said that all is fair in love and war would
have agreed that Lady Floria went too far.

She hobbled into Lady Harriet's bedchamber to feed the
younger girl's dissatisfaction and foster dissension, all in the
guise of friendliness. She read the gossip columns and
played cards with the chit. Harriet could barely read the
pips, but that made no matter; Floria cheated anyway. She
also convinced Harriet that she was so bored, nothing would
do but the doctor share their meals, too, and keep them company during the evenings when Woodbridge and his wife
were out enjoying themselves at some elegant affair or
other. Nothing loath, the ambitious young physician placed
himself at the ladies' service, fetching pillows for under Flo-

ria's foot, dimming the candles for Harriet's aching eyes. So agreeable was he, in fact, that Floria decided to convince Harriet to elope with him. His birth was nearly acceptable—for a desperate female.

Harriet would be sent away as soon as her father arrived, Floria told her. She'd be imprisoned in the country, never permitted to visit London again after her last escapade. Conveniently forgetting her part in the Vauxhall venture, Floria painted a dismal picture of Lady Harriet's future, using chub-faced Cousin Harold as the canvas. Harriet was convinced, but not as swiftly as the doctor, who thought he'd like marriage to a duke's daughter better than earning his own living.

Just one day before the party, Floria put her plans into motion. While Galen and Margot were attending a rout, she filled a portmanteau with silver candlesticks, no easy feat for a female on one foot. She stole Galen's silver-headed cane, too, before she limped back upstairs to shred the gown Margot had ordered from Madame Pauline. She hung it back in the dressing room, then hobbled to the attic level, where the boy and that convict were busy reenacting some battle or other, and found Galen's studio. Wrinkling her nose at the smell of turpentine and linseed oil, she defaced as many paintings as she could without getting any of the stuff on her hands. The best picture, the one Woodbridge was working on now, though, Floria took off its easel and packed away in her portmanteau, to sell. It would never bring her twenty thousand pounds, only a great deal of satisfaction. Not knowing that the chosen works were already at the framer's, she thought the viscount would be in Queer Street, since she also sent an anonymous notice to the papers, stating that part of the coming evening's entertainment would be Viscount Woodbridge's surprise talent. Another message said that Lady Floria Cleary would be leaving Town, where she had been sojourning with Woodbridge and his wife, to escort Lady Harriet Woodrow on her wedding journey, which was also a surprise.

Floria did so love a surprise.

Later, after the family and servants were asleep, she fed Margot's dog all the lobster patties that had been made in advance, and tipped out all the wine Fenning had brought up from the cellar. Then she led Harriet to the side door, where Dr. Hill was waiting with his carriage. Oh, and she set the library on fire.

Chapter Twenty-eight

Whoever said every dog has its day never heard one barking all night.

Lord Woodbridge tried to pull the pillow over his ears, but no mere sack of feathers could drown out the infernal noise. The blasted dog was so loud, Galen felt he would need a whole flock of ducks, all quacking at once. Since he'd just gone to bed after a shift outside Ansel's room, which was after an overcrowded, tedious affair where every scoundrel in the city wanted to simper over Margot's hand, Galen was not pleased. He tried to ignore the racket, but sleep wouldn't come with the very walls reverberating. Finally, Galen got up and stormed through the sitting room to rap on Margot's door before turning the knob.

She was awake, of course, tying the belt on her dressing gown.

"Devil take it, woman. Can you not control the beast? He'll have the whole household up next, and Lud knows the servants have enough to do getting ready for your wretched party."

"My party, is it?" Margot was just as tired and just as cross as he was, having lain awake wondering what her husband was doing for the last few hours. "And poor Ruff must need to go out. You are the one who keeps feeding him tidbits."

"Only to preserve my own skin, I swear."

Finding her slipper beneath the bed, Margot turned to her husband. The slipper fell out of her fingers. "You seem to have done a . . . a remarkable job."

Galen always slept in the altogether. He did not usually parade around his house in his pelt, but with so little sleep and so much noise, he'd forgotten to put on his robe. "Thunderation," he swore, grabbing up the first scrap of fabric that caught his eye, the paisley shawl Margot had carried that evening, and tying it around his waist. "My apologies."

Margot dragged her eyes away from his nearly naked male body, haloed in the light of the candle he carried, and tried to catch her breath. "I'll . . . I'll go let him out, shall I?"

"No, dash it. I am up, I'll go."

They both went. Ruff bounded up to them at the foot of the stairs, then tore down the hall, barking his head off, toward the library.

"You don't think he could have heard a burglar, do you?" Margot hurried after, shielding her candle with her hand.

"No, the man I have posted outside would have sounded the alarm. The red menace most likely spotted a squirrel or something, and he's yapping over his midnight snack getting away."

But Rufus was barking at flames starting to rise up the velvet draperies in the library. Without pausing, Galen rushed over and started to tear the heavy lined hangings off the window. Margot ran to help, but he pushed her away. "No, stay back." She helped anyway, pulling until the cloth ripped. While Galen folded the velvet over and over itself, trying to smother the flames, Margot grabbed the vase of flowers on the mantel and emptied that over the draperies, then she ran for the bigger arrangement in the hall they'd just passed. Galen was bent over, trying to gather the fabric into a wad to carry it out to the terrace, where sparks could not ignite the dry old books on the library shelves. "Open the—" he started to say when Margot heaved the weighty vase at the still-burning fire.

The water did land on the flames, extinguishing the last glow, but the flowers fell on Galen's head and back. The vase landed on his foot. "Bloody hell! What are you trying to do, woman, kill me and decorate my bier at the same time?"

He was hopping around, clutching his foot, and Margot's shawl came unknotted from around his waist. He picked it up and started to swipe at the damp petals clinging to his shoulders, which was, of course, enough to send Margot into nervous giggles.

"Think it's funny, do you, wench? You won't be laughing so hard when I get finished with you." He pulled her into his arms and held her as tightly as he could, kissing her cheeks, her brow, her eyes, in relief and reaction, and in gratitude for her quick wits, even if she had bad aim. Gratitude? "Dash it, I suppose I'll have to be thankful to the fleahound, too, now."

Margot shuddered in his arms, and not just because she could feel his bare body against the thin fabric of her night shift and robe. "If Ruff hadn't barked, I don't know what would have happened."

That got Galen to thinking. "I wonder what *did* happen. It's not as if a spark from the fireplace could have reached the draperies, nor a candle left carelessly burning." He padded through the flowers over to where the velvet had hung. Charred scraps of paper were still strewn on the singed carpet. "Someone set the fire on purpose. Thank goodness he didn't do a good job of it."

In a hurry before the doctor finished loading the bags and boxes that she and Harriet had managed to toss out the upstairs windows after drugging the watchman's wine, Floria had not given much thought to the act of arson. She knew the turpentine would do a good job of it, but her ankle was throbbing. She was not going back up those confounded stairs, nor scrabbling around looking for lamp oil. Her hand had closed on the decanter of brandy on the desk, and she'd almost poured its contents on the draperies, but decided she'd need it more if she was to spend the next few days in a carriage with Harriet and Dr. Hill. Instead, she'd grabbed up a handful of correspondence from Woodbridge's desk, hoping she'd taken something important, and lit the papers with her candle. She dropped the burning pages at the bottom of the nearest window before leaving. She could not have known that the draperies were still damp from being sponged clean just that afternoon, nor that the dampness in the air from so much rain had rendered the carpet harder to ignite.

And Margot and Galen could not know their unwelcome houseguest had left them such a parting gift.

"My stars!" Margot exclaimed. "Who could have done such a thing? Who would want to harm any— Oh, my God. My uncle!" In a blur of fabric she turned to fly up the stairs. Galen took the time to throw the sodden velvet out the door onto the stone terrace, just in case, before he followed her to the nursery level. He did not think Manfred Penrose would commit such a senseless crime, for it would avail him nothing. Besides, Galen did not think the dastard could have been in his house that night, not with the guard outside. His other suspicions could wait for morning.

Ansel was sound asleep, not even dreaming, that Galen could see. Margot was brushing the short curls off his forehead and straightening his covers, finding a metal soldier in the wrinkles. Ruff padded past Galen and leaped onto the bed, dug at the bedclothes, then curled up next to Ansel with a yawn, his ugly rusty head on the pillow next to Ansel's golden one. Large brown eyes looked up through scraggly eyebrows, daring Galen to order him off the mattress. The viscount made a fencer's salute. "You win, blast you, but you will not sleep in my wife's bed."

Ruff rolled over.

Lord and Lady Woodbridge agreed that no good could come of waking the household at this late hour, so they parted in the sitting room of their connecting chambers to get what few hours of rest were left before morning. Galen handed his wife the paisley shawl before he left, with a grin and a germ of hope. Margot's cheeks might be as red as the coats on Ansel's toy soldiers, but those blue eyes, ah, they burned a path down his body that could have ignited the entire house. His lady was interested, all right.

Neither Galen nor Margot could fall back asleep, both thinking they would rather be awake, together. They went down to breakfast early, to get a start on the last-minute preparations for the dinner party and the duke's arrival. As usual, they were the only ones at the table for what had become a pleasant part of every day, when they could make plans, discuss the day's news, and covertly study each other.

Today was not destined to be one of those quiet, taking-stock times.

A shout came from the hall. The egg man had discovered the outdoor guard tied and gagged under some bushes near the kitchen entrance.

A scream came from the kitchen. Cook had discovered that her lobster patties were missing, so she went after the dog with a rolling pin. Going to see what was the problem, Fenning discovered that the wine closet's floor was awash in His Grace's favorite year.

A shriek came from the Oriental Parlor when Mrs. Hapgood discovered some of the wedding gifts missing, including her favorite, a pair of silver chalices with swans etched in their sides, for loyalty.

A cry came from upstairs when Ella went to lay out her ladyship's gown for the evening and discovered the blue silk in streamers.

A howl came from the attic studio when Ansel discovered his lordship's paintings covered in a sticky, runny mess, and his own current painting, which was to be a wedding present for his sister and Galen, missing altogether.

Skippy Skidmore came, brandishing a newspaper, outraged that his best friend had never told him he had a hidden talent. The betting books were already filling with wagers as to the nature of the viscount's gift. "Lud, you ain't going to sing, are you, Woodbridge? Worst voice I ever heard."

Then the Duke of Woburton came, with the gout, and with another paper announcing his daughter's marriage.

They all ran up the stairs, except for His Grace, who stood in the hall, bellowing about his young daughter and his old wine. Harriet's room was empty, of course, except for a letter filled with melodramatic, melancholic misspellings, signed *The future Mrs. Dr. Hill.*

Floria's room was in shambles. What she couldn't pack, she'd shredded or smashed, including the furniture and the rugs. Across the lemon wallpaper, in Galen's yellow ochre paint, was written her parting message: *20,000 pounds.*

Margot could only shake her head at the destruction. "You should have given her the money."

"You should have strangled her when you had the chance," Skippy argued.

"Blast it, I told her I'd give the deuced dowry back to her father as soon as she left. It was Cleary's money, after all. The woman is a stark-raving lunatic."

Who had a seven-hour head start to Scotland.

Galen wouldn't consider going after Florrie, and he couldn't go after Harriet, not with the Prince coming that evening, along with fifty other guests, and his house falling down around his ears, which were still ringing with all the barking, bellowing, and bemoaning. The duke was in no condition to go riding *ventre-a-terre* to rescue Harriet from a fortune-hunting physician, especially after downing the only remaining bottle of his favorite wine. That left the Reverend Mr. Skidmore, who did not mind skipping the party, if he could place an informed bet on Galen's talent beforehand, to save his friend's sister. If he didn't make his fortune wagering on Woodbridge, Skippy could ask the viscountess to introduce him to some wealthy widows another time, if Margot could ever show her face in London after the debacle her dinner was going to be.

The cook was crying, the housekeeper was in a swoon,

and the duke was drinking. Ansel was trying not to cry, Margot was trying not to swoon, and Fenning was drinking. Galen was giving Skippy money, pistols, a fresh cravat, and a quick tour of his decimated studio. Ella was battering her husband about the head with a hairbrush for letting such a thing happen, and the dog was casting up his accounts behind the sofa. Nanny came downstairs wondering if she'd heard someone call her name.

Aunt Mathilda and Cousin Harold arrived to meet Galen's new bride.

Chapter Twenty-nine

Whoever said that love conquers all should have remembered that sometimes it needs a little help from its friends.

Margot thought of trying to wrest one of the pistols from Skippy before he left, so she could shoot herself. Dead was the only way she was going to get through this disaster. Then she decided she had to go with the reverend to Scotland, to support her sister-in-law when the brat was found. No, she really had to find a place to be sick. Rufus had already used the marble hallway.

Seeing his wife about to collapse, Galen put his arm around her waist, there in the overcrowded entry. "Don't fail me now, Margot Montclaire Penrose Woodrow," he whispered in her ear. "You are the most courageous woman I have ever met, and you have to keep on being strong a little longer. Ansel needs you. My father needs you. Most of all, I need you."

Margot looked around at the chaos in the hall, with guests and servants and Skippy milling about, getting in one another's way, tripping over the trunks and the sick dog and the prostrate housekeeper. She found Ansel in the confusion, frightened and bewildered at the maelstrom swirling in what he'd thought was a safe harbor. Margot saw His Grace leaning against the newel post, an empty glass in his hand. Ten years seem to have been added to the duke's face in the last hour, but whether that was at the loss of his daughter, the pain in his foot, or the sight of his brother's son, Margot did not know. Finally, she looked up at her husband, and what she saw made her stand taller, even if his arm was all that was keeping her erect at all. Galen did need her, not simply because no man should face the end of the world on his own, but because he was smiling, pleading with her to see the absurdity, and she was the only one who could smile back.

Galen needed Margot to be strong, therefore she was. If nothing else, she reasoned, her husband would have to join her in the country, for he'd never be able to hold his head up in Town again. She stepped out of the security of his arms and began to put her house back in order.

Skidmore was sent off, and Aunt Mathilda and Cousin Harold were escorted to their rooms to recover from the strenuous journey and the overset nerves. The trunks were hauled to the bedchambers, and Ruff was hauled to the rear garden. Servants were sent to replace the food that was either destroyed by Floria or Mrs. Shircastle's desperation, decimating every sweet shop, bakery, and victualer they could find. Fenning himself was driven to the various vintners, and Ella was closeted with two other Drury Lane wardrobe seamstresses, trying to complete a new gown for Margot. The stitching might be hurried, and the fabric might resemble something last seen on Desdemona or Titania, but Margot would have a gown worthy of a queen.

Mrs. Hapgood was revived with some of the duke's brandy, and the two of them and Margot got busy arranging the wagonload of flowers His Grace had brought from the country, while Galen and Ansel worked with the art restorers in the studio.

Since Margot had no time to replace the fire-damaged draperies, she had footmen tear down the rest of the library hangings. She replaced them, temporarily, with swags of white netting that fluttered nicely in the warm breeze from the windows that were opened to air out the smoke.

With Ansel in Galen's company, Jake Humber volunteered to tote the finished flower arrangements around, so Margot had him place a big urn over the burned spot on the library carpet. The rest filled the dining room, the music room, and the parlors, their scents overcoming any lingering odor from the fire.

Margot spent a great deal of time directing the hanging of Galen's paintings, which were more precious than ever with so many others damaged or destroyed, and a very short period of time having her new gown fitted, to Ella's dismay.

Luncheon was a hurried affair, thankfully declined by the Bath contingent, and the duke had finally stopped begging Margot for grandsons to succeed Galen as heir, instead of Horrid Harold.

After lunch, Margot gathered Ansel to help her practice for the evening's performance, which she had almost forgotten to panic over with so much else happening, while Galen and his father and Jake were closeted with Mr. Hemmerdinger and the Bow Street Runners. She'd worry about that conversation tomorrow.

Gracious, how was she to stand in front of all those connoisseurs and critics, knowing they were already thinking the worst of her? Worse, what if they did not come, not wishing to suffer the stain of scandal? Galen would be furious. Fenning would be mortified. Ruff and Harold would argue over the uneaten food.

"Margot, you left out a whole verse," Ansel complained.

"So I did, dearest. That must mean I need a rest. Why don't you come read in my room while I take a nap?"

Five minutes later, it seemed, Ella was shaking her awake. "Time to start getting ready, my lady."

A month wouldn't be enough time for this.

Dinner might have been sawdust and old shoes, for all Margot tasted of it. She never ate before a performance, anyway, and tonight those butterflies in her stomach were doing pirouettes and pliès. No matter, for Harold ate her portion. The ten other guests did their best to pretend the daughter of the house had not just fallen from grace, except His Grace, who glowered at them all from the head of the table.

The menu only vaguely resembled the one Margot had ago-
nized over for the past fortnight, and Fenning grimaced with
a headache from all the wine-tasting.

Instead of leading the ladies from the room after the meal,
Margot joined her husband and father-in-law on the receiving line, greeting the rest of the evening's guests as Fenning
intoned their names. Prinny's was not among them, to Margot's infinite relief. She just might survive her first entertainment, especially if her husband kept looking at her so
approvingly. He had certainly approved her sapphire blue
gown, what there was of it. Ella and the seamstresses
seemed to have forgotten to finish the bodice, or they ran out
of fabric, but Margot could only hope her guests' eyes were
on the diamond necklace, not her bosom. Of course she
could barely take her own eyes off Galen, who was more
handsome than ever in his formal midnight blue coat and
white satin knee breeches. She could have stared at him all
night. Unfortunately, her company expected music at a musicale.

The duke made a speech welcoming the guests and welcoming Margot to the family, then, to polite applause, Galen
escorted her down the aisle between the rows of chairs to
the pianoforte, only stumbling slightly when he saw who
was to be her accompanist. Ansel stood and bowed, and
Margot curtsied while Galen and his father took their seats.
Ansel began the introduction to her first piece while Margot
steadied her breathing and looked over the audience. Ansel
repeated the prelude. Margot kept staring at the small, gray-
haired man in the far corner, whose eyes flicked to Ansel,
her necklace, the priceless artwork, the nearest doors.

"Margot!" Ansel hissed, beginning her music once again.

She sang, without paying the least attention to the words
or her timing. She even left out that same third verse. Luckily, Ansel could follow her lead, and luckily, few of the listeners could understand the Italian love song.

At the end of the piece, Ansel stood and bowed again,
handing Margot a rose while everyone clapped. "Go sit by

Galen, *mon ange*. Tell him Uncle Manfred is in the back row."

Ansel almost flew to Galen's side, his face pale and his lip trembling. As Margot's usual pianist took his place, she saw the viscount glance over his shoulder, then beckon to Fenning in the doorway. He whispered something in the butler's ear, meanwhile keeping his arm around Ansel's shoulder. Then he nodded to Margot and smiled, as if to say she had nothing to fear.

Nothing was about all she could remember of her next selection. She stalled, thanking her guests for coming and inviting them to see her remarkably talented husband's paintings in the library when the concert was over. That wiped the smile off Galen's face, as he received curious looks from those nearby. His sudden anxiety made Margot forget her own trepidations, so she got through the long aria.

Fenning returned while the last note was still hanging in the air. This time, however, he whispered to the duke, who nodded and left the music room.

Margot's last piece was to be the ancient lay, "Prithee Fair Gallant," about a maiden begging her lover to slay her if he could not make her his bride. It never failed to bring a tear to the audience, but tonight Margot added a happy ending. "Thy love giveth breath onto me," she sang to her own husband. "Eternity be too short to spend with thee."

Galen came to her when she was finished and raised her hand to his mouth, turning her to face the enthusiastically approving audience. "You truly are magnificent, my Margot," he said for her ears only. "Finding you was the luckiest day of my life, dearest, and I truly—"

The words Margot had been aching to hear were interrupted by His Grace, stepping forward while the string quartet took its place. The duke raised his arms for quiet. "My friends, I have an announcement. I know you have heard rumors, but they are all false. My daughter has this day become affianced to the Reverend Mr.— Blast, what is the nodcock's first name? Surely it cannot be Skippy?"

Lady Harriet tripped down the aisle on Skippy's arm, both looking as happy as grigs. "It's Skidmore, Papa, but you can skip that part."

"Ahem. To the Reverend Mr. Skidmore, with my blessings, and the bishop's, I am sure. The wedding will be in the fall, and you are all invited. Oh, it was that unfortunate Cleary female who ran off with the doctor since no other man would have her. My daughter and her betrothed tried to stop them. Good riddance, I say."

Fenning and a squad of footmen entered with trays of champagne-filled glasses for toasts and congratulations. Skippy just winked and said, "A bird in the hand, don't you know." They didn't know if he meant his own engagement or Florrie's decision to get herself wed, one way or another, but Galen and Margot knew they would have to wait till later to hear the amazing tale.

The quartet was all tuned and ready when everyone finally settled back in their seats, but Ansel was missing. Margot would have leaped to her feet in the midst of the performance, but Galen held her hand. "Don't worry. He was exhausted from the excitement, so I sent him up to bed, with Jake Humber to guard him. Your uncle is still here where we can see him, and two Bow Street Runners in livery are watching his every move."

Margot relaxed at his side. Her part of the evening was over, thank goodness. She had only the rest of the concert, the supper, and throwing her uncle out, before she could have Galen to herself again, to hear what he had been about to say. She closed her eyes to listen to some of the finest musicians in the country, but all she heard was a dog barking.

"I'll kill that mongrel, I swear," Galen vowed. "This time I mean it. Things were going so well."

"But the barking is coming from the back garden, and you know Ruff would never have left Ansel's bedside when there was warm milk and—" This time she did jump to her feet and rushed past the startled guests to the door, Galen at her heels. Skippy and Harriet followed, as well as the duke, who was not letting his son-in-law-to-be out of his sight. The dowagers raised their eyebrows. Aunt Matty clutched her vinaigrette. Harold tittered. The quartet played on.

Margot was heading up the stairs to Ansel's room when Jake Humber staggered down the steps, blood dripping from his head. Harriet screamed and would have fainted into Skippy's arms, but he told her to stop being a peagoose.

"Damn, I like that boy already," His Grace commented while they waited for Jake to catch his breath.

"They got the boy!" he shouted from the second-story landing. "Some great hulk was waiting upstairs, and he clobbered me with a club, stuffed the nipper in a sack, and took off down the servants' stairs."

"The back garden!" Margot was already running, her hair coming loose and falling down her back. Galen shouted for Fenning to fetch help, pistols, and the gentlemen from Bow Street, but not to let Manfred Penrose get away.

By now half the guests were in the hall, watching this much more entertaining drama. The quartet's playing dwindled to a strum and a plucked chord before they gave up altogether and peered out the windows like the other half of the audience.

Margot and Galen and a handful of others ran through the kitchen, wreaking havoc on Cook's preparations for supper. She grabbed up her rolling pin and came after them, but no one was certain whom she meant to attack, so they ran faster.

Once outside, they listened for Ruff. With his mouth full of Renshaw's leg, though, the big dog could not make as much noise. The former pugilist was halfway over the garden wall, Ansel slung over his shoulder, but Ruff was not letting go.

"Good dog," Galen shouted. "We'll take over now, Ruff. Dammit, dog, let go so I can throttle the dastard. Margot, get back in case he has a weapon." Neither listened to his orders, so he leaped to the top of the stone wall and shoved. Renshaw screamed and fell, but Galen grabbed Ansel in the sack before he could get dropped, and lowered him to the waiting arms below. The footmen had Renshaw tackled, and Cook was bashing him over the head with her rolling pin. Ruff had let go of the bruiser's leg to lick at Ansel, who was covered in flour, the sack's previous contents. Fenning came running with a blunderbuss and a bald head, his wig having fallen somewhere along the way.

All the guests and the musicians were streaming out the library doors at the side of the house to see what was happening. A few of them even managed to notice Galen's paintings on their way, storing up every aspect of this gossip-rich evening.

"Don't kill him," Galen yelled. "We need him to testify." Renshaw was already babbling about Penrose and ransom notes.

But where was Penrose? The Bow Street Runners were hauling Renshaw to his feet and putting manacles on him. "We thought as how you'd want us to save the little baron, governor."

"Dash it, the dog saved the boy! You were supposed to be watching the uncle." Galen was halfway around the house by now, bypassing the servants gathered at the kitchen door. He ran back through the library, to the music room, which was almost entirely empty, except for Aunt Mathilda, who was clucking her tongue about the rag manners in London, and Horrid Harold, all twenty-five stones of him, sitting on top of little gray Manfred.

"Well, I thought the evening was a success, didn't you?" Galen was pouring a glass of wine for Margot. "Although I cannot imagine what we're to do for an encore."

Manfred and Renshaw had been carted off to prison, thence to Botony Bay, Galen hoped. Ansel had fallen asleep with his hand wrapped around Ruff's scrawny neck, and the guests had gone on to other parties or to their clubs, full of enough gossip to last the rest of the Season.

Lord and Lady Woodbridge were in their sitting room, in

their robes, both too tired and too stirred up to sleep. They were also too aware of each other. Margot sipped at her wine. "I . . . I suppose we should be going to bed. Tomorrow will be nearly as chaotic, with Harriet home."

"You'll manage, as you've managed everything else. Don't go yet. I was hoping we might have a private talk. We'll never get much chance, between my sister, your brother, and the rest of the household. Gads, do you think we'll have Skippy living here, too, now that he is leaving the Church?"

With the party over, Margot was not even sure where she would be living. "What was it you wanted to speak about?"

Galen rubbed his hand on the silk of her dressing gown. "I wanted to, ah, discuss the terms of our marriage."

Margot's heart sank. He was going to tell her that he wished to dissolve the marriage, one way or another. After so much public embarrassment, one more shock to Society would not matter to him, as long as he had his freedom. "I see. You want the contract to end sooner than the six months we'd agreed on?"

"Dashed right I do. Margot, I cannot wait six months to make you mine. I doubt I could last six more weeks. Six hours might be too—"

She was in his arms, pressed tight against him, body to body, separated only by two thin layers of fabric. "Six minutes?"

He cupped her face in his hands. "Sixty minutes, sweetheart. It will take me that long to tell you how much I love you, and to hear you say those words. You do love me, don't you, Lady Woodbridge?"

"Why, Lord Woodbridge, it's positively scandalous how much I love you. Sixty years won't be enough time together."

Their robes were on the floor, in six seconds.

Chapter Thirty

Whoever said that all's well that ends well, well, he said it all.